MW00676077

HOME AND AWAY

HOME AND AWAY

■ ■ ■ ■

A NOVEL BY

Peter Filene

Z

ZOLAND BOOKS

Cambridge, Massachusetts

First edition published in 1992 by Zoland Books, Inc.
384 Huron Avenue, Cambridge, MA 02138

Grateful acknowledgment is made to Random House, Inc. for permission to reprint excerpts from W. H. Auden: *Collected Poems by W. H. Auden*, ed. by Edward Mendelson. Copyright 1940 and renewed 1968 by W. H. Auden.
To Macmillan Publishing Co. for permission to reprint excerpts from *The Poems of W. B. Yeats: A New Edition*, ed. by Richard J. Finneran. Copyright 1928 by Macmillan Publishing Co., renewed 1956 by Georgia Yeats.
To CPP/Belwin, Inc. for permission to reprint excerpts from "Blue Moon" by Richard Rogers & Lorenz Hart. Copyright 1934, renewed 1961, 1962 by Metro-Goldwyn-Mayer, Inc. Rights throughout the world controlled by Robbins Music Corp. All rights of Robbins Music Corp. assigned to EMI Catalogue Partnership. All rights administered by EMI Robbins Catalogue. International copyright secured. Made in U.S.A. All rights reserved.
To Warner / Chappell Music Co. to reprint excerpts from "(Put Another Nickel In) MUSIC, MUSIC, MUSIC" by Stephan Weiss and Bernie Baum. Copyright 1949 (renewed 1977) and copyright 1950 (renewed 1978) by Chappell & Co, & Tro Cromwell Music, Inc. All rights reserved.

ISBN 0-944072-22-4

First Edition
Printed in the USA by Braun-Brumfield, Inc., Ann Arbor, MI
Composed by Books International, Deatsville, AL
Book design by Boskydell Studio

Library of Congress Cataloging-in-Publication Data

Filene, Peter G.
Home and away : a novel / Peter Filene. — 1st ed.
p. cm.
ISBN 0-944072-22-4
I. Title.
PS3556.I4254H65 1992 92-53831
813'.54—dc20 CIP

ACKNOWLEDGMENTS

With immeasurable gratitude to:

Laurel Goldman, Pete Hendricks, Peggy Payne, Linda Orr, Angela Davis-Gardner, and Georgann Eubanks, who accompanied me every word of the way;

Gary Richman, who was there at the start in the Looking Glass Cafe, and John Kasson, Peter Walker, Dorothy Filene, David Cooper, Rhoda Weyr, and Dorrie Casey, who provided invaluable guidance during the long passage toward completion;

my agent, William B. Goodman;

and Erica Rothman, who has been with me through doubt and delight.

To Erica

HOME
AND AWAY

PROLOGUE

I began with what Mom called "sweet dreams": the silver wrappings of chocolate kisses, the glossy yellow and red cartoons from Double Bubble gum, and the cowboy pictures on the underside of Dixie Cup lids. Then came colored pencils from Dad's office and all my baby teeth (since my German-born parents didn't know about the tooth fairy). Then stamps from England, Brazil, and all those other picturesque places Mom wrote to and her friends wrote back from; also Superman comic books; and of course the Sunday lists of major-league batting averages.

Dad saw the trend of things. "One morning, Lise, we wake up to find we have only one son at the breakfast table, because Murray cannot climb out over all the collections in his room." So my father spent a weekend measuring and sawing and hammering, with sawdust flecking the hair of his chest, until he finished the wall of cubbyholes. Seven rows from floor to ceiling, eleven from window to door, a total of seventy-seven cubbyholes. Every souvenir had its home, and there were empty homes waiting for the future. All Sunday afternoon I wrote labels in my best printing: BASEBALL CARDS; COMICS; DODGERS; DREAMS; and so forth, in alphabetical order, down to TOM MIX and YOYOS at my ankles. That was decades ago, when I was seven, but I still remember the tangy taste of those labels that I licked and pressed against the wood.

I say all this by way of introduction to the story of my biggest collection, the one from 1951, the one that grew larger than any of the others, even comic books, the one that ended my collecting career. The year I turned seventeen was the biggest year of my life. I never figured out which label to paste on the cubbyhole that held the collection I made that year. "Try MOUNTING CONFUSION," Ferg suggested one day, elbowing me in case I'd missed the joke, but I didn't think it was funny. Even now it's hard to laugh. (Of course my brother, Theo, is the one who's supposed to have inherited the Baum sense of humor.)

In 1951 I compiled old family photos; Dad's postcards from California, along with Arlie's from Paris; want ads and Korean War maps out of the *Times*; those accident photos that Foxx sent; Ferg's cryptograms; and the essays I wrote for English and history class, including of course the JRP, the Junior Research Paper.

It promised to become the best collection I had ever created—the collection of collections, the masterpiece. It spilled over the cubbyholes with a life of its own. Too much life, I began to realize. This wasn't the Dodgers' weekly batting averages or a little wooden horse on wheels. This was jobs and marriages, Communists beaten up in the streets. Before the year ended—before the Dodgers lost the pennant and after I was sure I had lost my father—I gave up the collection. Gave up my collecting career. And went on about the rest of my life.

■ ■ ■

I didn't know it at the time, but the 1951 collection began on the November night in 1950 when I lay half asleep and heard that argument through the bedroom wall.

"Not sign?" my mother yelled. "*Mein Gott*, what kind of fool are you, not to sign?"

"My name is my own," Dad yelled back.

I pressed my hand against my lips to stop them from trembling. My parents argued sometimes, but never like this, bitterly, as if they wanted to hurt each other. I pressed harder, against the edge of my teeth. "But how will we eat now?" Mom said. "You throw away your job like one of those baseballs of yours."

"Like a baseball? You are funny, Lise."

"This is no joke. No joke, Samuel."

"But I *have* my job."

"Until one day the boss says, 'Thank you very much, Mr. Baum, *auf wiedersehen.*'"

"Lischen, I tell you . . ."

The rest of his sentence was lost amid the creak of bedsprings, the hiss of water from the bathroom, the clapping of venetian blinds. And then I heard him say: ". . . a free country, isn't it?"

"*Na ja,* maybe not so free these days, as your friend Willy learned the hard way."

"Don't whip dead horses."

"Maybe Barbara could sit home like a silly wife while he ran around like a Communist cowboy. But I won't."

"Why must you always . . . ?"

"I won't be treated like . . ."

The noise gathered behind the wall. I couldn't stop it. My stomach hurt. I rolled and unrolled the blanket edge. Something—a shoe? a fist?—slammed against the wall.

"Is there no loyalty to me?" she said, in a voice thick

with rage or maybe tears. "You promised, Samuel. 'Never again,' you promised."

"Don't start that old business."

"Did it stop?"

The bed creaked.

"Why can't you give me for once what I ask?" she said.

Metal hangers rasped along the metal bar in the closet.

"Sign your name—is that too much to ask?"

The door handle rattled.

"Where are you going?" Her voice was suddenly high and timid, like a girl's, and I pictured her hands reaching out toward him.

"I'm taking a walk."

The bedroom door clicked and the front door clicked and the apartment turned terribly still. For an hour I listened to my own breaths, like someone buried under a ton of snow, until I heard the front door open, heard my father tiptoe down the hall to their bedroom, and I dared to fall asleep.

A month later he left again—really left. He sent a picture postcard from Arizona or maybe New Mexico, one of those square states out there.

Dear Murray,

Can you believe a New Year's Day with the sun so hot I'm wearing shorts? That's the desert for you. Look at the caktus picture on the other side.

When midnight came, I thought of you. Were you home eating *Pfannkuchen* like we used to? Or out with friends at a party? Then I remembered your midnight came two hours before mine.

I will write as soon as I reach Callifornia.

Love Dad

I tacked that picture over my desk, next to the Dodgers' schedule for '51 and Miss Moran's mimeographed homework assignments. After a few days, I got sick of looking at those barbed arms reaching across the desert. That was when I shoved the card into an empty cubbyhole. That was when my last collection began.

WINTER

1

Every morning Theo and I would grab our lunch bags and go off to school as Mom called "*Wiedersehen*, boys." Every afternoon when we came home she would call "Hello, darlings," in the middle of typing a letter or talking on the phone. Every day the *New York Times* was delivered, the mail was delivered, and Kenneth Banghart reported the NBC World News. Nobody mentioned that Dad was gone. At dinner the three of us would talk as if he had gone around the corner to the grocery store for a loaf of bread. After I did my algebra problems and memorized French verbs, I would talk with Arlie until Mom made me get off the phone, and then I would lie there in the dark, beside the ticking clock, feeling the wave of sadness wash over me.

One morning, a week after he left, I awoke from a dream about Dad and threw up in the toilet.

We were in Ebbets Field, in our usual spot behind first base, when a foul ball off Furillo's bat looped toward us. "It's yours, Murray," Dad shouted. I grabbed my glove, crunching peanut shells beneath my shoes as I stood and squinted happily into the golden sun. Down fell the ball, barely revolving, growing large, blocking out the sun, dark as Dad's blue flannel shirt, huge as his chest. "Help!" I cried, but he didn't answer, and then I saw that the seat beside me was empty.

"You have no fever," Mom said, stroking my forehead. "Perhaps one piece too many of my torte."

"Don't mention that word. Don't even spell it."

"You'll live." She leaned down to kiss my cheek. "I speak as a former nurse now, and not a mother. Sleep while I'm gone."

But I felt too awful to sleep. On the other edge of the country the sun hadn't arrived yet. People out there were still working their way through dreams. My father lay in his red pajamas—"like firemen wear," he had told us when we were still young enough to believe it. He was probably snoring, although he always denied it: "Humming, perhaps, but never snoring." My father was sleeping in Apt. 4, 2205 Cahuenga Blvd., numbers and names I already knew by heart, and a room I had never seen. It was as if someone had cut him out of a family photograph and pasted him on a blank white page.

When I closed my eyes, I saw Theo and me standing on either side of Dad, each of us holding one of his hands in the photograph that I had taken off my desk the day before and buried beneath the sweaters in the bureau drawer. Tiny ghosts. I hugged the pillow, trying not to throw up again. Was it worse to spit it out or hold it in?

Maybe I should have gone to school. But you couldn't go to school with your eyeballs red from crying.

Why? Why had he left? When was he coming back? Why didn't Mom talk about it? Why?

A car splashed through the slush in the street below. The refrigerator stopped moaning in the kitchen. Gus chirped in his cage in the living room, once, twice, and fell asleep. The apartment was unbearably quiet. I turned on the radio and let its voices carry me into the afternoon. "My True Story." "Break the Bank." "Young Doctor Malone." "Double or Nothing."

"That's absolutely correct, Margie." Applause. "Such a smart girl. And pretty, too, isn't she, folks?" Louder applause.

"Please, Mr. O'Keefe. You're making me blush."

On Sunday evenings at ten o'clock—"$64 Question" time—the four of us would sit around the living-room radio, holding our bells tightly so they wouldn't ring by mistake. When the question was easy, and all four of us shook the bells and shouted the answer at once, Gus would flap like crazy.

"Now for twenty dollars, Margie, can you tell me what's wrong with this sentence: 'We have nothing to offer but blood, sweat, and fears'?"

"*Tears*. It should be *tears*."

"Absolutely correct." Applause. "Now you decide if you want to try for forty dollars while we hear from Campbell Soups, the home-cooked meal in a can."

I flicked off the radio. Soup, sweat, and tears, your home-cooked kick in the can.

I propped one bare foot on the other and sighted down my shin toward the Snider photograph on the door. With my left eye closed, it was a straight line along Duke's muscled forearm to the top of his thirty-six-inch Louisville Slugger and then out to the gray sky beyond Ebbets Field. My big toe cracked faintly, like the crack of a line drive.

The apartment was too quiet.

"He's on a special assignment," that was all Mom had said. Mrs. Baum, how do you explain your husband's sudden departure for California? "He's on a special assignment for the publishing company." When do you expect him back? "I can't say." Special assignment: who but Theo would buy that?

The front door slammed. "Murray, I'm home."

"Hi, Sprout."

"I told you not to call me that."

"Sorry. One day I'll remember."

"Yeah, sure. One day you'll give me a Dodgers yearbook, too, like you promised me five years ago." He was chinning himself in the doorway.

"If you keep that up, your arms are going to hang below your knees."

"Eight. Nine. Ten." He fell to the floor, bounced to his feet, blew a pink bubble of gum, popped it. In his oversize baseball shirt, he looked skinnier than usual. "So how you feeling, Murray?"

"Okay."

"You don't look okay."

"Since when are you a mother?"

Then the phone rang and we ran down the hall, but he ran faster.

"Hello? Oh, nuts," he said. "Murray, it's for you. It's Arlie. Or one of your other girlfriends."

I grabbed the phone. "Hi."

"Hi."

"Hi," I repeated, pointing Theo out of the room.

"Were you sick today?"

"Nothing fatal."

"I missed you."

"I missed you more."

My girlfriend. I had never said those words aloud to anyone, including her. It wasn't exactly superstition; not-saying was a reminder that one day I could lose, as suddenly as I had gained, this wonderful girl. Light-blue eyes. Loose blond hair. I loved everything about her. Most of all, her voice: throaty, thick with undertones, occasionally hesitating before she delivered a phrase, as if entrusting you with it.

I tipped back the chair and cradled the phone against my shoulder. "Talk to me. Tell me everything."

"You first."

My news went by fast, since there had been only bad dreams and radio shows, and I couldn't tell her—not even her—about the dreams. Her news took longer: morning classes (French dull, biology duller, but after English, Miss Moran had sent get-well wishes to "my star student," quote unquote), lunch (meat loaf and string beans, and Linda said that Eileen said that Ruth Pearlman was going steady with that football player, Billy Biceps), afternoon classes, and homework.

I reached for a pencil and wrote on a shopping bag: *Alg, do last 10 probs on p. 106; read 1st 3 pgs of Gide essay, underlining every idiom; read ch 6 for Hist, three causes of WWI.*

"Here's the good news," Arlie said. "We complained that *Jude the Obscure* was deadly long and boring, so Miss Moran cut the assignment in half." Everyone had burst into applause, and then Miss Moran had blushed and given a twenty-minute lecture explaining Thomas Hardy's philosophy of determinism. "Not fatalism," Arlie said. "Not doom branded by God on your forehead at birth." Determinism said we make our own choices in life. Usually mistaken choices. "We write out our own doom," Arlie concluded.

"Cheery fellow. Thomas Hardyharhar."

A bell rang in the middle of her laugh, and Theo came at me, waving the egg timer. "Time's up, my turn for the phone."

Ardent farewells aren't easy when your kid brother is standing at your elbow. "I'll see you in homeroom," I said.

"Here's a kiss for you."

"And for you."

I should have started in on all that homework. Instead I walked through the apartment, room after room, as if I were looking for something. A column of comic books at least three feet high rose in the middle of Theo's room, surrounded by a tribe of little green robots. On the living-room table, Mom's typewriter lay under its gray plastic hood, and Gus sat motionless on his perch. The box beneath the mail flap on the front door was empty. Three pairs of high-heeled shoes stood on the bedroom floor, green and brown and black, all facing the same way, waiting for Mom to walk them somewhere. On Dad's desk there was a half-open scissors and nothing else.

But the hall closet was full of him: the padded shoulders of his everyday coat; the velvet collar of his coat for the opera and anniversary parties; the wide red scarf with *SJB* knitted into it. I knew Dad hadn't moved out, because his clothes were still hanging in the closet. Come to think of it, though, in southern California he wouldn't need winter clothes.

I sat at my desk and read a paragraph of *Jude the Obscure* over and over, listening for the sound of a key in the front door.

■ ■ ■

The music began inside my dream, breaking up an important conversation with somebody, and then I sat up in the darkness and heard the music coming from Mom's room. The green hands of the clock were folded over the number 1. The floorboards chilled my feet as I moved down the hall toward the half-open bedroom door. "Mom?" Closer. Louder. "Mom?"

Then the music was gone, and I heard only the rush of blood in my ears.

"Murray?" She was lying with a washcloth on her forehead. Her skin seemed one size too big, pulling loose from the jaw. "I fell asleep with the radio playing. Those pills, they're too strong. But I couldn't face a third night without sleep." She patted the bed. "Come talk with me." She tapped a cigarette against her thumbnail and lit it, all in one gesture. "In the old days I sat on *your* bed when *you* couldn't sleep."

"And you'd tell me the next installment of 'Captain Murray Marvel.'"

"He was rescuing the kaiser's daughter from the Apache Indians. Then you went into seventh grade and listened to those radio programs instead of me." She blew a slow stream of smoke. "It seems long ago. As if we were other people." She coughed and snuffed out the cigarette.

I yawned. She pulled the blanket over her arms.

"Do you think about him?" she asked.

"Yes."

"So do I. All the time."

"Yes, all the time." I sat rigidly on the bed—his side of the bed.

"But what could I have done to keep him here? Every night I ask What? What? All night. *Verrückt*." Her left hand took mine. "I shouldn't drag you into this. But you are my son."

I waited for more, but she remained silent, so I asked, "When is he coming back?"

"Who knows?"

"I don't understand. It's been two weeks."

"At sixteen, what does anyone understand? When I was your age, let's see"—her fingers counted against my wrist—"it was 1919, and the war had just ended. Like today, but this is America and that was Germany. Bombed-out buildings everywhere. No fruit, no meat. Only turnips, everything turnips, even marmalade made of turnips. All the cats in Berlin disappeared because people ate them. I wondered what had happened to the happy little life I used to have."

"What does this have to do with Dad?"

"*Ja, ja,* I'm getting there. Your father is a smart man, but sometimes he does not think ahead. 'Now, Lischen,' he says, 'in the words of my Polish grandfather, "Thinking will not make the sun shine."' But what do Polish grandfathers know about American loyalty oaths?" She pulled out another cigarette and held it, unlit. "You know what a loyalty oath is, Murray?"

"You swear loyalty to the government and say you've never been a Communist."

"Exactly. Well, last year his bosses asked him to sign such an oath, and he refused. He is no Communist. No traitor. No nothing. Yet he wouldn't sign. 'We left Nazi Germany to escape dictatorship,' he said, 'and I do not welcome it here.' That's all he said. *Schluss!* Finished. Nothing."

"But what about his right of free speech? In history class—"

"These are bad times for rights. Alger Hiss, those movie stars—read the newspaper. Any day the company may fire him, and then what? A bottle of milk is twenty-five cents now, and Theo drinks like a cow."

"But what does the loyalty oath have to do with his leaving?"

"It seems to be a kind of test they make for him, at least

so your father believes. 'Open up a California market for our art books, and we will not call you a Communist.' So now you understand?"

She took a pack of matches from the drawer. I watched her light the cigarette and exhale a stream of smoke.

"If that's all there is," I said.

Her lips tightened as she stared at me. I breathed as quietly as possible, waiting.

"All?" she said, stubbing out the cigarette in the ashtray. "People go along for years. Then they find out what's what." She closed her eyes. "Samuel had a friend I didn't like. For right reasons or wrong, what does it matter? I didn't like her. But he was stubborn about it, and we had arguments. Unpleasant arguments." She was looking at me again. "I speak to you, Murray, as a man tonight, which I hope is all right."

I nodded to keep her talking. I nodded, but I could barely hear her through the noise inside my head.

"Take a week in a hotel by yourself, figure things out, I said to him. But then the boss assigned him to the California market, so . . ." She smiled faintly. "So here we are."

"How long?" I whispered.

"Not a minute longer than necessary, I promise you." She yawned. "Any more questions?"

Why? Why? *Why?*

A second yawn. "Then sleep well, darling."

2

My upper lip felt red and prickly from the razor. Soon I'd have to shave twice a week. In the mirror, however, it looked like a regular pale New York winter upper lip. Actually, it wasn't my lip but the whatever-you-call-it just above my lip, with the little indentation.

"Put another nickel in, in the nickelodeon": I whistled my Friday-night theme song while I combed my hair. After I splashed on some of Dad's cologne, the whatever-you-call-it above my lip stung. Leo "The Lip" Durocher, Murray "The Lip" Baum. The white shirt hugged my chest, still warm from Mom's iron. Duke Baum. Preacher Baum. Pee Wee Baum. Before becoming enshrined in the Hall of Fame, I'd have to work with Red Barber on the nickname problem. Red Baum?

"Murray, this is the last time I tell you. It's seven o'clock. Now either come out of there or admit constipation."

"Mo-om, for Chri— for Pete's sake."

I took a last look in the mirror and opened the door.

"Oh, Murray, you look handsome," she said. "Except what's this?" The thumb, fueled with spit, zoomed toward my face. I ducked; she grabbed and rubbed. "Shaving cream! *Ach*, such a man. Next he'll be putting cigars in his coat pocket."

For a week now, ever since the night of the music, she had been the usual Mom again. Or at least she had been putting on a good act.

"I'll be home by midnight."

"Have fun," she said.

From his room, Theo shouted, "Don't do anything I wouldn't do."

I could taste the coming of snow. It was out there above Pennsylvania, sifting across the bleachers at Forbes Field, moving steadily eastward, churning the sky. I walked down Lexington Avenue close to the buildings, but the cold wind still managed to gust inside my coat and shove me into doorways. "All I want is loving you and music, music, music": I hummed myself toward Arlie, one block at a time. Sixty-third, Sixty-second, Sixty-first, Bloomingdale's. From the subway stairs came a warm sour breath, the leftover from rush hour. Fifty-third, -second, -first, and music, music, music.

The moment I stepped out of the elevator, I heard Foxx's voice. I walked through the open door and into Arlie's living room, and there he stood, with one hand raised high, addressing Arlie and Wendy (one of his countless dates) on the sofa. ". . . heads shaped exactly like bullets. Hey, Baum, we almost called the Bureau of Missing Persons for you, but we forgot your name."

"Funny as a crutch, Foxx," I said. He was wearing his usual black sweater, this time with a long white scarf.

"Actually, I'm funny as two crutches. Now where was I before I was so rudely interrupted?"

"At the Horn and Hardart," Wendy said. "With the Mafia."

I took Arlie's hands and stepped toward her, closing my eyes for a kiss.

"So here were these two enormous guys at the next table," Foxx said, "muttering like gorillas to each other." Arlie's lips touched mine. "Perfect thugs, straight out of a movie. Hey Baum, quit kissing Arlie and listen to me."

She turned toward him with a laugh. "Oh, Danny, you're such a spoilsport." Over her shoulder she said, "Guess what, Mur. Danny met up with Frank Costello at a cafeteria today."

Another of Foxx's bizarre stories. "And who is Frank Costello?" I asked.

"The famous racketeer," he said. "King of the underworld. Don't you read the paper, Baum? So here I am with my glass of milk and a book, trying not to look like I'm watching these bullet-headed guys with big shoulders and guns bulging under their coats. Now this man comes strolling up to them, with a thin cigar in his mouth and a very expensive coat and a familiar face." Foxx walked a few steps left, then right, his head cocked sideways. "For a moment I'm not sure, and then I know: Frank Costello!"

Foxx talked more than anyone I knew. Words came out of his mouth as if a little man were inside there with an electric typewriter.

"The two gorillas stand up with hands inside their pockets, and one gets a cup of coffee for Costello, and then they all lean their heads together to talk. I shift my chair a few inches in their direction, thinking I'm going to overhear names and dates, info that Kefauver and his Crime Committee will be glad to get. With a thousand-dollar reward for yours truly, of course. I'm reaching into my pocket for a pencil when I feel this hand on my shoulder, and this ugly voice says, 'Hey, kid, finish your milk and go.' The kind of voice you don't want to argue with." He ran his fingers through the mop of curls dangling over his ears. "So here I am, a thousand dollars poorer, and the Mafia lives on."

"Why, Danny, you could have been killed!" Wendy said in a mock Southern accent.

Arlie tugged on his scarf. "How do you always manage

to find an adventure out there?'' she said, smiling up at him.

''Just a knack,'' Foxx said.

''Let's go,'' I said. ''We're late for the movie.''

Why had I agreed to this double date? Arlie thought Foxx was ''entertaining,'' but I hoped we would lose him in the subway, or leave him at an all-night barber shop for a haircut. No such luck. All four of us ended up in the Loews Lexington balcony, with popcorn, Tootsie Rolls, Cokes, and Foxx explaining why *All About Eve* had been better on stage than on screen, despite Bette Davis, until finally Arlie leaned across me and said, ''Danny, hush.''

As Eve worked her guile on Bill and wooed him away from the aging Margo Channing, I began to feel depressed.

''Arlie,'' I whispered. The silver light of the movie trembled on her face, as if she were floating under silver water. ''Are you happy?''

She squeezed my hand. ''Shh.''

Afterward, we went back to her apartment, just the two of us. We embraced in our favorite corner of the couch, the one farthest from her parents' bedroom. I tried to match my breaths to hers. I pressed my face into her hair, inhaling the lavender-soap smell of her neck.

''What are you thinking about?'' she whispered. Mr. and Mrs. Thomas went to sleep early, but it was best to be careful.

''You.''

''All of me, or just the good parts?''

''All about Arlie. I'm taking notes behind your back,'' I said, ''with a tiny pencil and pad.''

She giggled. ''You're so clever.''

I kissed her. ''Aren't you glad to be alone, without them?''

"Sure." She traced a finger along my eyebrow. "But Danny's fun. You never know what he's going to do next."

"I don't want to talk about him."

She leaned back and looked at me, pressing her lips together tightly.

"He's a clown, Arlie," I said.

"I thought you didn't want to talk about him."

"Why do you flirt with him?"

"I don't."

"Look, Arlie, either you're dating me or you're not." My throat hurt. It was hard to be angry in whispers. "Well, are you or aren't you?"

"You've been mad at everybody tonight. You were even mad at Bette Davis."

"I hated the movie."

"Are you having your period?"

"Very funny."

She took my face between her hands and said fiercely, "What in hell is bugging you?"

"I just don't want anything to happen to us," I answered.

3

January 21, 1951

Dear Dad,

You wouldn't believe how hot it was yesterday. Sixty-two degrees, the radio said. During lunch period we played basketball on the *out*door court—Jeep, Bobby L., and some other juniors—and our shirts were like wash-cloths when we went to history class. Mr. Sklar told us to go out and find dry shirts. "This is not a locker room," he said in that ominous voice of his. "I want your brains, not your bodies." Mr. Sklar is a terror.

In assembly there was a hot and heavy debate on the draft. Some of the senior boys were worrying that the draft age will be lowered to eighteen and they won't get to go to college. Bobby L., on the other hand, stood up and said we ought to volunteer because it's a privilege to fight for America, but of course his father was a Marine. What do you think is going to happen, Dad?

I'm not used to writing letters to you. I picture you curling a finger in your hair as you read this. How are you? Thanks for the postcard of the movie stars' handprints in the sidewalk. Speaking of stars, last week I saw *All About Eve*. If you see George Sanders, give him my best wishes.

This weather makes me think of baseball season. Gil Hodges says he's looking forward to seeing the three of us at Opening Day as usual. Ha ha.

Miss Moran would give this letter a C– for incoherence. I better stop now before I do any more damage.

I miss you.

Love,
Murray

January 24

Murray and Theo:

I'm sorry not to write in so long. This new job keeps me busy, and so does loosing my way around this city. The picture on the other side, from an aeroplane, shows you how big L.A. is.

I feel funny without a coat in January. And the ocean is on the wrong side. And no one cares about the Dodgers. No, I haven't seen any movie stars, but I'll keep my eyes open.

I miss you my children allways, and love you very much.

Your Dad

February 5

Dear Dad,

Everything here is as usual. Black slush on the streets. Too much homework. I'm just getting over a cold. The good news is I got an 89 on a history test, which was second highest in the class (second to Ferguson—who else!). And I got another A in English Lit.

You didn't answer my question two weeks ago about the draft.

I'm sending you this obituary of Eddie Bettan, "the Dodgers' Number One Fan." Can you imagine seeing every home game for forty years? That's 3,010 games. And what did he get for all his loyalty? A television set and a trophy and an ovation at Ebbets Field. Someone should write a play called *Death of a Dodger Fan*, which would be like *Death of a Salesman*, except shorter and sadder.

When are you coming home?

Love,
Murray

■ ■ ■

The little yellow paper slid out of my looseleaf notebook as I settled onto the living-room rug. *As things would have it, we do not know what comes next:* that was what Ferguson had written on the note he handed me during history class on Friday. And here it was, Sunday night—homework night—and instead of doing my homework, I was rereading his sentence for the twentieth time.

As things would have *what*? And in any case, why

couldn't we know the next step? When I had questioned him, he had shrugged. "It entered my brain like lightning, a message in the dark," he said. And what did *that* mean?

I didn't have time to worry about Ferguson's messages. It was eight o'clock, and I had to write ten metaphors for Miss Moran before morning. Preferably ten excellent metaphors. After seven consecutive A's, I didn't want to break my hitting streak. *METAPHORS*, I wrote on the top line. I stared at the blank page; the page stared back.

"Murray, why don't I see your friends anymore?" Mom interrupted my trance. "Arlie hasn't dropped in for weeks now. And that nice boy Sol, and Jeep. Why don't you have a party?"

They hadn't been visiting because I hadn't been inviting. After all, what if one of them looked up halfway through dinner and asked, "Hey, where's your dad?" Glad you asked, Jeep. My dad just took off for California for a month or a year because he didn't want to sign his name. Pass the mashed potatoes. The next day, rumors would be running around Harrison High. The kid without a father. I'd walk down the hall and people would smile at me the way you smile at cancer patients.

I had told Ferguson about Dad and the loyalty oath. Then I was sorry I had, because he didn't seem very interested. "I can imagine," he said. Just "I can imagine"—that was all he said. Maybe Theo had the right idea; he told everyone, "My dad's in California," as if it were some kind of accomplishment.

METAPHORS. BY MURRAY BAUM. At this rate I would finish shortly before senior year began.

A lot of crunching and scraping was taking place across the room, where Theo sat on the sofa. He was scooping vanilla ice cream from a bowl with a pretzel stick while pretending to do his homework.

Mom sat in the easy chair knitting click-click-click at her usual supersonic speed.

METAPHORS. BY MURRAY BAUM. When Eddie Bettan died, we did not know what came next. He was always . . .

Crunch, scrape, click. "For God's sake, can't you stop that noise? I've got some homework to do here," I said.

Mom's mouth tightened in what Dad called patience ("Uh-oh, boys, watch out for patience"). "If you need quiet," she said, "work in your room."

"But it's Sunday night. We always . . ." I couldn't say the rest of it. Sunday night when Edgar Bergen and Charlie McCarthy talked to us through the red-cloth window of the big radio there in the corner.

"Now, Charlie, I'm disappointed in you, winking at that blond girl in the restaurant."

"Well, Edgar, I think you had a hand in it, don't you?"

"One more wisecrack out of you, young man, and I'll give you back to the lumberyard."

Mom would smile as she bent over her knitting needles. Theo, sitting on Dad's knee, would giggle, not always because he understood the joke but because Dad's finger was strumming his ribs in that spot under his left arm where he was ticklish. Every Sunday night at eight o'clock, until six weeks ago.

Theo dropped the pretzel into the dish and stood up. "We forgot to turn on—"

"Shut up, Theo." My arms trembled against my chest, trying to contain whatever was heaving inside there.

"But Murray"—he was walking toward the radio, smiling—"it's Charlie McCarthy time." An innocent smile.

"No!"

"Look at the clock."

I grabbed his ankle. "No, goddamn it."

"Hey, what's your problem?" He looked down, trying to shake free.

I tightened my grip. Dumbo! Acting as if life were hunky-dory, when any idiot, anybody who really cared, anybody who really cared about Dad . . . "Damn it." I toppled him. His knees thudded against my ribs; his elbow banged my skull. And then I was on top of him, straddling him, pressing all of my weight onto his belly, putting a fist where that smile had been.

"Stop it!" I felt Mom tugging at my shoulder. "Stop it!" she screamed into my ear. Then she grabbed my hair and pulled, one time, very hard.

I rolled off him, crouched on my hands and knees as I caught my breath, and slowly stood up. Theo lay whimpering amid a mess of pretzels, knitting needles, notebook paper, and ice cream.

"*Unverschämt!*" Mom poked me in the chest. "Apologize, or else."

"No. No," I screamed, and I turned my back on her. "How could you do this to him?" I shouted from the hall.

I slammed my door, dove onto the bed, and pounded a fist against the mattress. Then I lowered my face into the soft darkness of my pillow and began sobbing for Sunday nights as they used to be.

First there would be the bouncy Coke commercial, next the lumbering music for Mortimer Snerd. Now Dad's face would widen into that special grin. "Boys, it's time. Duh, duh," he said, his voice slurring, "duh, duh," his jaw swinging loose.

"Tell the people your name," Bergen said.

"Mortimer."

"Yes . . . Mortimer what?"

"Mortimer What. No, no, that isn't it."

"What is your *last* name?"

"Mortimer . . . um . . . gosh . . . Mortimer."

"Your last name."

"Duh . . . I know it as well as I know my own name."

Theo and I tried to imitate Mortimer, but only Dad could catch the dumb earnest rhythm. In the second hour of singsong prayer at Sol's bar mitzvah, there was Dad across the aisle, the yarmulke perched on his light-brown hair. When he sensed me watching, he had turned just a fraction, pushed his tongue below his lower lip, and wagged his jaw—"duh, duh"—so that among the hundred people watching Sol's tedious entry into manhood, only he and I had shared the Snerdish irreverence. Oh, Dad.

There was a knock on my door.

"Go away," I screamed into the pillow. But the knocking persisted.

"It's me, Theo."

"Go away."

The knocking stopped. "It's time to oil our gloves," said Theo.

The weekly ritual of oiling our baseball gloves, pounding the pockets a hundred times with our fists, and tying the hardballs inside so that we'd be ready to play when spring came. "All right," I said. I opened the door and we sat cross-legged on the floor, working on our gloves. Somewhere in the middle of a debate about whether Furillo or Snider had the better arm, I risked looking at him. His upper lip was puffy, and a red bruise trailed across his right cheek. "I'm sorry, Theo."

"Why did you hit me?"

"I don't know." I pounded the pocket of my glove a few times. "How can you forget Dad so easily?"

"I haven't."

"You act like everything's the same."

"Ouch." He ran his tongue along his lip.

"I said I'm sorry."

"Just because I keep going to school and getting my allowance and all, that doesn't mean I've forgotten him. Anyhow, he's coming back."

"How do you know he's coming back?"

"Are you crazy? Of course he is."

"It's been six weeks and . . . and two days."

"My prayers will take care of it."

"Your what?"

"Prayers. What you whisper when it's the bottom of the ninth and the Dodgers are behind by two and the winning run comes to the plate with Roy Campanella. He discards his warm-up bat, digs in his back foot." Theo's voice slipped into Red Barber's drawl. We had listened to that drawl for a million hours, and Theo had learned Red's every phrase and chuckle and pause. "That's when I cross my fingers, and if it's a really big game, I whisper a prayer, you know, to God. Mostly it works." He tossed me the can of neat's-foot oil.

It was almost funny: here was this thirteen-year-old kid comforting me as if I were *his* younger brother.

"Listen, Theo, this isn't some ball game. It's Dad. Things won't turn good just because you say a prayer. Dad left, and he won't come back until"—I shook my head—"until he wants to."

"But why wouldn't he want to?"

"Well, he and Mom, you know, they've had those disagreements," I said. Theo watched me with blank eyes. "There's that loyalty-oath thing."

Theo folded his glove and stood up. "Dad will come

home. All we have to do is be here waiting.'' He yawned. ''I got to get me some shut-eye, pardner, 'cause I got a long trail to ride to school in the morning.''

I stretched out full-length on the floor and stared at the ceiling. Was Theo acting dumb, or was he really dumb? Or was he smart to be dumb? I was so tired of trying to figure things out. As things would have it, nothing came next. *Dear Mrs. Bettan, I am terribly sorry about your husband's death and wish to join you in the bleachers for the memorial service.*

4

The elevator cables clacked and Frank the elevator man told me another of his ''seeing-eye dog'' jokes as we rode the seven floors up to home. But all I listened to was the gurgling of my stomach. A salami sandwich on rye, plus an Oreo cookie if I could sneak it past Mom. (''Ah, ah, is that a cookie I smell, young man? Sugar is not food.'')

She was in the living room talking with a man I had never seen. ''B. B. Wright. My pleasure,'' he said, shaking my hand while the rest of him—cheeks, chins, and belly—shook, too. ''A pleasure to meet you, young man,'' he said without a smile, and then he lowered himself into a chair.

''Mr. Wright has come to discuss some technical business,'' Mom said. ''So dinner will be a little late.''

''I'll eat a snack.''

''Some snack.'' She turned to Mr. Wright. ''The way this boy eats, I must buy an icebox just for him.''

No one joined her laugh. Mr. Wright was busy arranging papers, and I was backpedaling out of there.

B. B. Wright, Atty.: I remembered the copper name plate on an office down the hall from Dad's. Did his friends call him B.B., or just B.? I sliced the salami, spread the mustard and laid down the lettuce, cut the sandwich corner to corner, and slid a couple of Oreos into my pocket. What was he doing here? That dark-blue three-piece suit didn't belong in our living room; it was like a uniformed policeman come to report an accident. *Attorney* sounded more ominous than *lawyer.* I sat at my desk, chewing the sandwich and trying to decide whether to do French or algebra. Finally the front door clicked and Mom came in.

"*Tschia!*" She sat on the bed and clapped her hands. "Lawyer talk. I understand English and German and a *soupçon* of French, but lawyers talk a language of their own." She lit a cigarette, inhaled, exhaled. I wished she wouldn't fill up my room with smoke, but I didn't say anything.

"I called Mr. Wright after I read a letter sent to your father. Perhaps I shouldn't have opened it, but I'm the wife and there it was, from 'Mr. Hersey, Executive Vice President,' with 'please forward,' so I opened it." She blew out a thin stream of smoke.

"Was it about the loyalty oath?"

"*Ja,* when Samuel and those twenty others refused to sign, Mr. Hersey had a problem on his hands. He didn't want to fire twenty-one people. So he decided to 'save face'—that's how Mr. Wright put it—save face by letting the department heads sign in the name of everyone else. Then he sent this letter saying silence is not refusal. Silence is—what was his word?—silence is *consent.* Now if Samuel can keep his mouth shut, everything will be fine."

"So Dad's job is safe?"

"That's what Mr. Wright said."

"If only Dad doesn't call attention to himself?"

"I suppose so."

"Are you sure?"

"Must you keep asking questions?" She ground the cigarette against the side of my wastebasket. "I have to start dinner."

I opened the window and leaned into the night. Nothing but gray sky, gray skyscrapers, and the yellow roofs of taxicabs. I could stand here for hours shouting "Fire," and nobody would notice.

I tiptoed into the hall and looked toward the living room. Dark down there. Quiet. Too quiet. What if Attorney Wright was still sitting on the couch? But when I flipped on the lights, there was only the letter on the table, waiting for me.

January 4, 1951

Dear Mr. Baum:

This letter addresses two matters.

1. As part of our year-end review of employee performance, I have consulted with Mr. Philip Krulewich, Senior Vice President of Marketing, and personally reviewed your file. According to the records, nonfiction sales in your Middle Atlantic Region declined by 2.1 percent in 1950, in contrast to an average increase of 7.6 percent in our six other regions. Mr. Krulewich tells me that he discussed this matter with you twice and that you mentioned disagreements with Jacob Silver concerning advertising strategy.

It is my understanding that your consent to temporary reassignment in the California Region is an effort to resolve this situation. I trust that, with the benefit of a new perspective, you will eventually return to the Home Office on a more effective basis.

2. After consultation with the Board of Directors, I call your attention to the following statement, which, as of November 30, 1950, has been adopted as official company policy.

In the absence of evidence to the contrary, we assume that all employees have affirmed their loyalty to the Government of the United States by virtue of Section 18, Clause 8, in the contract which you signed when originally employed by this company. Furthermore, we assume that the signature subscribed to a loyalty oath by each Division Head constitutes an affidavit for all the members of his Division.

Sincerely,
Stanley L. Hersey
Executive Vice President

I laid down the letter. It was a case of mistaken identity. This Mr. Baum was not the man who was my father. Look closely: the nose, the hat, the wedding ring, they'll prove the error.

The letter was dated January 4, weeks after the argument with Mom in the bedroom. Had he already known he was leaving? "My name is my own!" Had he already known that someone was going to sign his name for him? When had he known? What else must he do to prove himself to the Home Office?

The questions ganged up in my head.

I wanted to crumple the letter and throw it on the floor.

I wanted Dad to walk smiling into Mr. Hersey's office and stand beside the other Mr. Baum. "Look for yourself, Mr. Hersey: that one is an impostor."

Snowflakes drifted against the windowpanes and melted in long streaks. I was talking out loud to an empty living room. Dad had been away for seven weeks. Forty-nine days he had not opened the front door. He was receding, smaller and smaller, too small for identification.

Back in my room, the wind had blown my desktop bare. Homework, envelopes, pencils—everything lay all over the floor.

■ ■ ■

The Knights of Buddy's Round Table met every Monday and Friday afternoon: Ferguson, Foxx, Sol, Bobby L., Jeep, and myself. The six of us sat around the red Formica table (which was not round but rectangular) in the back of Buddy's Grill on Fourteenth Street. Bobby L. invariably ate three hot dogs; after the second one he would look down at his belly and say, "If the table keeps moving away, I'm going to have to grow longer arms." Jeep specialized in Buddy's chocolate egg creams, no matter how cold the weather. When I had forty-five cents left from my allowance, I'd order a cheeseburger, medium rare. As for Ferguson, he had turned vegetarian in ninth grade and ate nothing at all. He sipped hot chocolate from a thermos and presided.

Usually he was the one—King Ferg—who devised the theme for the day: science fiction, Eddie Fisher, subway maps, Freud, whatever happened to pop out of that mind of his. But on this particular afternoon Sol set the agenda. He pushed aside the cups and plates and unfolded the newspaper. "I'm famous," he announced with what Foxx called his cocker-spaniel smile.

"Get appointed to the Supreme Court?"

"Next year. Did you guys hear about those teachers who got fired for being Communists? Well, my dad was their lawyer, and you can read his name right here on page fifteen of the *Times*."

Root beer bubbled into my nose and set my eyes watering. I could hardly see as we leaned over to look where his finger pointed. *Mr. Louis Cammer*. There he was, big as life.

"No shit," someone murmured.

"But your father lost," I said. "The teachers were fired."

"That's just the first round. He's going to file suit in district court and get their jobs back."

"Fat chance," said Foxx. "Once you've been called a Red, you're worse off than a mouse in a cathouse. That's a quote from my brother Frank, and he ought to know."

Bobby meowed, and Jeep laughed.

"Let me get this straight, Foxx," said Sol. A vein throbbed in his neck. "Are you saying my father's a loser?"

"Well, I wouldn't bet a dollar on the Pirates winning the pennant, either."

"What are you saying?"

The ice was clattering in my glass. Root beer sloshed over my fingers. I set it down carefully, looking around to see if anyone had noticed, but they were all too busy shouting.

"All I said was—"

"Who wants to bet on his dad?"

"You're on, Jeep. Here's my buck."

Then Ferguson stood up and silenced them with a hand. "I have an announcement," he said in his throaty voice. "Today is February ninth, and that's the first anniversary of the Round Table."

We looked at one another almost furtively. Anniversary? Tenth grade had gone, and eleventh grade had come. The Yankees had beaten the Phillies in the World Series. In a year we had eaten hundreds of hot dogs and hamburgers, gallons of mustard. The Formica table looked exactly the same, and so did Buddy over there in his greasy apron, but we were a year older. We tried to read in each other's faces how we felt about this chunk of time we suddenly owned in common.

"Happy anniversary," Sol said, shaking Ferguson's hand.

"If I knew this was coming," Foxx said, waving his straw like a baton, "I'd have baked a cake."

"Hired a band."

"Grandest goddamn band on Manhattan Island."

And then we heard Ferguson say "A band of brothers," and we turned quiet again. Anyone else would have had a napkin thrown at him, but not Ferguson. Light bounced off his rimless glasses as he surveyed us.

Sol smiled. Foxx chewed the straw. Bobby L. squeezed one bicep and then the other.

"Are we a band of brothers?" Ferguson repeated.

"You bet, and let's call us the Knights," Jeep said, stuttering with excitement. "We'll wear those silver jackets with our name sewn on the back."

"Kid stuff," Foxx said. "Not cool."

Jeep shrugged him off. "We could prick our fingers and drink the blood."

"Sicko!"

Sol raised the ketchup bottle to his forehead. "I swear to be loyal to my brothers of the Round Table. And I promise, on pain of death, never to reveal our secrets."

"Swear. Swear."

"Pain of death."

"Sign or resign."

Foxx was drumming on the table. "Sign or resign, the brothers so command. Sign on the line, the brothers—"

"No!" As I jumped up, my knee bumped the table. Ferguson's thermos tipped over, spilling hot chocolate over my hand, but I didn't feel the pain. "No, goddamn it."

"What's *with* you, Baum?" Ferguson was watching me while they sopped up the mess.

"You've got the right not to sign," I said. They were frowning at each other, ignoring me, embarrassed by me. "The right to your own name, for Chrissake." My hand was throbbing now, with hot, sharp beats of pain.

"Let's celebrate Sol's father," Ferguson said. "And all our fathers." As I bent my head to hide my tears, I saw his hand slide under mine, like a stretcher under a patient. "Does it hurt?" he asked.

Then we all were on our feet, holding hands and looking at one another across the soggy pile of napkins: Foxx and Jeep and Bobby L., and Sol holding my left hand, and Ferg holding the burned one.

■ ■ ■

Friday, Feb. 17 or 18

Dear Murray,

Your nice letters sit for days on the bureau, under your foto, right where I put my keys and *Taschengeld* (pocket money, if you remember) when I come home at night. So you see I don't forget you, even if I do not anser right away.

You ask about my work. I'm busy morning noon and night on this special job of finding a California market for our seriess of Art Books. I try developing lines to museum bookshops now, plus fancy gift shops, and of course the universities. Talking talking all the time, in one door and out the next. You will laugh: people here think I have a *New York* accent!! Maybe I lost the German when I hit that big bumpp in the road in Kansas, ha ha.

You ask also about the loyalty oath. This is very complicated business, Murray, more than I can say in a letter. Enough to say now is that I did not sign any oath because this is supposed to be America—democracy! But DO NOT WORRY: they promised I will not be fired.

Can you read my handwriting? Like chicken's footsteps in the dust, my school teachers used to say. I can hardly read my self.

I wonder how tall are you now. I am hoping to get back home as soon as I can, before you are seven foot.

Love Dad

"He writes like a chicken and spells like one, too." I looked up at Arlie as I finished reading.

"It's a cute letter," she said. "Especially that part about hitting the bump in Kansas."

"'Do not worry,' he says in capital letters. I wish people would quit telling me not to worry."

"I hate it when you get petulant."

"I'm not petulant. Whatever that means."

"Try grouchy, then. Or irritable."

"A regular Roget's thesaurus, aren't you?"

"First you piss on your father's letter, and now you're pissing on me."

"Arlie," I said with a little laugh, "girls aren't supposed to know words like that."

"Girls can say 'piss' if they want to."

"Just certain girls."

"Certain bad ones? There you go, pissing on me again." She punched the pillow. "I can say 'piss' in my own living room if I want. And on the street, in school, in my sleep, anywhere. Piss. Just like that. Piss. If you don't want to hear me, you had better go home. Piss. Piss."

A little feather floated between us, bouncing with our

breaths. "Arlie." I laid the feather to rest in her lap. "Can we start over?"

She folded her legs under her skirt. She stroked the feather against her cheek. "Well? Start."

I smoothed Dad's letter on my knee. "He doesn't really answer any of my questions. I must have read this thing at least ten times, and each time he seems to tell me less." I waited for her to agree, but she just raised her eyebrows and played with the feather.

"Coming home, for example. When exactly is 'as soon as I can'? That could be a week or a year."

"Maybe he can't be exact right now."

"But anything would help. 'Late February' or 'three to four weeks.'"

"Do you want him to make it up?"

"I want something to mark on the calendar. Where in hell am I supposed to put 'as soon as I can'?"

She shrugged.

"'Very complicated business'—that's what he says about the loyalty oath, as if I didn't know that already. 'I did not sign,' he says, as if I didn't know that, either. The only news is that he won't be fired."

"Good news or bad news?"

"Good news, of course." I looked into her eyes for a clue. "What else could it be?"

"Why don't you sound glad?"

"Listen harder. I'm glad. Of course I'm glad." I folded the letter, put it inside my pocket, and got to my feet.

"Hey, where you going?" she asked.

"Home."

"Just like that?"

"Bye."

The elevator sped downward, and my stomach lurched. I walked quickly across the lobby.

As I pushed the door open, the icy wind pushed back, snaking up my sleeves.

5

I had always been curious about what lay behind the door to the teachers' room. Now that I was here, though, I wished Miss Moran hadn't asked for this after-school conference. It was easy enough to stand at her desk among the other kids and check next week's assignment, but it was unnerving to sit alone with her in this quiet room with its upholstered chairs and its little refrigerator. She was so close that I could see the flecks of green in her hazel eyes and smell her perfume.

"I want to talk to you about your last paper," she said, spreading the pages in front of her. "'The shoulders leaned against each other, the sleeves were entangled. Inside the dark closet his empty jackets and shirts hugged in loneliness, waiting to be occupied again one day.'"

It was eerie, hearing my words come out of her mouth.

She turned toward me, smiling, and she pulled her long hair back from her cheek. "All the other students dutifully wrote a list of metaphors—a shopping list. But you wrote a little story."

"Thanks." I looked down at the green carpet. Brown and black stains ate into the fabric where coffee had been spilled and burning cigarettes dropped. Behind the door of their room, teachers were sloppy.

"'Hugged in loneliness.' 'The bittersweet fragrance of his sweat and cologne.' You have a sensual vocabulary that reminds me of D. H. Lawrence's early style. Have you done much creative writing?"

"Not really."

"Poems. I bet you've written dozens of lyric poems by candlelight."

"Sorry. Only essays and book reports. And of course the letters from camp that my mother is saving for posterity." Not much of a joke, but it made some laughter. Some breathing space.

How old was Miss Moran? When she had appeared in September to replace Mr. "Ancient Mariner" Cole, we had speculated like crazy. Twenty-seven, said Sol. Barely twenty, said Jeep with a leer. Twenty-four and just out of graduate school, look at that new shirtwaist dress, said Arlie. In the thickening copper light of late afternoon, Miss Moran looked younger one moment, older the next.

"Where I grew up, in farm country upstate, the only writing they did was on checks to the hardware store." She fussed with the sleeves of her jacket. "I want you to hear what no one ever told me. You're a writer, Murray."

Her hazel eyes were watching me intently. I could hardly breathe.

She spread her hand across my paper. "There's a power here. I hope you'll use it."

I saw my handwriting in the V-shaped spaces between her fingers. I stared with awe at those little blue words I had written two nights before. Suddenly I felt older, as if I had been lifted up and carried and put down in 1955 or 1960. My breath eased out of me, and my shoulders loosened. "I'll try," I said.

"Do, Murray." She pushed back her chair and laughed.

"Sermon's over. As my grandmother used to say after church, 'If that damn minister don't stop bellowing at us, one Sunday I'll walk in with earmuffs.'"

"Did she?"

"Probably. Last winter, at the age of seventy-seven, she was out there one night, five degrees above zero, chasing a fox out of the chicken coop."

I felt more at ease now that we were past my metaphors. "I never had any grandmothers. They died in Germany before I could meet them."

"You mean . . . ? Because of . . . ?" She pressed her fingers against her lips.

"I still can see that yellow telegram trembling in my father's hand. It arrived a week after the war ended. Both his parents had died in a concentration camp. Years before." I pulled at a piece of skin along my fingernail. "They'd been killed years before, but he didn't know it until that afternoon."

"How awful he must have felt!"

I thought of my father as a son who had suddenly lost his mother and father—letting go of whatever hope he had held on to through the war. My father crying.

Then I was telling her about Dad, all sorts of things about Dad before he left. She laid her cheek against her palm and watched with eyes that seemed never to blink. The shadows lengthened across the rug as I talked and talked until there was no more to be said.

I stretched and looked over my shoulder, and the window startled me with its blackness. "Oh my God, I've got to get home."

As I stood up, she folded the essay and slid it into her purse.

■ ■ ■

Mr. Sklar was in his teaching position: left foot propped on the open desk drawer, left elbow propped on his knee, right hand aiming the chalk at us.

"Memory is a kind of history, working invisibly and privately inside your brain. Written history is memory turned public. It's outside your brain, set out on a page for all to see. To write history is to objectify memory. Do you understand? And you, Simon"—he threw the chalk a yard to the left of Simon's head—"either destroy that love note from Josie or I'll read it aloud." We listened to the tiny shredding sounds, biting our lips so as not to laugh. The green walls around us were full of little white chalk marks.

Other teachers could be soft-soaped or sidestepped, but not Mr. Sklar. You heard the rumors as soon as you entered Harrison High. He assigned a book a week; he flunked half the class (the previous spring he had flunked two thirds); he threw chalk. That was what you heard in tenth grade, the year before "American History Since 1865." It was like the distant roar of an oncoming locomotive. In eleventh grade it—he—arrived, brilliant and bellowing.

"Historians objectify memory. But that doesn't mean they write the truth. As Voltaire remarked with only slight exaggeration, 'History is a pack of lies.'" Mr. Sklar swiveled to write *Voltaire* on the board. "Right now, of course, none of you pubescent puppies has the slightest notion of what I'm saying. That's because you haven't tried to be historians. Well, ladies and gentlemen, now you will try. It's time for the JRP—the Junior Research Paper."

We groaned. One girl made a noise like a nervous horse. Ferguson drew lopsided windmills in his notebook. Foxx whistled the first bars of the "Marseillaise," and Sklar, without turning, said, "And you, Foxx, plan to write yours in French, I suppose." Thin laughter.

The JRP! It counted a third of your total grade. Legend told of students who had had to rewrite their whole JRP, some of them twice. I felt my stomach clench—but not altogether in fear. There was that certain excitement you feel as the audience settles into the red velvet seats, the houselights dim, the chitchat subsides, and the curtain twitches once and begins to rise.

"You're smiling, Baum. Would you kindly share the joke with the rest of us?"

"No joke, sir."

"Sheer mindlessness, then?"

"Broadway, sir."

"Broadway?" His eyebrows popped up; his lips tightened until they became almost invisible.

"You know, at the theater . . . opening night . . . that time just before the director finds out whether his play will be a hit or a flop."

He and I watched each other across the rows of desks. Doomed. I waited for the flying chalk.

But instead he said, "Not bad, Baum." He turned and wrote on the board, *Dress rehearsal: May 15. Opening day: June 3.*

"Choose any topic in the last fifty years of American history," he said. "Do research, write a first draft, and then write a final draft. On June third the curtain rises. Or else"—he tossed the chalk into the wastebasket—"it's curtains." The bell sent us scuttling from the room.

"Hey, Mur, for the hundredth time, you comin' or not? You in a trance?"

"Yeah. No." I looked down at Jeep. "Go on without me."

I didn't want to go and talk out loud at Buddy's. I wanted

to hear from whatever was banging inside me. The moment before the play.

I stumbled into the bathroom, flipped down the lid in a stall, and sat and stared at the green metal walls.

Annie Abrams is so round, so firm, so fully packed. Have a lucky strike, boys.

Joe Dimadgio can't hit shit.

You can't spell shit.

Can too: S H I T!

The penciled messages climbed over each other. *The $64 Question? You're holding it in your hand, moron. The mentality of students at Harrison High is moronic and disgusting. Takes one to know one.*

I put my fists over my eyes. Broadway, sir. Not bad, Baum. Take a lead off third, take a step, and another, and before Maglie believes what you're doing—before *you* believe it—you're running toward home, head down and arms pumping, racing the ball that Maglie's fingers have just thrown toward the fat glove of Wes Westrum, who crouches above the plate, guarding it, waiting for that ball, as you lift and dive with both hands stretched prayerfully straight out. The kneepads scrape your shoulder, the ground jars your ribs, dust fills your mouth, but all you care about is whether you got there before the ball. "Safe," bellows the umpire. *Baum steals home*, that's what Dad will read in his morning paper.

Over the pounding of my pulse I heard the flush of a toilet far away downstairs, and then nothing. No voices, no footsteps, no bells. The big building was deserted. Dead. How long had I been sitting in this cubicle? The green walls shimmered for a moment before they came into focus. I took a pencil from my pocket and found a space above Dimadgio. *Stealing the Past*, I wrote. Then I crossed it out.

Double or Nothing. I crossed that out, too. *Truth or Consequences.*

Not bad, Baum. I nodded at myself in the mirror, smoothed my hair, and shouldered open the bathroom door. Far down the hall, blue fluorescent light leaked under the door of Room 411.

He looked up from his book. "Keeping late hours, aren't you, Baum?" His black eyebrows curled over the silver rims of his glasses.

"I came back to tell you my JRP topic. I'd like to write the history of my family." The eyebrows bounced dangerously. "You said we could do anything from the past fifty years, didn't you? Well, my idea is to look at family letters and then interview some people and put together my family's history." I sucked in a long breath. Now for the tricky part. "What do you think of this title? 'Truth or Consequences.'"

He cocked one eyebrow. The dark eyes held mine and wouldn't let go. Finally: "Not bad, Baum."

That seemed to be the end, so I started to walk out.

"'Truth *and* consequences,'" he shouted after me. "*And!*"

SPRING

6

The weatherman was wrong again. Scattered clouds, he had promised cheerfully on WOR this morning. But after huddling for thirty minutes in the lobby of Rockefeller Center, Arlie and I knew he had lied. The rain spilled steadily out of the sky. So much for ice-skating.

"If only we lived on a tropical island," I said.

"They don't ice-skate in Tahiti."

"At least we'd be warm. Imagine lying on the beach, just the two of us, hot and brown, smeared with suntan oil."

"Come on, I've got an idea," said Arlie. She pulled me into the rain, and I chased her uptown, over and through puddles, until we revolved through the door of the Museum of Modern Art and went dripping and squeaking up the marble staircase.

"Tahiti," she said as we sat down on the bench in front of Gauguin's painting. "Stretch out upon the soft sand," she whispered into my ear. "The orange sun is baking your body. Palm trees creak in the breeze. Brown-skinned, big-lipped women kneel beside you with soft hands, singing mysterious songs." Her breath blew warm in my ear. The paint seemed to stir upon the canvas. Patches of yellow and thick green and muddy brown rubbed against each other.

Her hand found the skin under my collar and pulled me against her mouth, against her tongue. When we stopped kissing, I bunched my raincoat in my lap to hide my hard-on.

She giggled. "I'm glad I'm not a boy."

I looked toward the Gauguin so she wouldn't see me blush. "I'm glad you're not a boy, too."

Our giggles exploded into whoops—unmuseumlike whoops. As the guard advanced toward us, we beat a retreat past Monet's waterlilies.

A week later I learned you can't duplicate ecstasy. "It's Saturday morning and raining," I said to her on the phone. "Meet me in Tahiti at half past noon."

This time a class of Hunter College girls was studying the Impressionists for a term paper. No kissing on the beach today. Abstract Expressionism seemed to provide the only room for privacy. Hand in hand, we stared into Jackson Pollock's conglomeration of black dribbles over white dribbles over gray. A black strand of oil oozed down diagonally through webs of white, lurched up under patches of pale blue spattered with flecks of orange and red—blood droplets—and then abruptly raveled into glistening black threads that curled every which way, weaving and clotting. Spiral upon spiral of dabbed, dripped, splotched paint, five feet eight inches high by eight feet eight inches wide. "This is crazy," I said.

"No, it isn't."

"I dare you to tell me what it's about."

She spread her fingers across my forehead and squeezed. "Turn off your mind, Murray. Forget the names of things."

I was leaning against her fingers, trying to forget the names of things, when a familiar voice surfaced beside me. "Well, well, if it isn't Mr. and Mrs. Pollock."

"Foxx! How do you happen to be here?"

"Sheer luck. Plus a hot tip from your girlfriend."

"You told him? Oh, Arlie."

Before she could reply, Foxx said, "Hey, kids, how about a quick splash in Monet's flower pond, and then let's go to this café I know where we can get wonderful espresso." He wrapped his white scarf around our necks.

"Espresso," Arlie said. "If I ever go to France, I'm going to sit in cafés all day drinking espresso." She unwound herself and stood up. "Come on." She stretched both hands toward me.

"But you . . ." I cleared my throat. "I promised I'd be home by four."

"It's only one-thirty."

"Well, by the time we get to this café . . ."

By now her hands were inside her coat pockets. She looked down at me through narrow eyes, gave a slight shrug, and turned away.

". . . simply marvelous," Foxx was saying as I caught up with them at the stairs. "This friend of mine named Pierre, who plays in a jazz band, says they'll perform my opera free of charge for a week, just to get it off the ground. Then if we can—"

"Opera?" I said. "I thought you were doing vaudeville."

"Actually it's kind of an operatic vaudeville."

"Do you ever stick to one story, Foxx?"

"When my imagination fails."

I waited until they stopped laughing. "See you around," I said, and I pushed through the revolving door. The rain had given way to flickering, lukewarm sunshine. The weatherman had lied again.

Halfway down the block I turned and watched them recede: a girl with golden hair and a boy with a long white scarf who walked as if he had exciting appointments waiting around the corner.

■ ■ ■

When I got home, I arranged my desk with a semicircle of math book, poetry book, French book, history book, and sharpened pencils. I kicked off my sneakers and sat in my chair at the center of that semicircle, ready to dive into homework and disappear. Wanting that pure black concentration. Ready. If only I could get past the cheerful music coming through the wall.

". . . right out of my hair . . . right out of my hair, and send him on his way." Mary Martin was driving me crazy. Theo was driving me crazy. For a week now, ever since his teacher had taken his class to a *South Pacific* matinee, he had been playing the album and humming Ezio Pinza deep and Mary Martin high, shampooing his hair every night. "I'm gonna wash that man . . ."

"Hey, wouldya turn it down?" I yelled. But of course he couldn't hear me because he had turned it up. He didn't hear my knocking, either, so I pushed open his door.

He was lying on his bed, his hands behind his neck. "Isn't it beautiful?"

"Beautifully loud. I'm trying to do my homework."

"Listen to this part. Just imagine, one enchanted evening, when you see a stranger across a crowded room and her eyes turn toward yours. Then you will know, really truly know, she's the one for you."

"You're as horny as Kansas in August."

"What's that mean?"

"Forget it."

"How did you fall in love with Arlie? Was it across a

crowded room?'' He pulled me onto the bed, and comic books crunched under my leg.

''Jesus, you're nosy.''

''Come on, I need some older-brother wisdom.''

''You mean the birds and the bees.''

''No, I know all that stuff already from Jerry Robinson, who's in the ninth grade. I want to know about 'in love.' Does your heart beat faster when you see Arlie? Do you ever, you know, *sing* stuff to her?''

''Sing? I don't sing to her. I don't talk to her. I don't anything. For God's sake, stop talking about her, wouldya, because . . . because . . .''

''Hey, forget I asked.''

''Just turn it down so I can do my homework.''

But in my room, everything was gibberish: quadratic equations, Yeats, and false French cognates. *Blesser,* ''to wound''; *dame,* ''lady''; *formidable,* ''marvelous''; *friction,* ''massage''; *sympathique,* ''nice.'' I pushed back the books and laid my cheek on the desk. The wood was hard and cold. The black grain rippled toward my eye in tight patterns. I heard an ocean noise, a rhythmic splash and hiss.

Why hadn't she phoned? Who should be the first to phone? What if I called and she said goodbye? Better not to phone. Unless she was waiting for me to phone first. Was that why she hadn't phoned? My cheekbone hurt where it pressed against the desk. I had to think of something better to do.

Dear Dad, I'm sorry I haven't written lately. What a lame beginning! Even the handwriting was lame, limping below the line. I balled up the page and threw a hook shot off the rim of the wastebasket. *Dear Dad, If you were here tonight you'd be singing ''Bali Ha'i'' and shampooing your hair.* I balled it up: off the rim.

Dear Dad,

Yesterday I got my light-blue jacket out of the hall closet. You know what that means? The season's about to start. Only 154 games to the Series.

But something else is about to start, too: the Junior Research Paper. Twenty pages, and one third of the grade. You can bet we're scared. People are even planning to go to the Public Library (the BIG library) for special books. Guess my topic: "The History of My Family." It sounds kind of crazy, but Mr. Sklar approved it. I'm going to look through those old letters in your bedroom closet, and talk to Ernst and Tante Lotte. And Mom, of course. When you come home, I'll interview you, too. (That sounds funny—like I'm Edward R. Murrow or something.)

When are you coming home? I miss you.

I took out the red crayon. It was so much shorter now. The red Xs marched like Communist battalions across my wall calendar. Eighty-five, now eighty-six Xs since the winter morning he had given me a hug and said "Be good" and stopped over to grab the two big suitcases. After which there was only the blankness where he had stood.

When I was a kid I used to run to the front door to meet him coming home from the office, and I'd stand inside the silky darkness of his overcoat, where he held me safe.

But one morning your coat opened up a space too blank to live in. The red crayoned words slithered across the bottom of the page. I didn't remember writing them. The scissors shook as I cut off the bottom of the letter. Should I put this ragged strip into the wastebasket? Or into a cubbyhole labeled BLANK?

I took Kaiser Wilhelm out of his cubbyhole and stroked the smooth mahogany flanks, the white straw mane. "This horse was mine as a boy," Dad had told me on my eighth birthday. "Be kind to him, talk to him, feed him sugar on Sundays." Old and loyal Kaiser Wilhelm. One glass eye was scratched. His metal wheels squeaked as I pushed him across the desk. But his right foreleg kicked the air as boldly as ever.

"I pace upon the battlements and stare. . . ." Five poems to be read for Monday, and I had read half of one. "Yeats is a passionate poet," Miss Moran had told us. "Read him with your heart as well as your brain."

"For I would ask a question of them all." I paced around my room. Down the hall. Around the living room. "Good night, Theo. Good night, Mom. No, not sleepy yet." I stood in the kitchen, with the cold of the linoleum floor rising into my bare feet. I picked up the phone and put it down again. I picked up the phone. GRamercy 6–5046.

"Hi," I said. "It's me."

"Hi," she said.

"Why didn't you call, Arlie?"

"I feel on trial."

"Come on, Arlie."

"If I don't give you a big enough hug, or if I laugh at someone else's joke or talk to Dan, you . . . accuse me."

I shifted the phone to the other hand.

"I really care for you," she said, "but . . ."

"All I want is for us to be happy."

"You're asking too much."

"I'll do better. Let's spend a day alone together and then—"

"I think we need a vacation from each other."

"You want to end it?"

"There you go again. Murray, please! We've only known each other for six months, and we—"

"Five and a half."

"Whatever. We're too young for this."

I felt the little muscles throbbing next to my ear.

"Murray?"

"Okay, I give up. You take a vacation."

"Damn it, Murray."

"I love you."

"I'm sorry."

I held the phone at arm's length. It made no sound. It was empty. My feet were very cold. She hadn't even said goodbye.

I lay on my bed, my arms crossed rigidly on my chest. She said and I said and she said and I said. Mom and Theo filled their rooms with happy breathing. On Forty-ninth Street Arlie slept inside her breathing, and Foxx over on the West Side, and Dad under the warm sheet of orange California. Everybody but me was afloat in easy sleep. Why me?

Not fatalism, Murray—determinism. Hardy says our lives are made by our own choices, usually mistaken ones.

Did I choose to love you? How do I choose to unlove you?

A sound began in my throat. Arlie! I tightened my arms against my ribs to stop the shuddering.

I didn't want to cry. If I cried, I would never stop.

I needed something to hold on to. I closed my eyes and reached into a cubbyhole, any cubbyhole.

TOM MIX—good choice.

The Tom Mix Magnet Ring. The Lucky Horseshoe Nail Ring, made out of one ingeniously twisted ordinary nail. The Magic Cat's-Eye Ring, which burned with a green fire deep in the pupil. The Periscope Ring, with which I used to spy around corners and over windowsills on Theo and

Mom and Dad. The Photo Ring, which neither Dad nor I ever figured out how to operate. The Tom Mix Signature Ring, in case I wanted to verify that a check or a letter from Tom Mix had really been signed by him. The Slide-Whistle Ring, which always set off Gus and perhaps every other parakeet in midtown Manhattan. And of course the Decoder Ring, with which I decoded the secret messages that Tom Mix entrusted to all of us sitting by our radios across America just before he told us to eat Instant Ralston and shouted farewell. The ring glowed in the dark so that we could finish decoding under the blanket if our parents forced us to go to bed. It glowed with a gentle radioactive green that faded slowly, so slowly, as I drifted into sleep.

▪ ▪ ▪

I woke up to the sound of rain and the desire to punch Foxx. Heavy, cold rain. Rain so heavy and gray that the street lamps were still burning. The drains made a nasty gargling sound. It was the curl of his mouth that I wanted to punch; I imagined slamming my fist so hard against those pink lips that for days they would be swollen, clumsy, ugly, and he wouldn't be able to smile, wouldn't be able to talk. The subway windows were steamed up. The school hallways were slippery, and the classrooms smelled sour from the wet wool sweaters, wet rubber raincoats, wet chinos, wet hair. The rain drummed without pause into the afternoon, and the street lamps burned yellow through the grimy air.

"Hey, Mur, how's the old art lover today?" Foxx shouted as the six of us crossed Fifteenth Street.

I reached for his arm to spin him around and within range, to get it over with. But my books spilled loose and splashed into an oily puddle. "Shit!"

A woman grabbed my shoulder and glared at me. "Filth! Don't you have a mother?" she demanded.

They were still laughing as we heaped up our coats in the back corner of Buddy's. "You should have said, 'Lady, be kind to me. I'm an orphan.'"

"Found in a wastebasket in Penn Station."

"Living at Buddy's on leftover hot dogs."

"Bet you a buck you can't eat six today, Bobby."

"Put your money where your mouth is."

Ferguson set down his thermos, dried his glasses with a large white handkerchief, and then arranged them over his ears. "Hey, orphan, why the tragic face?"

I shrugged.

"You want some of this hot chocolate?" he asked.

"No thanks, I ordered a root-beer float." I went back to patting my books with paper napkins. Ferg blew into the plastic cup and sipped, blew and sipped. The meat on the grill spattered while Buddy, humming along with Nat King Cole on the jukebox, flipped the patties high. I couldn't see through the steam on the front windows, but I knew the rain was still falling out there.

"Clear the table," Jeep called as he and Sol and Foxx shuffled toward us, balancing cups and plates on palms, wrists, and forearms, with forks sticking out of their shirt pockets and white straws cocked behind their ears like cigarettes.

"I tell you," Sol was saying, "in a year Mantle's going to make you forget DiMaggio ever played."

"Bullshit. No one's ever going to forget DiMag'. Fifty-six straight games, .325 lifetime."

"He's old. He's history. Mantle's only nineteen and hitting .550, for Chrissake."

Ferguson looked up from his hot chocolate. "But as the

rabbi said, the roses of spring training may become the onions of summer."

Bobby L. waved his Coke. "But as the rabbi's wife said, did you see the neck on that rookie? With a neck that thick, oy, I'd love to see the *important* part of him, is what she said." He licked the mustard off his hot dog.

"You wanna wash down that mustard with a bottle of ketchup?"

Our elbows could hardly find room on the table. Plates of half-eaten hamburger buns rested on other greasy plates and wadded napkins and somebody's plaid scarf. Jeep was tracing his name in the mound of salt that remained after his unsuccessful attempt to balance three shakers on top of each other. Sol's umbrella, the blue one that his mother made him take on rainy days, leaned against his chair and clattered to the floor every time Bobby L. reached for the mustard. Jeep explained that he was drinking vanilla egg creams instead of chocolate because he wanted his acne to clear up before the spring prom, but Foxx assured him that no girl was short enough to dance with him anyway, though Bobby L. said he knew of a place renting out midget girls for half price, and Sol said the Knights of the Round Table would chip in and buy him a pair of Thom McAn elevator shoes, whereupon Jeep began squirting egg cream at us through his straw until Buddy hustled over, his apron flapping, and said he was going to throw us out and keep us out for a week unless we piped down. I stirred the ice cream around in my root beer, not thirsty, making a soupy mess, waiting for the right moment.

"Gentlemen," said Ferguson, holding up a newspaper, "listen to what I found this morning in, of all places, the *Daily News*." He straightened his glasses and began to read so quietly that we had to lean in on our elbows to hear him.

"'Three runaway Pennsylvania girls, spree-bent in a race against an atomic doomsday they expect any time, eluded police today in a cross-country chase. They ran away from their homes in the Pittsburgh suburb of Lebanon four days ago, leaving behind a note saying they wanted to see the world "before an atomic war blows it up." The girls are all in junior high school: Olive Christian, 15; Louise Kelley, 14; and Josephine Kelley, 12. After driving the Kelley parents' car, they spent Sunday night in a Columbus, Ohio hotel.'"

"I don't believe it," Bobby L. said.

Ferguson held the article out toward him.

"I don't believe that atomic stuff," Bobby L. said. "They just wanted to blow out their valves, is what I think."

Jeep made motorcycle noises in his throat. "Too bad those chicks didn't need a chauffeur."

Ferguson smiled patiently. Foxx hummed a little tune as he piled sugar cube on sugar cube, building a white castle.

I pictured them, Olive and Louise and Josephine, in knee socks and ponytails, speeding westward on big highways, eating candy bars and french fries and thinking about atomic war. "You really believe them, don't you?" I said to Ferguson.

"All I know is what they wrote."

"The Bobbsey Twins meet the atomic bomb," Foxx said. "That's one crazy story."

"Going to make an opera out of it?" I said.

"Could be. The Bobbsey opera."

"The Bobbsey bebop opera," said Jeep.

"With a chorus of the Hardy Boys."

"Bobbsey Girls and Hardy Boys. Boom kaboom."

They were whooping now. Ferguson folded the newspaper and looked at the ceiling. Olive, Louise, and Josephine sped steadily west, chewing candy bars and chatting about diets, boyfriends, and Gregory Peck as they gazed through the dusty windshield at the world before atomic war blew it up.

"Hey," I shouted. "Shut up!" And they did, all at once, all of them staring at me. "I've got something to say to you guys. To Foxx." He raised his eyebrows. "Arlie and I broke up." No one moved. No one spoke. "It's over. Done. Finished. We talked and talked and didn't get anywhere. So we're finished. Arlie and I. Done, for Chrissake." The sugar cubes tumbled and clicked and scattered madly as my hand swerved toward Foxx. "So you got her, big mouth." He was smiling. Actually smiling. "Shitface! Shithead!" I shouted. I was ready to punch him at last. I was on my way toward those lips of his when Ferguson suddenly appeared in front of me, his eyes behind the thick glasses looking straight into mine while someone behind me wrapped his arms around my chest.

"Sit down," Ferguson said quietly, his eyes never blinking. I shook my shoulders, trying to loosen those arms. "Sit down," he repeated even more quietly, "before it's too late."

For another moment I defied his eyes. Then my body slid down through Sol's embrace and I sat slumped in the chair. I had lost my chance. Lost everything. They were all looking at me, and I wished I were a thousand miles away.

"Ah, Baum, Baum, Baum." It was Foxx, drawling and chuckling. "You poor schmuck. For a guy who's supposed to be some kind of whiz in English, you've been writing the stupidest soap opera I've ever heard. What in the world makes you think I've taken your lovely Arlie away from you?"

"Saturday at the museum, she—"

"She nothing. We nothing. Only you, Baum, in that soap opera of yours."

"But you went to that café and—"

"Listen, pal. I think Arlie's beautiful and intelligent et cetera, but that doesn't mean I do anything more than give her a kiss hello, goodbye. Which hardly adds up to adultery, does it?" He tossed a sugar cube from hand to hand. "Even in soap operas." He pitched the cube high and caught it in his mouth. "Anyhow, love takes up too much time." He smiled as he crunched the sugar between his teeth.

"Hey," I said. "I'm sorry."

"Don't apologize. Just think of me the next time you're lying between her legs."

"Jesus, Foxx, don't you ever—"

"Brothers." Sol was raising his glass and saying, "It's five o'clock and time to go. Hail to Brother Baum."

"Once again a bachelor like the rest of us."

"Rain or shine, may you prosper."

"And hit .365."

"And grow a thick neck."

7

I realized it was April Fools' Day when I tasted the salty Colgate toothpaste. Mom realized it when she found the large white box marked *Perishabel Food: Open Imediately* and the frogs leapt over her arms and to the far ends of the apartment. At breakfast Theo explained that he had spent Saturday afternoon wading through creeks in Central Park, scooping up frogs.

We laughed loyally. Even when my toes exploded the balloon inside my shoe, even after I found my underpants in the refrigerator and an ice cube melting on my chair, I laughed loyally. After all, Dad had made April Fools' a "high Baum holiday." In Germany, he would say, "such lovely nonsense is *verboten*. Only in America." He would laugh until the tears ran into his mouth as I tried to pick up the nickel nailed to the floor, or Mom sat on the whoopee cushion and blushed, or Tante Lotte shrieked at the plastic spider in her glass of white wine. After Theo and I discovered the Third Avenue Magic and Fun Shop, which he plundered every March 31, he would laugh just as hard when tomato juice gushed down his shirt from a dribble glass or he tried to cut his knockwurst with a rubber knife. "Wonderful," he gasped. "If only I could have played such tricks upon *my* father." Only once did he not laugh: when I cut the front page of the *New York Times* into paper dolls. "The *Times* is no joke, Murray. Never mistreat it again, do you hear?" Yes, I heard. In fact, I made sure never again to smear jelly or splash milk on the newspaper that was so precious as to cause him, for the first time in my life, to reprimand me.

This year Theo carried on the tradition single-handedly with frogs, toothpaste, and other surprises. Spooning around the plastic eyeball in my Rice Krispies, I wondered, with loyal but sinking heart, what the rest of the day would bring.

"Seventeen down, six letters—'legendary monarch.'" I was halfway through the Sunday crossword when the phone rang. Arlie! She had changed her mind! I raced down the hall and could hardly hear the voice over the beating of my heart. "All aboard for Pittsburgh, Cleveland, and *Kook*-amanga.

"Dad!"

"Well, who did you think it was? Jack Benny? Happy April Fools'." His voice came loud and soft and loud again, hisses and booms, as if buffeted by vast winds, but it was certainly his. Sunday Dad. As soon as I closed my eyes I saw him, in his floppy blue flannel shirt, one red slipper dangling from his big toe as he sat in his favorite chair. Sunday Dad humming "Take Me Out to the Ball Game" behind the raised pages of the sports section. His unshaven cheeks made sandpaper sounds against my fingers.

". . . right along the beach. You would have loved it."

What was he talking about? "Dad."

"You needn't shout, Murray. I hear you plain as day."

"Dad," I shouted. "I miss you."

"Me, too. I've been thinking I should fly home for a visit when my work lets up. *Oy gevalt*, the work here you would not believe. But I . . ."

On Sunday, Dad played games. Checkers when we were young, with him marching his kings across the board to the beat of triumphant clicks of his tongue. Later, chess, in which he would exchange bishops or risk rooks with inspired strategies that usually backfired. If Mom was out at the grocery store, there would be hide-and-seek, with Theo and me counting loudly backward from twenty-five and then finding him under Theo's bed or behind the winter coats or, once, underwater, fully dressed, in the bathtub that he had filled an hour before.

". . . and school?"

"Dad," I called into the winds between us. A whole continent of winds.

Theo tugged my elbow. Mom stood behind him, tracing clocklike circles in the air. "Everyone else wants to talk now, Dad. I love you."

"I love you, too."

On the calendar over my desk, the first red X stepped into the white page of April, the ninety-third X. Ninety-three divided by seven equals thirteen and something. Nothing was coming out even.

Their voices carried down the hall, too far away to be more than strings of sounds, first Mom's voice thick and serious, then Theo's thin and fast, then nothing at all. Dad had hung up and gone back to whatever he did on a Sunday in California.

"Murray," Mom called from the kitchen. "Please set the table. Ernst and Lotte will be here any minute."

As if I could have forgotten, when she had spent all morning banging pots and pans and talking to herself about gravy. Turkey, mashed potatoes, brussels sprouts, red cabbage, gravy, lemon meringue pie—the works. The kitchen counters were littered with bowls and greasy spoons.

"Why brussels sprouts?" I asked. Just thinking about them, those green leaves rolled up into sour little balls, made me wince.

"Ernst loves them," she said.

"Everyone else in the world despises them."

"Two sprouts won't kill you."

"Have you checked the death rate in Brussels?"

She laughed as she bent down to find something in the refrigerator.

"Really, Mom, you cooked brussels sprouts for him last week. And the week before that. Isn't that enough?"

"Ernst is an old friend." Her voice sounded peculiar inside there.

"At this rate we'll be eating sprouts every night."

Her face was red as she turned to me. "What should you care, Mr. Smart Aleck?"

"I was only joking."

She thrust a handful of silverware at me. "Go joke to yourself setting the table."

Sunlight slanted through the tall water glasses and moved in rippling currents across the white tablecloth. In early afternoon the dining room was at its best. The blue wallpaper deepened, and the rug was flecked with gold. Knife and spoon to the right, fork to the left, napkins rolled up inside their wooden rings. I knew every move by heart.

Lotte was an aunt, Mom's younger sister, and after so many years Ernst was practically an uncle. All my life one or the other or both had been dropping in for Sunday dinners, birthdays, holidays, or other family times for these people who had no family of their own. They filled the apartment with bouquets of roses, old jokes, and German accents. This Sunday was no different, except for Dad.

First came Tante Lotte with a whoosh of perfume, swooping upon each of us with hugs that lasted a little too long. Then Ernst, shaking hands with me and Theo, kissing Mom on the cheek, his black shoes squeaking as he walked. His fingers carried the faint chemical smell of freshly developed photographs—Ernst's perfume. Suddenly I knew what I wanted from him today: facts, dates, ideas, meaningful episodes, stuff that I could put into the draft of the JRP.

"Turkey!" Lotte exclaimed as we took our places and Ernst rolled up his sleeves to carve. "Did I ever tell you the story of our father when he carved the duck?" Theo rolled his eyes, and Mom shook an index finger at him. "I was four years old. This was back in Berlin in the days when our family still had a backyard. Vati was carving the duck, just as you're carving, Ernst, and I sat beside him just as I do here. My mouth watered, because I loved duck, loved it like candy. Oh, if only I hadn't eaten so much candy, I wouldn't be so fat today." She spread her fingers across her belly. "In any case, I watched him carve and I said—now remember, I was only four years old—'Vati, where is Hugo?' which was the name of my pet duck in the yard. 'I couldn't find him this morning.' Vati stopped carving and looked at me for a long, long time, not saying a word, until I understood. We were about to eat Hugo! I burst into tears, and to this day I have never eaten one more bite of duck."

Lotte looked around the table with a smile of astonishment. "Not one bite. But turkey is not duck. That slice looks good and lean, Murray. Just right for your fat tante."

The bowls circled the table from hand to hand, steaming, depositing untidy mountains of food upon our plates, silencing us for a while. I covered the two brussels sprouts with ketchup and waited for courage.

"Lise, you have outdone yourself," Ernst said. He put his fingers to his mouth and flung a kiss at her.

"You are easy to please."

"I suppose. A bachelor like me, living from one canned meal to the next, forgets food that has been made by a woman's hand."

"You should have married," Lotte said. "Theo, why are you looking under the table at my big feet? Yes, marry, Ernst. My years with Max, God rest his soul, were too short, but they were good."

Ernst smoothed the silver curls over his ears, adjusted the pearl cuff links. "There were a few women who caught my eye from time to time, but it was never the right moment."

"When is it ever the right moment?" Mom said.

"*Touché*, my dear." He raised his fork to her in a kind of salute.

Lotte was midway through another potato when the alarm clock shrilled beneath her chair. She jumped up, she shrieked, she flung her fork, she cried, "Fire!" and Theo cried "April Fool!"

"Call the firemen!" said Lotte, holding a water glass high.

"No fire, Lotte. Just one of Theo's jokes," Mom said, smiling grimly as she bent over to pluck potato from the rug.

"Nothing to worry about," Ernst said, stroking Lotte's arm. "Come, sit down and tell us about your hospital."

Lotte stared at the alarm clock and then at Theo, and with a slow shake of her head, she sighed. "It's so sad, so sad. Some mornings I barely have it in me to go to work. But this week there was good news. A lovely young man, Albert Schoenfeld, who they thought had cancer, had only an ulcer. Such a nice young man, Mr. Schoenfeld, he gave everyone flowers—the doctor, the nurses, even me, the receptionist. When I asked him, he said no, he was no relation to Karl Schoenfeld who was our second cousin, Lise's and mine, a well-known lawyer back in Germany. Poor man, he died in his office of a stroke, only fifty-two. Ach, this lemon pie is irresistible. Lise, how is it you stay so slim?"

"I wish." Mom slapped her hips. "More and more I am like a pear."

"Nonsense," said Ernst. "To me you are a perfect banana."

She giggled and blushed and rose from her chair. "Oh, what do men know about fruit?" Giggling harder, she nearly spilled the potato bowl on her way to the kitchen.

"Now, children." Lotte leaned toward us with a whisper. "Tell me quickly what is with your father."

"Lotte, *lass es sein,*" Ernst cut in.

"But she tells me nothing. Of course I don't ask, because I don't want to make it harder for her, poor Lischen, who must wonder what mistake she has made."

"Enough, please."

"Picture me, Ernst. I sit in my apartment and think about everyone who is no longer here—my Max, and my parents, and Karl Schoenfeld, so many, and now Samuel, too—while no one tells me what's happening."

"What's happening, Lotte, is that we are enjoying an April Fools' dinner and you are growing a bit fatter." He stood behind her, one hand on each of her shoulders, as if he were squeezing her thin. "Boys, it's time to clear the table."

I wondered if it was the right time to interview Ernst. Alarm clocks and bananas didn't seem the setting for historical research. But neither had my thirteenth birthday party, and it was then—before the annual photograph, as he helped me knot my tie—that Ernst had mentioned the family he had lost at Auschwitz. Parents, sisters, a brother, an uncle, on whom he could put only names, not faces, because the family album had been burned along with everything else. "Perhaps that is why I'm a photographer," he said as he finished with the tie. I saw my face reflected in the lenses of his glasses, white and shy and young, as he said, "*Mazel tov,* my friend," and shook my hand.

When is it ever the right time? After dessert on April Fools' Day, I took Ernst to my room. He tipped back in my desk chair, his vest unbuttoned, his thumbs hooked under his belt, golden light coiling down the watch chain, and listened to my description of the JRP.

"I'm envious," he said at the end. "When I think of the history they made us study in *Gymnasium* . . ." He shook his head. "Emperors' death dates. Three explanations for Caesar's victory. The Schleswig-Holstein question." I shook my head in time with his. "And today I can barely recall if Schleswig-Holstein is a country or a cow."

He smiled, and I smiled back as I held the freshly sharpened pencil over the new notebook. "To begin with, tell me about Mom and Dad."

"Just like that, 'tell'?"

I nodded and wrote *Ernst, April First* neatly at the top.

"But Murray, tell you *what*?"

"When you met them, where they lived, what they did. Everything."

"I've known your father since 1933 and your mother since 1924—half a lifetime. 'Everything' is too much." He pulled the watch from his vest pocket and wound it. "Remember, I am a mere photographer, who is used to focusing on things before my eyes, a few concrete things at a time."

It was like an invitation. It was as if he had told me to open the drawer, reach under the woolen sweaters, and bring out the photograph he had taken of me and Theo and Dad. "Start here," I said, placing it on his lap.

He removed his glasses and held the picture close to his eyes. For a long while he made little noises in his throat, and then he said, "Ah, Murray, you always ask so much."

"I want to know."

"Do you?"

"Why shouldn't I?"

His lips nibbled the air, holding a little conference with himself. He scanned the cubbyholes, row after row, and shrugged. "Let me study this photograph at home and I'll write something about your family. Not the truth, but at least a sort of truth."

Nine years ago Dad and Theo and I had stood hand in hand in hot white sunlight, squinting toward Ernst's camera. Now we lay prone in his palm, seven inches long, smooth, motionless, squinting up toward the white ceiling of my bedroom.

"Why did he leave?" I asked quietly.

"Who?"

"Dad." The photograph was trembling. "Why did Dad leave?"

"Who knows exactly?" He looked at the picture and laid it facedown on the desk. "Maybe not even Samuel knows."

"Guess for me, Ernst."

He looked stern, almost angry. "And then what? You'll take my guess and make it a truth? You'll fold it and put it into one of these little wall-boxes of yours." He began to rub his glasses with his handkerchief.

"Ernst, please. The loyalty oath. The job in California. Tell me what's going on."

Without glasses, his eyes were slits. "What's going on?" he said. "Every night for weeks now, your mother and I have discussed what's going on." His eyes surfaced again under the thick lenses. He folded my hands between his. "Who are we to judge, Murray? Who are we to say he should have signed or not signed? I can't help remembering the Jews who stood up to protest in Nazi Germany and disappeared before morning—but they *really* disappeared. They didn't phone home on Sundays."

He stroked my cheek, stood up, took the picture, and left me without a word. Without even saying goodbye.

8

April lurched forward like the Lexington Avenue IRT Local. Forty-second Street, Fifty-first, Fifty-ninth, each day blinking against the windows and skimming into the darkness behind us. Sixty-eighth, Seventy-seventh. In the darkness ahead waited the JRP Draft Day—Dread Day. Every afternoon in class, Mr. Sklar counted the days left: thirty-nine, thirty-eight, thirty-seven. Every week Mom asked, "So how goes the family history?" But I couldn't get moving.

Too many assignments. Ten math problems a night, and three perplexing poems by Yeats, and fifteen French sentences using the conditional tense (*-ais, -ais, -ait, -ions, -iez, -aient*).

Too many interruptions. Tante Lotte phoned to say she had poison ivy on both arms after a weekend in the Catskills. Ernst came for dinner but said nothing about the photograph. Mom came home in tears, saying, "I see my first crocus of the season, and then on the radio I hear they will send the Rosenbergs to the electric chair. Oh, their poor children! What kind of a world is it, Murray, that we make crocuses and orphans?"

Too many ups and downs. Arlie smiled as we passed in the halls and offered a breezy hello. Hello, I said. How can you smile? I thought. How dare you smile as if nothing hurt inside you when our eyes meet? As if you had already forgotten.

The Dodgers lost the season's opener, then won and lost,

took four in a row and lost three in a row and won three in a row. Fortunately the Phillies were doing no better, so we were only a half game out of first. Nevertheless, at this rate . . .

Draft Day loomed larger and larger. Thirty-four, thirty-three, thirty-two. Since that inspired afternoon in the school john, what had I accomplished? Other than giving Ernst the photo, nothing.

"I'm stuck," I said to Ferg as we walked out of history class. "Completely stuck."

"It's just a batting slump. Keep swinging, and the hits will come."

"A goner. I should tell Mr. Sklar I'm quitting."

"Nonsense. Come along with me to the Public Library."

"Why?"

"Yours is not to question why. Yours is but to follow the rabbi." He broke into a trot. I had never seen Ferguson move so fast. His legs swung sideways as much as forward; one hand clutched his books and the other his thermos. His buttocks churned under his corduroy pants. After half a block of this, he slowed to his usual pace, and thirty minutes later we were climbing that wide stairway between the stern stone lions.

In the card-catalog room I decided to look under *I* for Immigrants and *G* for Germany. What the hell, just keep swinging. But neither *Immigrants' Income* nor *The Immigrant's Day in Court* sounded very useful, and *Immigrants: A Lyric Drama* by someone named Percy MacKaye sounded just plain strange. Batting oh for three, I moved on to *G*. Most of the books weren't in English, of course—*Deutsche* this and *Deutsche* that—but I did manage to find a few like *Germany from Versailles to Danzig* and *Germany Then and Now*. In the end I decided to go with Frederick Schuman's

Germany since 1918, all 128 pages of it, hoping to bunt my way on.

After I copied the call number, author, and title on the little slip, I joined Ferguson in the Cs, where he was looking for information on conscientious objectors in World War II.

"It's like seeing the war inside out," he said in that foggy voice, while his fingers clicked through the cards in the drawer. "These COs were Americans who fought against the war. Fought nonviolently, of course. Because they wouldn't use a gun, they were put into prison. They were locked up while the men who shot and killed were given medals. Crazy, isn't it?"

"How did you ever stumble onto this topic? I mean, I've never even met a CO."

He hunched over the drawer, clicking the cards. I thought he hadn't heard me. "Ferg?"

"My father was a CO." The cards clicked and clicked.

"Your father? Jesus! Did he go . . . ?" I didn't dare finish.

"A minimum-security federal prison. Kind of like a college dorm with locked doors, he says. For fifteen months."

"Jesus." Mr. Ferguson was an accountant, nearly bald, who blinked a lot and whose stomach sagged over his belt. Mr. Ferguson had gone to jail for fifteen months. "Jesus Christ, Ferg."

Finally he was looking at me. "Don't worry." He pinched my cheek. "As Campanella said—or was it Ecclesiastes?—every batting slump turns around."

The librarian, a supremely bored young man with acne, folded our call slips into the pneumatic capsules, and whoosh, they were sucked into the copper tubing and clattered toward the library's faraway stacks. In fifteen minutes some other bored young man would deliver the books to our seats.

"Hey, Ferg, imagine a system of these pneumatic tubes all across the country. You put a message into the tube in your living room, press the right combination of buttons, and off it goes—like an airmail mole. Ten minutes later it spills out into someone's living room in Connecticut or somewhere."

"Would you really want these capsules dropping onto your living-room rug at all hours of the day and night, thudding like—oh—like gigantic mole turds?"

"Shh, for God's sake."

"This is a *public* library, Baum. We are the public. Ergo, we have the right to say 'mole turds.'"

I hunched my shoulders and turned away so that no one would think I was with him. He pursued me, a gleam in his eye. "*Mole turds.* Simple one-syllable words." I back-pedaled, and he pursued again. "Mole turds. Turds mole." And louder—"Turds mole!"—while people stared, until finally we were out in the marble lobby, where the guard told us to quiet down.

"You are so innocent, Baum."

"And you are so crazy, Ferg."

"Just a little, my friend."

Cold water gushed from the mouth of the tiny lion. Arlie had discovered this drinking fountain one afternoon months ago, back when we were first falling in love. "Turds mole!" The fierce whisper ambushed me. I choked, giggled, and sprayed water onto the floor.

"Can't hold your water, Baum? Come on. While we're waiting for those books, let's find something to eat."

As we walked down the hallway, our sneakers lapping along the marble floor, I felt light and poised, like Jackie

Robinson dancing sideways off the third-base bag, ready to steal home.

■ ■ ■

The first part of the letter was handwritten, almost illegible:

> Dear Murray,
>
> Here are some thoughts upon the photograph you gave me. I'm not sure they are what you want. Certainly they're not quite what I expected. But here they are, whatever they may be worth. I hope they help in your search for "the truth" of history.
>
> Love
> Ernst

The rest was typed, single-spaced, with almost no margins:

> The sun was unnaturally demanding that afternoon. In March it burned like June through my gray-felt winter hat. I shot three photographs, quickly, before you boys wilted inside those jackets. Samuel would not wilt, of course; his handkerchief bloomed always fresh out of his coat pocket. Even from where I stood, I caught a whiff of that cologne of his.
>
> This photo that I hold in my hand, the one you loaned to me, is the third of the series. I will prop it against a vase, because in a moment my fingers will begin to stiffen again. A photographer whose fingers stiffen, and whose left eye clouds behind a cataract: some photographer!
>
> What does the photo show? A tall man with two boys clutched in his hands like bouquets of flowers. They look directly at you through the emulsion of the paper, just as they looked at me on that March afternoon through the

lens of my camera while I tucked my chin and nudged the three figures into place on the screen and shot once, and again, and again. Since then, they never look away.

But to begin with the facts: I hunched over my Leica as I had on so many occasions with Samuel, Lise, and their boys. Almost the official family photographer. How did I—high-fashion photographer, aging bachelor—fit with this family of picnics, baseball games, and comic books? But love makes its own chemistry, you know. I loved those boys, and before them I loved the man who fathered them, and before him I loved the woman who became his wife and their mother.

But I promised you facts.

Fact: the man towers in the center—axis of this threesome looking at an invisible fourth, myself. (There was no fifth because Lise stayed home with one of her migraines.) On either side of this dark pillar stands a boy, one hand wrapped within his father's, the other dangling down. It seems a symmetry until you look more closely and detect certain differences.

For example, the boy on the left, whom I belatedly introduce to you as Murray, wears a little-man's suit. The boy on the right, Theo, wears pants that pause above the knee. What's more, a large handkerchief blooms from the paternal pocket, and a small imitator blooms from Theo's. But none from Murray's. Notice also that Theo and his father stand together in a pool of darkness; their sleeves blend into a single sleeve where the photo was underexposed. Murray stands on their shoreline, a sixteenth of an inch apart. Measure with your finger that sixteenth of an inch.

Murray: the bright one; the one who does not smile or even squint; who seems to wait as an observer being observed by the photographer.

And Samuel: I look steadfastly into the eyes of this man

who looks at me with his nonchalant smile, his ears carving semicircles out of the sky ("ears the sun shines through," he used to say), his tie and his right foot angled to the side as if blown by a lusty wind. Now, nine years later, he has disappeared, and all I see is the 5 x 7 black-and-white souvenir of him. He has walked out of the frame; the bouquet-children hang in midair.

I don't understand it. I don't understand it at all.

Facts: three photographs, March 4, 1942, Kodak Plus-X, 1/60 at f5.6, developed for seven minutes in D-76 mixed 1:1. Slightly overdeveloped. Printed on Kodak Medalist Paper, grade 2, developed in Dektol mixed 1:2, and fixed for seven minutes.

▪ ▪ ▪

"Have you made any great discoveries in our family history?" Mom asked while she was washing and I was drying the dishes.

"Don't ask."

"I could have told you, darling, the Baums and Nadelmans did nothing to put themselves in the history books. No Bismarcks."

"I know that. All I want is some information, some anecdotes. I'm going to interview Tante Lotte."

"She'll give you enough anecdotes for five JRPs." She handed me a bowl. "Ernst says he wrote you a memoir."

"He told you?" I felt annoyed. I had wanted it to remain between the two of us, man to man.

"Why shouldn't he?"

I shrugged. "He gave me lots of beautiful words, but nothing definite in the end."

"That sounds like Ernst, all right."

"The historian depends upon evidence, Mr. Sklar said.

But all I have to go on is what Ernst and Lotte choose to tell me. I'm in trouble. I should change my topic to Woodrow Wilson or the Depression—something normal."

"Well, I may have something that can help." She held a dish over the sink, watching the film of water slide off. "Have I mentioned to you the letters in my closet?"

"What letters?"

"Your father's and mine. And some other persons' we used to know. Here, this is the last dish."

"From when?"

"Starting the day we met. We wrote back and forth in our courtship, and also later. Your father was quite the gallant writer, let me tell you, even though he couldn't spell." She looked down as she dried her hands on her apron. The muscle at the corner of her jaw throbbed. Then she faced me. "And there are long letters from me. Who knows, you may find some—how do you call it?—evidence."

"Terrific, Mom. Can I use them?"

"You may come upon some difficult things."

"Written in German, you mean?"

"That, too."

"Don't worry, I'll figure them out. Or I'll ask you."

She had a serious, almost stern expression on her face. "You want to be a historian?" She nodded slowly. "Here's some history for you."

"What will Dad say? These are his letters, too."

"He's not here to say, is he?" She took my hand. "Come."

I opened the closet in their bedroom. Blouses and jackets and shirts shouldered each other like a crowd of people playing Sardines. They smelled of cigarettes, mothballs, the grass of summer picnics, roasted peanuts.

"Up on the shelf," Mom said. "Stand on this chair."

I put one foot on the chair, grabbed the lip of the shelf,

and rose into a musty twilight. The minute hand of the Big Ben Westclox glowed a feeble green. The other hand slumped at the bottom of the glass, broken off years ago when Theo threw me a forward pass across the living room and I didn't catch it. Woolen mittens and scarves tickled my wrists.

There it was, the fat chocolate-brown folder with the black shoelace cinched around it. LETTERS, LISE AND SAMUEL, 1933–, the label said. I recognized Mom's handwriting from notes to teachers and letters to me at summer camp.

"Murray? Are you dead from mothballs?"

"I found it."

The folder was heavy. The chair wobbled. She stretched her arms up toward me. "Oof! What heavy thoughts we had when we were young!"

I stepped down and out into the light of the bedroom. The folder stood on the floor between us, brown mottled with streaks of darker brown, bulging against the shoelace. The accordion pleats were cracked with age.

"Are you sure it's all right for me to read them?"

"All I ask, Murray, is that you do a good job."

"'Tell the truth,' that's what Mr. Sklar said."

"The truth." She pointed the toe of her shoe toward the label. "*Ja,* I think you'll find the truth of Lise and Samuel lying inside there." Her shoe nudged the folder. It tipped against my ankle with a crumpling sound. She turned and hugged me until her earring bit into my cheek. "My historian."

As I carried the folder down the hall to my room, I felt like one of those messenger boys with floppy caps, delivering urgent messages.

I found a pencil, spread some index cards on the desk, and untied the thick black shoelace.

27 April, 1933

Dearest:

It is three-thirty in the morning. I hope you are asleep. I, too, should sleep, but after such a time together as we had, I can't. I am not sorry or upset. Just happy and thoughtful—as I have every reason to be.

Her familiar handwriting moved evenly across the page, falling into the center fold and climbing out, dark-blue ink on light-blue paper, moving in the middle of the night happily, thoughtfully, as she composed the first letter she ever wrote to him.

I think especially of all that we talked about. Pleasure and happiness. My former life—the life I lived before you came—had much pleasure and not much happiness. Now I am ready to live the other way around. I believe it is the right thing to do, even though hurting somebody's feelings. Understand?

My queer guy, I think of you and make a wish: you shall never be sorry about being in love with me—neither today nor in the future. This is not only a wish but a promise.

Although I am not sleepy, I am dreaming already—of that soft curl of hair upon your forehead, of your dark green eyes.

Yours,
Annelise

PS: I graduated University Hospital in Berlin and got a three-years training as a nurse. This is to answer your question yesterday.

Excuse my bad writing, but I am in bed. And also, to write in English is difficult.

Underneath the blue page lay a large white sheet, the letter he wrote her three days later from his apartment on his side of the city. The handwriting rose and fell as if traveling over a bumpy road, occasionally running into blotches of black ink where he crossed something out.

4/30/33

Darling:

I read your note over again and tried to understand what you say between the lines. I think I do. On the other hand, may be we should ~~nicht~~ not understand everything, some Romance should be left, and Romance could be distroyed by two much understanding. As my Polish grandmother used to say, Love has its own language. Well, ~~maybe~~ we will have a long time to learn each other, if I may be permitted such a hope.

I hope you had a fare week, got some rest. By the way, to be awake at 3 in the morning, that is not permissable, let it never happen again, please. (Ha, ha, a joke.)

Samuel

So it was true: he couldn't spell even then. And even then he told you when to laugh at his bad jokes. But in other ways he didn't quite sound like himself—declaring ideas with those capitalized nouns.

Beneath this white page lay another, dated simply "Midnight."

Annelischen—

I love you! Nothing else is important! I love you! That is all I wish we said tonight on the telephone instead of compli~~katted~~ diskussion about right and wrong, and soon and later.

I love you. Do you hear, *Liebling*? What else needs saying?

"My queer guy." "*Liebling*." "Annelischen." Was this really what they called each other when I wasn't there, discussing deep into the night the differences between pleasure and happiness as they began to fall in love? I felt as if I were meeting my parents for the first time.

Liebster Samuel:

Lass das schimpfen, es ist spät aber ich muss mich noch eine kleine Weile mit Dir unterhalten, although "not permissible," *ehe ich ins Bett gehe.*

Two weeks later it was her turn again, another blue page, but this time with a thicket of German that stretched halfway to the bottom before it finally turned into a language I could read.

Darling, I just remembered to write English, as we promised to each other, "an American couple," you say we must be. *Aber ist schwer, nicht wahr, wenn es so spät ist und ich müde bin.* Oh no, German again. You are laughing at me, I am sure. But dear man, you laugh so lovingly I do not mind.

This letter will not be long. It is not like the *New York Times* you read to me on the picnic blanket, with "all the news that's fit to print." What is there to say but those little words I whispered into your ear, joyfully, in that cottage last weekend. I wish your head lay next to mine tonight—and the rest of you, too.

Liebster, viele viele zaertliche Liebe und einen Gute Nacht Kuss.

Deine Annelise

My fingers were slippery with perspiration. As I dried them along my shirt sleeves, I felt the stiffness in my shoulders, as if I had been bending over these papers for days. I should have been taking notes on the index cards, but I couldn't stop reading. I wanted to go to the kitchen and get a drink, but I didn't dare stop, in case something happened while I was out of the room. Cottage! Little words into your ear! All that between one letter and the next!

5/15/33

My dear:

It is amazing that all of a sudden you appear in my life, that we take a hold of each other in such a way without any prepparation. I told you I believe in "Instinkt" more than anything.

So Dad felt it, too, the "amazing" rush of events. And he, too, sounded breathless, trying to catch up and pin one of those capitalized nouns onto what was happening.

Life is strange, isn't it? And women are especially, if you will pardon my saying so. But happiness, however strange and amazing, is happiness, and I put my trust in it. You called it "my fatalistic Optimism," which is truely positive.

These four weeks were wonderful, and beyond them we will see as Life goes on. Give it time, and we have time!

(Yes, we shall be an American Couple. We shall read the *New York Times* and, who knows?, go even to baseball games!)

In the next three letters there was more German, and gossip about people I didn't know, and worries about paying for rent. After such loud exertions of romance, they seemed to be biding their time, content with everyday news. The only excitement came later in May, when Ernst made his first appearance in one of my mother's letters:

> The moment I reach home, the telephone rings, Ernst saying he had done a big job for Bloomingdale's and was "rich"—for one week rich, anyhow. We must all three have dinner and champagne on Friday at a fancy restaurant, he says. With Ernst it will always be excitement and generosity, just as it was when I knew him back in Weimar days. He has been such a good friend to me, and now to us. I wonder which woman will catch his attention long enough for him to marry.

Then she returned to daily matters, with a long paragraph of complaints about her housemate Trude: unwashed breakfast dishes, wet stockings hung in the kitchen, etc.

> Sometimes I think I should not live with anyone, woman or man, because I make things hard with my—*wie sagt man das?*—impatience. (I looked in the lovely little Duden dictionary you gave me. Thanks again.)

That was in mid-May. The next letter came a month later, this time not from the other side of Manhattan but from halfway across the country, from the Grand Hotel in Chicago. The paper was creamy white and parchment-stiff, with the initials *G* and *H* embossed in gold. It had the look of an official document, but his handwriting ambled across it with the usual unevenness, ending in a large lumpy heart with their names inside.

June 3, 1933

My darling,

Would you believe this fancy-schmancy hotel, with nine towels in the bathroom?

On the train I thought to myself: I travel three thousand miles from Germany to a foreign country with less homesickness than I go eight hundred miles from you. "Funny," as Americans say, but of course there are reasons not funny at all: Hitler has stolen our homeland. Fortunately you make New York seem like a home.

That is another way of putting the question I asked you on Tuesday. Please, Lise, take all the time you need to consider your anser. For such a life, long anser. I can hold my breath for days.

I must go now to the editors' meeting downstairs. I'm learning many names and faces and American phrases at this busy conference, "you bet."

During the next year there was no letter or note. Nothing. Silence. But of course I knew what she had answered. Precisely because she had answered yes, because they had married and Trude had taken her wet stockings and moved out so that he could move in, they talked across the breakfast table instead of writing. It was strange, how they disappeared as they got ready to become my parents. The closer they came to me, the more they went out of my reach. But this history I knew by heart. Marriage, December 2, 1933. Move to 237 East Seventy-ninth Street, March 1934. Somewhere among the next letters in this chocolate-brown folder, I would be born.

The first hint appeared on July 26, 1934, as he wrote on stationery from the Claridge Hotel ("The Skyscraper by the Sea"), in Atlantic City, New Jersey.

Darling:

Hello from Atlantic City. The window is wide open and the sound of the ocean enters like a symphony.

It is a new but nice experience to go away on a business trip, have a wife at home, and call her long-distance. I think every once a while one needs such a day of rest, off the routine, with time for reflexion. I hope you didn't feel lonsome. But after all, you are not alone anymore! I don't know how to think in terms of three of us, may be because I am only a man, and women are more suited to pre-thinking. But I am glad—you know it.

Thanks for the "love note" and chocolate hidden in the suitcase. It really was a surprize. You always get me with a surprize.

Many kisses to you, and you both.

Your S.

My darling man,

I picture you when you open your suitcase and hold this love note and the chocolate. Surprise lights up your face with a smile.

Our first night apart since thirteen months, do you realize? I could try to enjoy my freedom by singing those Schubert *Lieder* you don't like and cooking for once brussels sprouts that you don't eat, and even smoking a cigar such as I used to do when I felt "dangerous."

No, I want none of these—only you. I sing lullabies to our child, but he (she?) seems not to be listening inside there. I talk to you, but you are too far away.

Now that I have grown married to you, I am incomplete without you, my darling. Come home quickly.

Your Annelise

■ ■ ■

That was me they were writing about, me curled inside her stomach while she sang a lullaby and didn't smoke a cigar

(Mom smoking a cigar? My mom?). When Dad came home from Atlantic City and hugged her at the door, I floated between them and was hugged too. When they lay in bed, exchanging murmured stories of the past three days, I lay between them, an invisible eavesdropper. Of course they didn't know me then, didn't even know whether I was a boy or girl. I was only a fistful of life—no, even smaller: a finger, a fingernail.

Seventeen years later I lay on my stomach, an eavesdropper on the letters spread across the floor, overhearing accents as familiar as the corners of my teeth against my tongue: "my darrling," "that is not permissible."

There they were, pieces of paper older than my body. The words that Mom and Dad had scribbled across these pages mentioned me before I had a name. Before I ever was! Between the lines, I became. And when I turned the page, I emerged from Mom's belly into the light. Finally they saw me, finally they named me, and I became Murray. What was I before? Myself, but not Murray. A bulge of her belly. Living with Mom, within Mom, so entirely *within* that she could write about me yet not see me.

My fingertips rubbed a whispering sound across the page. *Measure with your finger that sixteenth of an inch,* Ernst had written. "Forget the names of things," Arlie had said.

Forget the names of things. What's left to remember, then? How do we speak to each other?

Dear Dad. I pulled the chair closer to the desk.

I've been reading the letters you and Mom wrote to each other in 1933 and '34, back in the very beginning. It's a little eerie, overhearing the two of you, if you get what I mean. But it feels good, kind of like listening in on the conversations between you and Mom in the front seat as we drive on Saturday mornings to the beach.

A tear splashed on the page. I hadn't even been aware I was crying until some words drowned right there beside my thumb.

Should I rewrite the page or leave it like this? I left it.

Through the deep water of sleep I heard Mom: "all I want is" and "what wife would not" and "why can't you," wide mouthfuls of words, extremely urgent, expelled by someone drowning or saving someone drowning. "Never again," she cried at the brink of no more breath, "never again," angered and afraid at all this possible waste.

But in daylight the phone lay quiet in its black cradle and Mom said "Good morning, darling" in her usual voice, smiling, spooning two poached eggs from the boiling water, so perhaps it had been a dream. Another oceanic dream.

9

April sped into May. Only fifteen days left to the JRP Draft. Fourteen, thirteen, twelve.

The Dodgers lost three and won one, lost and won, sinking to fourth place, but I barely had time to keep score.

Arlie asked how I was doing and I said "Fine" and she said "I miss our phone calls" and I banged into the homeroom door.

"You what?" I asked, holding my elbow.

"Our phone calls," she said. "Just because we stopped dating doesn't mean we have to stop talking." The hot pain surged up my arm. She made it sound so easy, in that beautiful voice. "I've got to go to class now," she said.

"No time," I said to Mom when she told me to clean my room. "No time," I said to Theo when he suggested playing handball in the park.

"I don't have time for a party," I told Foxx.

"Everyone has time for a good time," he said.

"But I don't have a date."

"This is a no-date party. I'm inviting thirty girls and fifteen guys. And you." He tapped my chest. "You won't regret it."

But after an hour of eating popcorn with Sol at the edge of the lights-out living room, analyzing who was dancing with whom and how close, I began to regret it. I should have stayed home writing questions for my JRP interview with Tante Lotte the next day.

I wiggled my toes inside the stiff black leather shoes, brushed popcorn kernels from the sleeve of my tweed jacket, and smiled at the girls who squirmed past us with little smiles and "excuse me"s.

"Whom you going to ask to dance?" I asked Sol.

"I'm thinking about it." He grabbed more popcorn. "What about you?"

"I'm thinking about it."

Foxx's place was filled to the brim. In the kitchen, guys debating Giants vs. Dodgers. In the dining room, couples holding hands, trios gossiping, singles eating pretzels and trying to look busy. Along the hallway, a line of girls with pocketbooks outside the bathroom. Behind a closed door in the back bedroom, Foxx's mother. And in the living room, these interlocked pairs of dancers.

The Artie Shaw album ended and Richard Rodgers began: "Blue moon, you saw me standing alone." Foxx folded Lisa's—or was it Zoe's?—arm against his chest and seemed to be nibbling the curls at her neck. "Without a dream in my heart, without a love of my own." His other hand journeyed down her back, lower, lower. "And suddenly there appeared before me." His thumb and index finger connected in a circle, and when I looked up, he winked at me.

"Old Foxx is doing his foxy number," Sol murmured.

"You sound jealous."

"Damn right."

One evening in tenth grade, when the two of us were walking home from a movie, Sol had confessed he had never kissed a girl on the mouth, whereupon I had confessed the same. Since then, of course, I had kissed Arlie's mouth often, but Sol—sweet Sol—still had virgin lips.

"So, when are you going to dance?" I asked.

"I'm thinking about it."

I was holding my wristwatch to my face, trying to read the time, when Jeep jostled my arm. "Hey, Mur, I've been looking everywhere for you. Guess what I just heard from Eileen."

"I give up."

"She says Ruth wants to dance with you."

"Ruth Pearlman? Get off it. She's still got the hots for Billy Biceps."

"Wrong again. Eileen is Ruth's best friend, and she told me, totally confidentially, that Ruth came tonight with 'ulterior motives,' if you catch my meaning."

I remembered the moistness of her fingers when she borrowed my pen after math class that day, and the shimmy of her bangs when she tilted her head to say, "Thanks, Mur-ray," inserting that slight, interesting pause between the two *r*s. "See you tomorrow, Mur-ray," she had said as we faced each other, holding algebra books and ulterior motives against our chests.

Before I could talk myself out of it, I crossed the living room and asked Ruth to dance.

Her hand was smaller than Arlie's, curling like a sleepy kitten as we danced. Our feet moved slowly, so slowly, carrying us toward the dimmest corner of the dance floor, where we hardly moved at all, pressing cheek against cheek less and less shyly. Her breath blew against the skin of my throat. She was shorter than Arlie, so I would have to bend my head to kiss her. But the song ended before my lips dared shape that ulterior motive, and her "thank you" stepped discreetly between us. I wanted her to pronounce my name again, but she didn't. Before I could ask her to dance again, the music stopped and a game of Charades began. And after that Sol whispered to me, "I danced with that one over there, Lianne, the cute one, can you believe it?" The one who aimed at him a smile that shone with braces and adoration. And after that Foxx sang his long ballad, "When Batman Married the Robin of His Dreams."

Shortly before midnight I asked Ruth if I could take her home. "No," she said, and she stood on tiptoe to kiss my mouth, soft as a breath. "No, I don't think so," she said, leaving me to wonder for hours, as I lay in bed, half undressed and half asleep, what *did* she think? Should I listen to her lips or her tongue? Or both? Or neither?

■ ■ ■

The most important thing Tante Lotte told me for the JRP was the thing she *wouldn't* tell me. "My tongue has run far enough," she said, pressing a finger and thumb to her lips and turning an imaginary key.

That came after lentil soup, mushroom omelet, four rolls, strawberry jam, chocolate torte, and two hours of reminiscences, none of which mixed very happily with last night's popcorn and lack of sleep. But I struggled to digest all her food and words, just as I struggled to swallow my yawns, because the JRP needed all the help it could get.

"Everything is waiting for you," she said, and she ushered me between the bulky upholstered chairs and the tables of glass knickknacks, past the umbrella stand and the crimson-beaded lamp, into the kitchenette. "You sit here, which was Max's chair." She turned to the stove, stirring and scraping, sending puffs of steam into the few rays of sunlight that squeezed through the ivy across the window.

We began with lentil soup and November 23, 1935, the day she walked down the gangplank onto the sidewalk of America and into the arms of her sister and brother-in-law. "There you were, little Murray, one year old, sleeping peacefully in your carriage while the boats whistled and taxis honked like crazy." For a month she lived with us, unfolding the canvas cot every night in the living room, folding it every morning before going to hunt for a job along with the other job-hunters of the Depression. The red pencil with which she circled want ads in the *Times;* the smell of the polish every night on her only decent pair of shoes; the butcher down the street who spoke Yiddish to her German while grinding a pound of "chuck" for dinner; Dad putting his hat on top of the refrigerator ("'Keep a cool hat and a cool head'—such a comedian, your father"); little Murray sitting on the potty with a picture book on his knees ("'Already a scholar,' your mother said as she asked Ernst to make a photo, but he said that was not fair to your dignity"); the green chewing gum of the other secretary in the little insurance office where she first found work for $14.60 per week—every sound, smell, and color from sixteen years ago survived fresh and fragrant in the warehouse of Tante Lotte's memory.

As she juggled soup plates and eggs and silverware between stove and table, she talked and sighed and talked, urging me to eat, please eat. Whereas with Ernst I had had to coax, with Tante Lotte I had to try and catch up, scribbling madly with my right hand while clumsily forking omelet with the left.

Detail by detail, my younger parents materialized. Mom filled the apartment with the smell of red cabbage and apple pie, with newly sewn and ironed curtains, with the tap-tapping of her typewriter sending letters to European relatives, and with wicker baskets of laundry still warm from the launderette down the street. "I tell you, Murray, your mother was one hundred and ten percent *Hausfrau*. Seeing her in that apron, you would never believe she once wore a flapper skirt and silk stockings."

Whereupon Lotte slid back a decade and across the ocean to Weimar Germany. The most beautiful legs in Berlin—that was my mother's reputation. And with it came parties, dances, and boyfriends, as many as there were nights in the week. The Nadelman family used to joke that they needed a doorman, a diplomat, and a doctor: the doorman to direct all those boys into the parlor; the diplomat to keep peace among them; the doctor to cure their broken hearts. "For Lise was never satisfied long with any of them. A few, with their broken hearts, turned to me, the little sister," said Lotte. Among these was a shy young man named Max who, ten years later, in America, became her husband, "may he rest in peace." She blew a kiss toward Max's portrait staring down at us, his mustache thick and serious.

I swallowed the last of the omelet. "Did any of those boys want to marry Mom?"

"Nearly every one of them, or at least that is what she said to me when we sat in the parlor after the parties, with our high-heeled shoes kicked off, rubbing each other's toes. Sometimes, let me say without meanness, your mother exaggerates the truth. So perhaps she invented a few marriage proposals. But as a fact, because they told me with lumps in their throat, I know of Franz Grossman and Stefan Weiss, and Arnold something-or-other, and I suspect Ernst, although he denies it to this day."

Franz; Stefan; Arnold. I scribbled down the names of these Germanic strangers who had wanted to be my father. And for a moment I felt a little dizzy, a little scared, writing this might-have-been history. A few tiny changes, an *n* instead of an *m*, a *t* instead of a *u*, an *f* instead of an *l*, and *Samuel* turns into *Stefan*.

"Tell me what Dad was like when you met him."

He had been thin, taller than she expected, with a large nose and large ears ("Ears to hold up my hat," he liked to say), talking with taxi drivers and shoeshine boys, anyone who could teach him American slang. He left in the morning with the *Times* folded under his arm and came home with a handful of red roses. "Such a husband he was," Lotte said, shaking her head. In restaurants he remarked to the waiter, "Isn't my wife beautiful?" Walking along the street, he held her hand like a teenager. In the middle of the Great Depression he made everyone laugh and forget their troubles. "Who needs Jack Benny," they used to say, "when we have Samuel Baum?"

Lotte was talking over her shoulder while, wearing yellow rubber gloves, she washed the dishes. "However, he wasn't always the comedian." There had been times when he was a *Luftmensch*—an "air person"—floating off into his thoughts, disappearing into silences. One would look across the Sunday dinner table and catch him staring upward as if listening to some remote voice. Instead of standing in front of the radio to conduct the NBC Symphony Orchestra ("kibbitzing Toscanini"), he would sometimes sit silent on the couch.

I licked the chocolate from my fork. "Why do you think he was silent like that?"

"*Mein Gott*, child, I'm no psychiatrist, just a sister. Silent is silent, who knows why? Perhaps that business in 'forty-six changed him. Max always said so, and Max was a wise man."

"What business in 'forty-six?"

She peeled off the gloves in two swift motions and looked at me through narrowed eyes. "*En presence des enfants.*" She twisted her finger and thumb against her lips. "My tongue has run far enough. Let me wrap a piece of torte in wax paper, and you take it home for Theo."

■ ■ ■

The section of the folder labeled 1946 was thick with opera programs, Mother's Day and birthday cards, a picture postcard of Rhinebeck, N.Y., on which Mom had written *I miss you,* letters from her about weather and food and Theo's broken finger, and notes from Dad about weather and work. If there was anything that belonged to "that business in 'forty-six," it was in three letters and, maybe, a small white card that fluttered into my lap and that said, in smeared blue ink, *Never again.*

April 29

Dearest Lise,

You would not recognize Willy and me. After four days not shaving, we look like real Maine fisherman. Don't worry, I will shave before I get home. Willy says Barbara will love his furry face. I wonder.

Weather is cold but not wet. We wake up with the sun, fish all morning, walk the afternoon, drink beer and eat hamburgers and talk at night. Like the old days when Willy and I were Scouts in the Schwarzwald.

Think about this for an idea, Lischen: a camp this summer, for us and a dozen of "our gang." This is Willy's idea, and a fine one I think. We rent a big house in the country, where the wifes and children stay all week and the men come out weekends. With the War over at last, we deserve a vacation. All of us will share the meals and the rent. Evenings we will talk politics or read plays or sing and dance under Japaneze lanterns.

Think on it. Talk with Barbara and others of our friends (although I cannot imagine Ernst out in the countryside!).

I miss you and the boys. I'll be home on Sunday in time for Edgar Bergen if this old Ford doesn't have a nervus breakdown.

Love Samuel

The second letter was typed on the stationery of the Commodore Hotel, 131 E. 42nd St., New York 17, N.Y. Two creases furrowed the page where it had been folded open and shut, open and shut. The circle of a coffee-colored stain almost obscured the bottom lines.

Sept. 11, 1946

Dear Samuel,

Although I don't wish to talk with you right now, I am thinking of you very much as I type this. I think of you (and us) more than I can bear. My head aches with a terrible migraine from smoking too much and trying to find a way out of the mess we're in.

The camp was not for me. I understand that now. For me the best holiday is a family weekend at the beach, or reading at home while you take the boys to a baseball game. But you jump into every crowd, shout as loud as the loudest, swim and sing with everybody beyond midnight.

Perhaps I am somewhat to blame, then, that you seek companionship with others. But companionship is not what I saw that evening through the cabin window. You may say it is a friendship with her, but I cannot help believing it went across the line.

Which is why I sit smoking in this hotel room, trying to find how I will manage to forgive you. As soon as I do, I will come home.

Annelise

The third was a green and red striped "Happy Holidays" card.

December 29, 1946

Dear Lise and Samuel,

Thank you so much for the lovely flowers and the get-well card you sent Willy. They meant a lot, believe me.

He is getting steadily better. But for a few days it was rather frightening. Although the scar was healing nicely around those eight stitches, his mind was not. As I sat by his bed, he would talk half in German, half in English, forgetting names—he who was always such a factual man. Fortunately all that is over now, and every day he is more himself.

He'll have to give up his "politics of the street," though. Doctor's orders. At least the police did that much for us.

When will we see you again? We haven't seen you even once since Labor Day, except that night at the hospital.

Fondly,
Barbara

Willy Jacobs. Villy Yacobs, as it was pronounced in German. He sat with a knife on the porch steps at the camp. I was only eleven years old, small for my age, and Willy seemed dangerously big. The black corduroy shirt creased across his chest. Black hair clustered like iron filings at the vee of his shirt. The muscles of his forearm churned as his jackknife worked against the wooden dowel. The shavings curled ahead of the knife, spilling onto his legs. His eyes never rose from the knife as he talked in those long sentences. When he wasn't talking, he was whistling some marching song, always the same song, pumping one bare foot up and down.

Barbara Jacobs. All summer I watched her blond hair swaying against her shoulders as she crossed the lawn, and her long tanned legs slicing the sunshine. One afternoon I glimpsed her right breast as she swung open her blouse to nurse the baby. Among all those gargly German voices filling the rooms and telephones and croquet lawns of the camp, I could always distinguish Barbara's straight-edged Kansas accent. "My American beauty queen," Willy called her, until she made him stop.

Willy and Barbara and Dad and Mom. They stood arm in arm on the rubber raft, mouths agape with laughter, Mom's free hand flailing to grab a handle of air before they toppled into the lake. Arm in arm they stood in the blurred photograph that used to be on Dad's desk. I used to stand there and listen for the huge splash of four laughters that would happen—had happened—a split second afterward. Where had the photo gone? I hadn't seen it in years.

Willy talked in long sentences, punctuating them with rough little barks ("*ja, ja*") when he got excited, which was often. I understood only half the words and never understood what they added up to. "Until the workers learn to undo the corporate subsidy that grips their consciousness, *ja*, that fits hand in glove with the government's so-called welfare, *ja*, which in fact is little more than another capitalist disguise, ever since the so-called New Deal put into effect the permanent poverty of the underclass who . . ." Something like that.

When I ran along the porch with a book, heading for an afternoon under my special tree, I passed him carving wood and unwinding his sentences while Dad leaned against the wall with a glistening bottle of beer, muttering, "You bet, Willy, you bet." When I returned, wondering how the Hardy Boys would free themselves from their sinister kidnapper, there was Willy, loud and indignant, with wood shavings ribboning his hairy legs, and my father and some of the other men saying, "but, *Mensch,* look at the facts!"

Once Willy pointed the knife at me. "Hey, Murray, hold up a moment. You're a bright boy, so answer me this. Would you rather be a rich factory owner or a poor worker?" Hours later, I had an answer. But on the porch I stood paralyzed, looking at Dad, who finally patted my shoulder and said, "Best to be a shortstop, right?" The men's laughter released me from Willy's trap. I hated him after that. Ja Ja Jacobs, I called him to myself. I didn't want Dad to say "You bet, Willy," or play Ping-Pong with him at night under the Japanese lanterns. I felt sorry for beautiful Barbara and her nursing child. Someday when my skinny eleven-year-old arm had thickened with muscles and my voice had changed, I would confront Willy on the porch and pronounce the answer that would leave him speechless.

But I lost my chance. On the last night of summer, an uproar broke out. Loud, spiteful chunks of words, familiar voices twisted strange and vicious, out there where the grown-ups were dancing under the red and yellow lanterns after I had gone to bed. Not for a young boy's ears, and so my parents had never explained and I had tried to forget. All I knew was that Willy and Barbara had disappeared from our lives. Now, five years later, they emerged from the chocolate-brown folder, a sudden ripple of blue lines written across the surface of 1946.

Fondly, Barbara.

Swim and sing with everybody.

Through the cabin window.

Never again.

The rest of the story lay elsewhere. Somehow I had to dive into the white sixteenth of an inch between those blue lines. The faceless, wordless, white surface. Like the back side of a photograph. Blank.

I crayoned another X on the calendar. One hundred and fifteen days since Dad left. Seventeen days until the draft of the JRP. I was drowning in time.

A point of pain began to pulse behind my left eye as I lay on the floor beside the documents of 1946.

10

Fifth-period study hall wasn't heroic enough. I needed to be far away from giggles and pencil sharpeners and the wet little pops of bubble gum if I was to subdue the JRP.

The library was cool and dry and silent, as if it had been closed to the public for a hundred years. I climbed the creaking stairs to the balcony, the wooden rail sliding smooth as oil against my palm. Up here the ceiling was barely higher than my head. The smell of leather and dust thickened as I went past painting and literature and finally entered history, the Dewey Decimal 900s, and found a little desk at the end of the aisle by the window where I could settle down to my task.

TRUTH AND CONSEQUENCES, I wrote at the top of a clean sheet of paper. A few minutes later, after nothing else happened, I erased the words and wrote, in smaller letters, *That business in '46* and *Willy*. Again nothing happened, not even when I added *Dad* and *The camp* and drew circles around each of them and lines connecting circle to circle.

"No answers without questions," Mr. Sklar had said after class when I told him I was lost.

I laid out a fresh sheet of paper and wrote at the top, QUESTION. After the word hovered there for a while, unanswered, lonely, I added an *s* and a numbered ladder:

QUESTIONS: 1. ______________
2. ______________
3. ______________
4. ______________

But nothing stepped out onto those hopeful rungs.

"No one said it would be easy," Mr. Sklar had said in a soft voice—too soft for me to be sure whether it carried sympathy or menace. "Your suspects won't simply reach into their pockets and hand you their secrets."

On a new sheet of paper, using the edge of my French book, I drew vertical and horizontal lines. Then I began to fill in the blanks.

DEEDS	*TIME*	*SUSPECTS*	*MOTIVES*
Marriage	1933	none	love
Ernst's photo	1942	1/16 inch	?
Dad's silence	1946	"that business"	?
Commodore Hotel	Sept. '46	"her"	to forgive
Willy's scar	Dec. '46	police	?
raft photo disappears	?	?	?

The sixth-period warning bell rang. I had worked for an hour to produce a page of tiny boxes that were filled with either cryptic phrases or question marks.

I stared at the words until they disintegrated into useless letters: *d, si, p.* I leaned close and squinted between the words until I saw nothing but white. Somewhere under there lay the answers. I pressed the pencil against the paper until the point snapped. Until the shaft splintered.

■ ■ ■

"*Mein Gott,* Murray. Must you slam the door like that?" Mom looked up from the typewriter, her hands poised in midair.

"It slipped."

"What's wrong? Did the Dodgers lose a tournament?"

"Won't you ever learn? They play games, not tournaments. When's dinner?"

"Dinner is after I finish writing to my second cousin Konrad in Israel. And after you apologize for being rude."

"I'm sorry." Halfway down the hall, I stopped and listened to the typewriter's steady clacking, punctuated by the cheerful little bell. In a hotel room five years earlier, that same machine had produced another letter. Those same fingers. This woman. "Mom," I said aloud. But she didn't hear me. "Mom," I shouted, and the clacking stopped. "I need to ask you some questions tonight."

It was almost ten o'clock by the time Theo and I had washed the dinner dishes; and I had helped him write his essay on volcanoes ("Why would anyone live at the foot of Vesuvius?" he asked. "To make their life interesting," I replied); and Mom had made our lunches; and I had stood in the bathroom shaving my upper lip and chin, including a new area beside my left ear, and practiced in whispers asking Ruth to the movies Saturday night, even though the next day was already Thursday, which at least meant I wouldn't seem desperate for a date ("Hi there, I just happened to be thinking . . . " "Hello, would you happen to be . . . ?" "Ruth, you're the very person I . . ."); and, finally, I had written down and crossed out one question and another and another about 1946. By ten o'clock I realized I was afraid to know what had happened in 1946, but now it was too late. The secrets owned me now.

"So, my darling, ask already." Mom glanced up while the knitting needles clicked in her lap.

"What are you knitting? I like the color."

"A scarf for Mark, the boy who delivers groceries. He looked so cold this winter when he stood at the door."

"Mom, we're heading into summer now. Who needs scarves?"

"For Christmas. Must you fidget like that? Your leg runs a mile sitting down."

I wedged it under the coffee table. "But how do you know Mark will be delivering next December?"

"Then I give it to him in July. Murray, are we here to discuss my knitting?"

"Of course not." I consulted my yellow pad: Willy? That 1946 business? The Commodore Hotel? "Of course not." I drew an arrow out from *1946* and an arrow from the arrow. "Actually, I'd like some help on the family history. Some information."

"Whatever I can, my historian. I want your paper to be a success, you know."

"Okay, let's begin after the war. Can you remember what you were doing back then?"

"The second war, you mean? Well, that would be V-E Day. Who could forget that day? When the announcement came, Samuel and I danced to Glenn Miller records for hours in this very room." The knitting needles slowed. "But a week later came the telegram from my mother. The first news we had received from Berlin since 'forty-four. My father was dead of pneumonia. And I remember thinking, the bombs and the Nazis did not get him, but pneumonia did." She stopped knitting and sighed. "Two days later, your father got his telegram, about his family, their deaths in the camps. A week of telegrams."

I waited until the knitting resumed. "Mom," I said, clearing my throat. "Let's move on to 1946."

The needles paused. "Nineteen hundred and forty-six? Yes, why not?" They began to click swiftly, methodically.

"There were only a few letters."

"Mmm."

"But a lot seems to have been going on."

"Mmm."

No one said it would be easy.

"Willy Jacobs, for instance," I said softly.

"*Ach,* him. Mr. Troublemaker. What does he matter? He's not family."

"One of the letters mentioned he got into some kind of trouble with the police. What was that about?"

"All right, if you must know. . . ." She gave me a glance while the needles kept moving. "Willy was a big shot in the electrical workers' union, always proclaiming himself a 'friend of the vurrkers,' off every night to 'vurrker' meetings. One night he made remarks to a policeman outside the union hall, however, and he ended up unconscious on the sidewalk."

For a moment I thought she was smiling, but her head was bent, so I couldn't be sure.

"No permanent damage, but maybe it knocked some

sense into Willy. Or maybe it finally got Barbara to put her foot down and make him pay attention to his family." She shrugged. "Who knows? When they moved away, we never saw them again."

"Where did they go?"

"Who knows? Connecticut. What do the Jacobses matter?"

What did they matter? In that photograph on the raft they had been locked arm in arm with my parents, laughing.

I leaned forward, trying to see Mom's face beneath the thick rim of her hair. "Weren't you all good friends?"

She looked up at me. "Not exactly." She set her knitting on the couch. "It's a long story." She pulled out a cigarette, lit it, and dropped the match into the ashtray with a little click. "An unpleasant story. If you'd rather not hear it, Murray . . ."

I turned to a new page of my yellow pad.

She took in a long breath of smoke and let it out in little puffs, with her eyes half closed. "We used to be friends. Willy and your father since boyhood back in Germany. Then the three of us over here. Then all of us, after Willy sat in a bus beside that beautiful Kansas girl and, boom, in one month married her. She was much younger than we were, but it didn't seem to matter."

Mom looked up at the ceiling, blew out smoke, shook her head. "Such fun we had together. Bridge and beer on Friday nights. Dances in the union hall. Jones Beach. Double date, Samuel used to say. You know how your father likes American talk. Double date."

It felt strange to picture Mom and Dad as a couple, double-dating. Teenagers were the ones who went out on dates; parents were supposed to stay home.

"Then came the camp." Mom ground the cigarette against the ashtray. "Samuel made it sound so wonderful. Just think how happy we'll be, he said, we German refugees, if we make a summer home together. A *Brüderschaft*. Everyone embracing everyone in true socialist fashion."

She made a wet noise with her tongue. "Understand, Murray, I tell you this only because of your paper."

"It's all right, Mom." A shiver of dread ran up my back—or was it excitement?

"One hot evening late in the summer," she said in a somber voice, "I passed by a cabin window and saw two people in an embrace which . . . lasted too long. I didn't want to believe what I was seeing. Samuel and Barbara, her blond hair shining in the lamplight."

I was staring into her dark eyes, feeling that moist summer heat in my face, seeing that yellow window in the darkness.

"I walked in the meadow for an hour," she said, "trying to get hold of myself. When I got back to our cabin, he was in a chair, reading. 'I saw you and her tonight,' I said. 'We need to talk,' I said. 'Why must everything have words?' he said. His usual."

She picked up the pack of cigarettes and tossed it onto the table. "What was I to do? After days of this, I went off to a hotel. 'Some time on our own,' I told him, 'will help us find a solution.'"

"'Find how I will manage to forgive you'—that's what you wrote him from the Commodore."

She stroked my arm. "'Manage to forgive'? Well, that's what happened. After three days, a porter came to the door with an armful of roses and a card saying 'Never again.' Immediately I jumped into a taxi and came home."

"But what did he mean?"

"'Never again.' What else can it mean? That's plain English, isn't it? 'Never again' means never again. Surely that's not too much to expect from one's husband."

She stood up, straightening her skirt at the waist. "An unpleasant story."

"At least it came out all right," I said. She made no response. "Didn't it?"

She looked past me and clicked her tongue. "*Na ja,* we shall see."

"But Mom, I thought—"

"It's bedtime."

I let myself be hugged.

"How tall you are!" she said.

I looked down at the white line that parted her hair like a scar. She smelled of smoke.

I am incomplete without you, she had written to Samuel the first time he left, before I was born. She had hidden chocolate and a love note in his suitcase, for him to find while the ocean made a little symphony outside the window.

"When's Dad coming back?" I asked.

"Don't be too angry with him."

■ ■ ■

The Dodgers had the bases loaded in the bottom of the ninth, down by two runs. I was lying in the dark with the radio beside my pillow when I heard, mixed in with Red Barber's drawl, two German voices at the front door. One was Mom's, but the other wasn't Dad's, although it was very familiar. As soon as I turned off the radio, I recognized that measured phrasing, that throaty tone: Ernst. Back and forth went the German sentences, playful as tennis, while I didn't understand what they were saying in the doorway at

12:15 A.M. When the lock finally clicked and Mom, finally alone, passed my doorway with a whoosh of perfume and silk, I pretended to be asleep. And when I really did fall asleep, in every dream we lost in a different way: strikeout, ground out, double play.

11

Dear Rabbi Ferg:

Have you considered the question of drowning in time?

Sincerely,
Turds Mole

I had sent this note during English class. After lunch I opened my desk and found his reply taped under the lid.

Dear Turds Mole:

I have no time to consider your otherwise interesting question of drowning in time.

Sinkingly,
Rabbi Ferg

I grabbed his elbow as he came shuffling out of the biology lab. "I need to talk to you," I said. "I think the JRP is affecting my mind."

"Your mind has certainly turned un-Murrayish. Batting slumps, drowning in time—what next?"

"Seriously, how about a talk?"

"Definitely. How soonly?"

"This afternoonly?"

"Better yet, come to my house for dinner."

His house! He had never asked me to his house before. An invitation to the inner court!

I waved goodbye, wheeled, and collided with Ruth. Books spilled from her arms. "Goodness' sake, Murray." She held my wrist to keep her balance. "First you don't talk with me for a week, and now you knock me over. What next?"

"Oh, Ruth!" I bent down and collected the books.

"That's my name," she said, smoothing down her bangs.

"Ruth." Was I doomed to repeat myself forever? "I liked dancing with you last week, didn't you?"

"Yes, I did, Murray."

"And I'd like to go out with you, would you?"

"Yes, I would." The pause might have continued for hours as I tried to figure out what next, but she rescued us. "Saturday night?"

"Saturday? Oh, Saturday is fine. A fine day, Saturday."

"I have to go now." When she smiled, a dimple bloomed in her cheek. "Call me." When she walked, her rear end went bump, bump.

Bump bump. Turds Mole. I felt like shouting.

■ ■ ■

The front door to Ferguson's inner court was an ordinary front door: black, dusty, with a silver rectangle inscribed *A. & D. Ferguson.* Ferg turned the key and beckoned me forward. One step, two steps, and I entered light so intense that I had to lower my head and push my way through. Spotlights blazed against the white-tile floor and white-plaster walls, which blazed back. White, pure white.

"This is my mother's art gallery. Yes, everyone stares at those Picassos, but I like this little Chagall best."

Imagine carrying your lunch bag of tuna-fish sandwiches past Picasso every morning. Imagine sitting at night in front of Chagall's flying purple cow, doing your algebra homework.

"Come on upstairs, Murray. You can look at the pictures later."

The marble stairway rose, curved once, and glided away under a crimson carpet. More paintings; a grand piano; a jade plant taller than me; a chandelier bristling with silver bulbs.

"Let's go upstairs to my room."

"Upstairs"? How many more ups were there in this painted palace? I climbed behind my friend, giddy with light and height.

"Hi, Mom. I want you to meet Murray."

"Allen has mentioned you often. I'm so pleased to meet you at last, Murray." Her fingers were thin, like her voice. Red roses leaned out of a glass vase on the glass table where she had been reading glossy magazines. Her hair was short and somewhere between yellow and orange. "Allen, dear, your father and I are going to the Smithsons' for drinks tomorrow. And of course you're invited, too."

"Anything special?"

"Mr. Smithson's brother is back from India, where he made a movie on Gandhi."

India. Chagall. I felt as if I'd walked into the middle of a Broadway play.

"Sounds good, Mom. Come on, Murray, let's go to my room."

Finally the world became almost familiar again. The textbooks on his desk were the textbooks on my desk; the sneakers and T-shirt on the floor were the sneakers and T-shirt he had worn to school the day before; the pajamas on the chair were green, like mine. On the wall a framed certificate proclaimed in black scrollwork, *Arthur Ferguson, National Spelling Champion, 1922.*

"He has a photo-perfect memory," said Ferg, following my glance, "so it was hardly a contest for him. He won with laryngitis."

"From spelling so much?"

"What?" Then he smiled. "No, with the *word laryngitis.*" And then we were laughing together. "You want some licorice?" he said, opening a tall glass jar thronged with black and red stalks.

I shook my head as I settled onto the floor. "Your house is great. Fabulous."

"Well, like the poet says, 'Take our greatness with our bitterness.'" He sat against the bed and swung the licorice like a pendulum. "Yeats—the poem we read last month for English. Yeats describes his home, the paneled doors and polished floors, the galleries lined with portraits of ancestors. Then he says, 'What if those things the greatest of mankind consider most to magnify, or to bless, but take our greatness with our bitterness?'" He bit into the licorice and chewed slowly. "I may not have a photo-perfect memory, but at least I can remember things that rhyme."

Ferguson had never before said so much all at once. I felt flattered, even though I had barely understood a word of it. I took a stalk of licorice. "Any bitterness that you see, will not unrecognize you to me."

"Yeats?"

"No. Baum." A little laugh bubbled out of me.

"Murray Butler Baum. I bet you could write poems if you tried."

"Like those notes you send me."

"Those aren't poems. They're graffiti. Graffiti from the

men's room in Saint Ferg's Cathedral." He waved the stub of licorice. "Just like that one, for instance. Nah, that's easy stuff, Mur. The hard stuff is the long line, the long haul."

We sat quietly against the bed, fingering our shoelaces. Quietly and comfortably. I wished we could be oiling our baseball gloves, but I doubted Ferg had one. "Do you ever wish you had a brother?" I asked him.

"Sometimes. Mom gave me a dog when I was five or six, but he left too much fur on the rugs. Black dog and white rugs. We gave him to the maid."

I tipped my head back. "Wow!" I exclaimed as I looked up at the glossy black map of silver stars spread like a canopy above us.

"I bought it at the planetarium, just to remind me. The heavens wheeling overhead, the huge electric voice of the narrator—it was like religion, except it was true."

Side by side we sat against the bed, our faces tipped upward. Our mouths made soft little sounds as we bit and chewed a fresh pair of licorice sticks. Cherry this time, sour-sweet. When I half closed my eyelids, night moved into the room and the stars began twinkling and shifting up there a hundred light-years away. I watched them for a while. Then I began to tell Ferg about that evening at the camp at the end of the summer of 1946.

"It was Labor Day, and the grown-ups were on the lawn drinking beer and dancing under Japanese lanterns, celebrating the 'vurrkers.' I was in bed listening on the radio to the scores of the doubleheaders. Musial hit three for nine, so I got up to find Dad because he really likes 'Stan My Man.' As I walked barefoot down the porch steps and onto the lawn, I heard Willy shouting, 'Every man lays eyes on my beauty-queen wife, which is bad enough. But no one must lay hands on her, no one. No one lays my wife,' and he went into a slew of nasty-sounding German words. My feet were turning numb with cold as I crouched at the edge of the light.

"I heard Dad saying things like, 'Willy, you're a brother to me, Barbara is like a sister.' Willy began to say 'Bullshit,' over and over. Then I heard two women, not screaming but hissing. Like geese. 'Slut, blond slut, baby at one breast and men at the other.' 'You are so quick to criticize, why don't you try to love him?' My mother and Barbara, hissing.

"'I hate the camp, I hate the camp.' Was Mom saying that, or was I? All I know is that suddenly I felt myself rising, and I smelled the sweat of my father as he gathered me into his arms. 'Son, you do not belong here,' he said, and he carried me back to bed while I whispered into his shoulder, 'I hate the camp.' His arms scared me with their anger. In bed, trembling, I told him about Stan the Man, but he only said, 'Forget this bad business, Murray.'"

The stars shifted and reshifted, making my eyes water. I took a deep breath and turned to Ferguson. "Well, what do you think?"

He shook his head.

I pressed my lips until they ached, fighting not to say it, but finally I needed to breathe. "Do you think Barbara and Dad were . . . ? The business in 'forty-six was . . . You think they were having an affair, don't you?"

Our eyes met, shifted away.

"Say something, Ferg."

"Look, it's not always—"

"I can't believe that about . . . my own father."

"Why not?"

"He's my father."

"Suppose he isn't perfect. I mean, who would want a father who's really perfect? Can you—"

"Jeezus!" I jumped at the sound of the buzzer.

"That's the signal from Molly in the kitchen. Dinner-time."

I laughed. "My mom shouts,'Dinner, already,' and your Molly rings buzzers. Amazing."

"We should exchange lives for a week."

■ ■ ■

What kind of love
holds you up
beside the wrong ocean?
How do you spend your Sundays
always three hours after ours?
Do you tell yourself jokes?
Or have you saved them
like pennies in a cup
for carfare home?
Do I dare ask
so many questions?
So many questions.

I began it as a letter, but it came out a poem. It lay on my desk under thickening dust because I had no cubbyhole for poems.

Dear Murray,

It's April 22, a long while since I wrote you. My work keeps me busy, but I'm not as tired as before. Now I "know the territory," as we salesmen say. Soon this assignment is done, I hope, because California does not fit me.

Theo sent the fotos of his Julius Caesar play and he looks like an excellent Emperor. You are probably as tall as George Mikan now. I can't wait to see both of you when I come. Me, I look the same except a little thinner from no home-cooked *Apfelstreuselkuchen* that I always love too much.

Did I write you of the car I bought? A blue DeSoto. Used, but not much used, by the widow of a movie star who died. I drive around town feeling almost a movie star myself.

If you go to Ebbets Field, shout for me at the umpires, okay?

Much love from your Dad

On the back of the envelope was another message: *M: I just found this letter after a week in my pocket, which Mom calls my* "Jüdische *Postbox." Sorry!!!*

May 2

Dear Dad,

Your letter arrived today after hiding in your *"Jüdische* Postbox." The new car sounds beautiful.

Spring weather has come at last, although I haven't had much chance to enjoy it because the JRP keeps me so busy. I'm learning how to "ask the right questions," as historians say. While reading through the family letters I thought of a few for you. Please give me your answers as soon as possible, because D Day (Draft Day) is coming close.

1. What were you doing in Germany in the 1920s?
2. How did you find a job when you came over here?
3. What do you remember about the camp in 1946?
4. Why was Willy Jacobs knocked unconscious?
5. What happened to him and Barbara afterward?

I haven't seen even one Dodgers game so far, but they

seem to be doing all right without me. Robinson's hitting .412, in case you haven't been paying attention.

Love,
Murray

The picture-postcard sunset lay upon the ocean in pinkish-reddish splotches, as if tons of fruit had capsized.

On the other side, the caption said, *The gorgeous Pacific from Highway One.*

And Dad said,

Dear Murray,

In anser to your questions: Yes. No. I don't remember. Yes. Probably not. But seriously: I anser you when I have more time to write.

Much love,
Dad

It lay around my room for a few days. Then I threw it into the wastebasket because it made me so angry. Then I pulled it out and stuck it in the PICTURE POSTCARDS cubbyhole, because I had never thrown away anything of Dad's.

■ ■ ■

It was a First Date, which meant that unlike Fred Astaire and what's-her-name dancing in *Royal Wedding,* we kept bumping into each other, Ruth and I, verbally speaking, as we ate cheesecake in a restaurant after the movie.

"Sometimes I wonder whether boys have souls," she said. "I know boys have minds, but I wonder about their souls, because they only seem interested in, you know, sex."

I kept chewing while I made a quick search of my mind

and face to see if any sexual desires were showing. Finally I said, "That's not fair."

"Exactly. It isn't fair that we always have to protect our bodies and our reputations against you."

"I mean it isn't fair to accuse all boys of single-minded lust for your body. Boys have more than one mind." I put the fork to my mouth and discovered it was empty. "What I mean is, have I laid a hand on you yet, Ruth?"

"Thank you, Murray." Her fingers tiptoed along the inside of my wrist. "I think you're so . . . sensitive." Perspiration was pooling in my armpit, and I couldn't remember whether I had used deodorant after my shower.

"Thank you," I said. "Do you want more cheesecake?"

"I'd love to, but I'm watching my weight."

"What are you watching?"

She shifted her shoulders, her breasts, her hips, one at a time. Before she could catch me staring, though, I looked away from this wonderful commotion. "Oh, you're just too thin to understand," she said. "Someone like me has to watch every bite because otherwise I'd wake up one day and . . ."

"You look just fine to me."

"Let's stop talking about me."

We talked about Fred Astaire dancing on the ceiling. She talked about Peter Lawford, who, in case I hadn't noticed, looked a lot like the tenth-grade art teacher. I talked about Orson Welles in *The Third Man*. When neither of us could think of any other movie actors to talk about, we talked about our brothers and sisters.

"My sister is taking ballet lessons and hating them," Ruth said, "because she's at that age, fourteen and a half, when all she thinks about is boys. Next year I'm going to take acting lessons. My dad promised he'd pay for them if

I'm really serious, which I am. My mother says that's ridiculous, 'Do you want to be poor all your life, Ruth?' But I don't care about money. What I want is to step into the life of someone else, Shakespeare's Cleopatra or Ibsen's Hedda Gabler. Step inside her personality as if I were wearing her clothes. I'll walk onto that big stage and . . ."

I followed her far-flung gaze and saw the waiter watching us through half-closed eyes. On some invisible radio, Teresa Brewer was singing, "All I want is having you and music, music, music," In some room high above the city, Ferg was hearing about Gandhi.

"What are you thinking, Murray?"

"I'm thinking I like it that you have big dreams."

She leaned over and planted a kiss on my mouth. "Thank you." Freckles made a narrow path down the dim valley between her breasts.

Later, outside her apartment door, she stood on trembling tiptoe while my fingers supported her shoulder blades and her breath warmed my cheek and my lips pushed against the push of her lips until, for just a moment, her tongue vaulted past the tip of my tongue, wet and urgent.

"Don't forget me, Murray."

On the way home, I met each pedestrian with a smile, hiding Ruth's stiff memorial behind a casual hand.

12

Mom had been preparing dinner all day. Gradually the apartment filled with meaty smells, glass and silverware sounds, and then the guests: Lotte, Ernst, and two new ones—or rather, two old ones, very old, the Silbermans from Cleveland.

At first I didn't remember Franz Silberman. This man, whose skin was pulled cellophane-thin over his face, seemed more like the ghost of that Franz Silberman. "It was 'forty-one when I was here, so you were perhaps four or five years old," he said.

"Seven. And you were a banker."

"I still am a banker. And you used to be a small boy, Murray. I held you upside down until pencils and marbles fell from your pockets."

When we shook hands, his fingers felt weightless.

"After you heard I was a banker, you turned to your mother and said, 'Did Mr. Silberman get his name because he was a banker, or did he become a banker because he was named Silberman?' Oh, you made us laugh." But now his laugh was a slow wheeze that collapsed into coughing.

His wife hurried over. "Your pills, Franz, you want your pills?"

"No, darling. Please, no fuss."

"He tires easily, you know," she told me above his head. "After such a long train trip, he should rest."

"Murray does not need medical reports, Hannah. Now please leave us men to talk politics and smoke cigars."

"You must not give him a cigar," she commanded me. "The doctors have absolutely forbidden it. And don't tell me, Murray, you already smoke?" She backed away, wagging one finger.

From across the room, where he was talking with Theo and Lotte, Ernst gave me a little salute, which I returned. He had never mentioned his letter about the photograph, nor had I. It seemed to have formed a pool of silence between us.

Mr. Silberman was tugging my elbow. "She suspects I hide cigars inside every book." He winked at me.

Instead of winking back, I said, "You know, I still have all those cigar bands you gave me." Dozens of shimmering circles of paper, embossed with tiny golden crowns and the profile of some West Indian prince, filled a cubbyhole on the top row, between BASEBALL CARDS and COMICS.

"Cigar bands without cigars? That's like a bikini without the woman inside. But at my age I suppose a man has lost the right to complain." He opened his palms and raised them above his ears, as if testing for rain. He seemed like a little boy who was too shy to make friends.

"Would you like a tour of the collection in my room?" I asked. He gave me a crooked smile, and behind Mrs. Silberman's back, we slipped into the hallway. He came only to my shoulder, but he moved with surprising speed.

The cigar bands delighted him, rustling among his fingers. The comic books bored him. The forty dice, of all sizes and colors, held his attention briefly. The Dodgers yearbooks, interviews, preseason forecasts, postseason totals, etc., mystified him. "Basketball I barely understand after fifteen years in America," he said, "but baseball surely no German can decipher. Except for your father. I remember Samuel in 'forty-one listening to baseball on the radio, but I mean *serious* listening, like to a speech by Churchill." He shook his head and looked down into his lap, at the cigar bands. "What comes next, Murray?"

Next came Dixie Cup lids, with Dale Evans and Roy Rogers yellowed by years of sunlight. I skipped dreams. I had never let anyone—not even Arlie—read those, and anyhow there were only three. The elephant-tusk cubbyhole was empty, as it had been since the time Dad read me the *Just-So Stories* and promised, maybe, a tusk for Christmas. When would Mom call us to dinner? The tour was turning sad.

My Friend Flicka: the personally signed letter from Mary O'Hara, thanking "Dear Master Baum" for the letter telling her I was eight years old and had read *My Friend Flicka* nine times. Enough. I wanted Mr. Silberman to go back to the living room, where he belonged, back among the grown-ups.

"We are both bankers, Murray: you with these safe-deposit boxes, and I with my vault in Cleveland."

He winked at me, and despite myself I winked back.

"But what is this? Oh, *mein Gott*—the horse!" Cigar bands fluttered to the floor as he reached for the small wooden horse. Gently he held it with one hand under its chest, stroking its straw mane, stroking its lustrous brown nose. "Kaiser Wilhelm. I haven't seen him since . . . probably thirty years now." The skin of his face seemed to stretch even more tightly as he stared into the eyes of the horse. "You were such a beautiful creature, Wilhelm. We rode you like princes."

"Rode him?"

"I rode many horses as a boy, but never one more majestic than him."

"Rode a wooden horse?"

"Wooden?" He looked up, still stroking the mane, and his mouth wrenched into some expression I couldn't read. "Your father never told you about 1918? The death of the kaiser?"

I shook my head. "Tell me."

Mr. Silberman sighed. "Samuel's not here to be asked. And if this cancer has its way, I won't be here long, either. So . . ." He took a long breath.

"Your father and I were best friends throughout our

youth. Even then I was the smaller and more cautious one. Even then the banker, *ja?*" The horse jiggled beneath his hand. "Every day we played marbles and cards, football in the street, and horseback riding. Your grandfather, Morris Baum, owned horse stables before the war—the first war, I mean. Of course automobiles were coming fast, but the best families of Berlin still took pride in their horses and carriages, and the best of the best families bought theirs from Weintraub and Baum, which was your grandfather's firm.

"Then came the war, and the old life ended. Four years later, half the young men were gone, the empire was gone, and also the horses. Herr Baum gave up horses for the cement business. One he would not sell, however: a tall mahogany-colored stallion he had ridden for ten years, named Kaiser Wilhelm. Of course, after the war the name was a kind of joke. A bad joke. Have you learned in your school about the German revolution of 1918?"

"When the emperor was overthrown?"

"Smart boy. The Weimar Republic replaced the empire. But before it arrived, there was great uncertainty. Would the kaiser remain as a figurehead? Would the army rule? Or the conservatives? Or the socialists? Most radical were a group called the Spartacists. They held meetings and marches all over Germany, calling for a people's republic. Imagine: a people's republic! Samuel and I and many of our friends went to those meetings—secretly, because our parents would not approve. We told them we were going to the theater. Off we would go from our suburban houses to downtown Berlin, past all the bombed-out buildings and all those legless young men who sat like old men on the sidewalk, begging. Horrible. Horrible. The Spartacists promised to build a democracy on that rubble, and we believed them and wanted to help." He shrugged one shoulder. "Well, we were young."

"Franz? Murray? Come to dinner."

"In a minute, Mom," I called out.

"Quickly, then. One afternoon we rode to a Spartacist rally, I on my bicycle and Samuel on Kaiser Wilhelm. It was the largest gathering yet, perhaps several hundred people in the square. Potsdammer Platz. The sun was warm on our heads. We felt so happy, Samuel and I, waving at each other from our high seats, laughing like children. Then we heard a thunder. It didn't come from the sunny sky; it rolled between the buildings along the pavement behind us. Over our shoulders we saw the helmeted policemen, the armored cars. Row upon row. Dark. Large." Mr. Silberman was looking out my window. "I couldn't believe what was about to happen. I turned to Samuel and I watched the smile clinging to his mouth, like a light that went out slowly, even when the motors roared and the police charged past him toward the speakers' stand. Then came the gunshots, and Kaiser Wilhelm shrieked, jumped sideways, and fell flat against the pavement. The sound of a big ripe fruit. Somehow Samuel flipped away, and there he stood, looking down at the horse. *'Was soll ich ihm sagen? Was soll ich ihm sagen?'*—'What shall I say to him?'

"'What are you talking about?' I screamed.

"Police and Spartacists were fighting across the *Platz,* twisting in the dust, but all of that seemed far removed from us, as if it were a story happening to someone else. We were in our own terrible little story, Samuel standing above the Kaiser, I holding for dear life to my bicycle. *'Was soll ich ihm sagen?'* he said again, and I screamed: 'Samuel, for God's sake, you can't say *any*thing to him, he's dead. Get on my bike and let's go home as fast as we can.' Perched on the bar, rocking between my arms as I pedaled home, he said, 'No, what shall I say to Father?'"

Mr. Silberman paused, looking into the face of the wooden horse, shaking his head softly.

"What happened?" I asked.

"Samuel never told me. Something awful, I'm sure of it. He was a different boy after that."

Another pause. He was drifting away. "How different?" I said, almost shouting.

He rubbed a knuckle under his nose. "*Na ja,* how to put it? After those two said whatever they said—and believe me, Herr Baum could put terror in your heart just by twisting his mustache—whatever they said, afterward Samuel laughed too much. He never spoke of the horse. He never spoke of any griefs or worries. He would only permit us to laugh."

"Franz! Murray! Come now, before the turkey turns into sandwiches."

He held out the horse to me. It felt warm and moist. I looked down, but there was no blood seeping from the smooth wooden flank. "Wait. Tell me the rest," I pleaded.

Mr. Silberman grasped the edge of the desk, pulled himself up, and leaned heavily on my shoulder. "I thank you for listening. When one is old, no one listens anymore. They just take away your cigars." I thought he was going to hug me, so I turned toward the door. But he pulled me back with bony strength. "Murray, your father means no harm."

I looked into this parchment face, wondering how it could ever have been young, looked into the yellowing eyes for miniature pictures of my father on horseback. Then we shook hands.

During dinner I had trouble pushing food past the tiny

obstruction in my throat. As I did my homework, it remained wedged there. Toward midnight, when I wanted someone to talk to me, it had grown too thick for me to make myself heard.

Dad? Damn you, Dad, what else haven't you told me?

■ ■ ■

What else? Scared father, laughing father, silent father—more fathers than I knew—were all arriving out of the past. An unruly crowd.

I was sitting upstairs in the school library again, working on the JRP.

Dad

loyalty oath

Mom

Kaiser Wilhelm
& Dad's Dad

"means no harm"

Willy

Dad Mom, Commodore

Barbara

Willy & the police

They had escaped their little boxes. They ambled across the page, this way and that, refusing to line up.

Only eight days to D Day.

I kept recalculating, looking for a more innocent answer. Mom plus Dad divided by Barbara and Willy equals what? Nineteen forty-six?

"When you look too closely at a photograph, you merely

see the grain," Ernst once said. I held the page at arm's length. Turned it sideways. Turned it upside down.

"Do you remember how I held you upside down until pencils fell from your pockets?" Yes, Mr. Silberman. But then you told me about the horse's falling like dead fruit under my father, who gave me a wooden corpse and never said it had been alive.

Willy falls to the sidewalk with secrets.

My right foot was asleep. I wiggled it until the blood surged painfully again down there.

Eleven-fifteen in the morning. Time was running out. Mr. Sklar was waiting.

My story begins when I was born, in 1934 at 237 East . . . Scratch that. *My story begins nine months before I first saw the world, when Samuel and Lise Baum . . .* Scratch that, too.

Eleven twenty-eight. A new sheet of paper. *My family's story began before I did. In fact, I arrived only in the middle of it, which is why I have only the slightest notion of how it went. In fact . . .* Mr. Sklar isn't laughing. "Cute, Baum. Cut the cuteness."

I balled up the page and dropped it on the library floor. Other historians seemed to have no trouble doing the job: there they were, fat and leather-bound, shelves of them. Yet I couldn't get past the second sentence.

Eleven forty-six. Four minutes to the bell. I chewed my knuckle.

The history of my family is the history of secrets. My father hides the death of his father's horse and hides his feelings for a woman named Barbara, and now he hides in California. My mother hides beneath forgiveness her feelings about my father and Barbara. My aunt hides what she knows about my father in 1946 and pretends she isn't jealous of my mother. My parents' friend Ernst hides his feelings in his darkroom. Barbara and Willy have fled whatever they did in 1946 and live underground somewhere in Connecticut.

I hurt, deep down, where something in my chest had burst. I shouldn't have written these words. I had no right. But each breath came a bit slower now, and the pain subsided. Right or wrong, this paragraph was where I must begin.

Twelve twenty-nine. I had missed lunch. I was nineteen minutes late for math. Everybody would stare, and Mr. Winogrand would fuss, but it was worth it.

$(4a + 5b)(9a - 6b) = ?$ Quietly I joined my classmates at the blackboard to perform quadratic equations. "I'm drowning in secrets," I whispered to Ferg.

"You all right, Mur?"

"I'll tell you about it at Buddy's."

I waited for an opening amid hot dogs and root beer and Bobby L.'s belches and a huge debate about whether the trade of Minnie Minoso to the White Sox would help the Sox more than the trade of Gus Zernial to the Athletics would help the Athletics.

"Gus and Minnie, Minnie and Gus?" Foxx said. "This sounds like Walt Disney's breakfast table. Gus and Minnie, Minnie and Gus? No, no, no." He stood up, one fist churning the air. "It's Minnie and Mickey as sure as my name is Foxx. Yes, Minnie Minoso meets Mickey Mantloso, they fall in love and ohhh, one warm night in the empty stadium they *do it*, way out there in center field, Minnie and Mickey making major-league love, oh yes, and he never takes off his cleats."

Foxx swept an invisible cap to his chest as he bowed to our applause. Root beer bubbled out of Sol's mouth, Bobby L. screeched with laughter, and even Ferguson rocked back and forth, making silly sounds.

"Zernial, Zernial, Zernial," someone chanted. Zernial, Zernial, Zernial.

For a wonderful moment I knew nothing but Buddy's Grill, loud and stupid and sweet as a cherry Coke.

13

By this time of the evening there were only three of us left in the newspaper room of the Public Library: the old man smelling of urine, who snored into the collar of his coat, the brown-smocked librarian who perched on his stool flipping the pages of *Collier's*, and me.

Electrical Workers. See *United Electrical, Radio and Machine Workers.* I leafed through the *Times* index for 1946, copying dates and page numbers. A thousand names blurred past me, but I cared about only one: Willy Jacobs.

February, September, October. Dust puffed out of the three volumes as the librarian laid them before me. "Heavy," he grunted. "I'll bring you November and December in a minute."

February 27. There they were, on the bottom of the front page. Eight hundred striking employees of the General Electric Company were parading before the plant's gates in Philadelphia, defying an injunction. At 8:00 A.M. fifty mounted policemen galloped into the crowd of marchers, with nightsticks swinging. The strikers ran up onto the lawns of homes and down side streets, shouting "Cossacks" and "Gestapo." Seven men were arrested; one received hospital treatment for cuts.

Gestapo! Cossacks! I could read the words only in a

German accent. Somewhere in that mob, Willy had taunted the police, raising one fist like a flag. The other hand had hid the jackknife inside his pocket, just in case.

Had Willy mentioned Philadelphia while the wood shavings curled around his ankles? I couldn't remember. It didn't matter. Whether he had been there or not, this melee had taken place in February, months too early for his scar of eight stitches.

On to September 9 and Milwaukee, where two factions of the CIO United Electrical, Radio and Machine Workers Union clashed at the annual convention. Former president James Carey proposed a ban on Communists' holding union office, and Local 119 urged delegates to "oppose communism, fascism and all other totalitarian forms of government." On the other hand, Local 1421 called for closer U.S. cooperation with "our great ally," the Soviet Union.

I pictured Willy standing at the lectern in the convention hall. The gray hairs curled over the vee of his shirt. "Whoever votes against this resolution, *ja,* votes against world peace. Make no mistake, comrades. If the vurrkers of this country . . ." The pudgy policemen in the aisles shifted their weight from foot to foot, slapping billy clubs against their palms.

I saw the scene as clearly as I saw the green lampshades dotting the library tables. He might have been in Philadelphia; he had surely been in Milwaukee. I knew it, somehow I knew it, but his name didn't rise to the surface of these pages, so I couldn't prove it. Canny Willy, hiding out. I hunted him into October and November. I turned the large pages, the stiffening, crackling pages, yellowing like skin. I hunted him, peeling one layer, and another, November, December.

On December 20, 1946, at union headquarters on Schermerhorn Street in Brooklyn, the Communists won reelection in Local 475, but where was Willy? The corner of the page tore off as I turned angrily through the next issue. Ten issues. Nothing. The UERMW vanished from 1946. Willy Jacobs had never appeared. But I knew he was there, walking down Schermerhorn Street with the other comrades in their flannel shirts. Silvery breaths puff from their mouths as they discuss "our great ally, the Soviet Union." Turning up the headquarters steps, Willy confronts John Dillon, mutters something with a sneer, gives him a shove, or perhaps Dillon shoves, or perhaps they accidentally knock elbows in the narrow doorway. "Hey, we don't want no rough stuff!" "You get what you deserve, fink!" And then the pair of cops moves in: "Okay, you guys, shut up and move on!" Willy whirls, hunches down, and says, "You may have an Irish face, but you're Gestapo inside!" Or perhaps simply, "Shut up yourself!" It all happens in a split second, and Willy sags to the ground. The men growl and then subside, backing off, because the cops are big and it's not a good time to make trouble. A friend of Willy's wraps his coat around his bleeding head until the ambulance arrives. A small, quick incident; a small, quick wound, only eight stitches. Too small to make the *Times.*

"Time to go, fella." As the librarian shook the old man's shoulder, the snores turned ragged and stopped.

Willy was there on Schermerhorn Street; he must have been there. But in these pages he had left no trace.

■ ■ ■

"Hey, Murray." Theo beckoned me into his room with a whisper. "Close the door."

"What's up?" I stepped over the phonograph, moved the

comics from the chair, sat down, and jumped up again when the gong bleeped. "Jeezus!"

"Don't worry, that's only the electric-eye burglar alarm."

"In case a burglar sits in your chair?"

"And reads my comic books with mayonnaise on his fingers, like Pat Parks used to do when I thought he was my friend."

I leaned against the windowsill across from his Duke Snider poster, the twin of mine. "So what's all the whispering about?"

"Mother's Day. Dad says he wants us to keep the whole day free for the surprise he's planning for Mom."

"Dad? When did he say that?"

"On the phone tonight. You were at the library."

"Why didn't you tell me?"

"I *am* telling you. Hey, don't get mad."

"I'm not mad." While I was reading through dead newspapers, the two of them had been merrily talking away.

"You have that mad expression in your eyes."

"Just tell me what Dad said, damn it."

He threw the pillow and told me that Dad was flying in on Saturday night, nine o'clock sharp. So have the band waiting at La Guardia, Dad had said. And don't forget (Dad had said after Mom got off the phone), Sunday would be Mother's Day, and he happened to have an idea, a perfectly wonderful idea, of how to celebrate. There was no use in guessing, we would have to wait until Sunday.

Dad was coming home. I flicked my wrists, swung smoothly, looked toward the rooftops 450 feet away. Sunday Dad. Coming home. Surprise! Just like a year ago on Mother's Day morning, when he had stood in his maroon silk robe beside the mannequin in *her* maroon silk robe and we had all watched Mom's eyes widen with tears ("*Aber Du,* Samuel, the robe from Lord and Taylor's window, but darling, too expensive!"). And the Mother's Day morning in 1948, when the bathtub had brimmed with red and yellow tulips that he had hidden overnight on the fire escape. And the Mother's Day in 1947, when we had sailed all afternoon on the boat around Manhattan while the little band played German songs and Dad conducted with an umbrella.

I pulled the bill of Theo's Dodgers cap over his eyes. I didn't know what to do with my hands or my jaw, they seemed so loose. Saturday, 9:00 P.M.: three days and one hour from now, three times twenty-four, seventy-two plus one.

"What else did he say? Did he sound excited? How long did you talk with him?" After five months, we were down to seventy-three hours.

"Hey, Murray, where you going?"

My feet took me bouncing into the kitchen. (If I knew you were comin', I'd have baked a cake.) Rye bread, slice of ham, American cheese, mayonnaise (hired a band), mustard, and a pickle, *two* pickles (grandest band in the land), square it up and cut from corner to corner in one deli motion (zap-a-doo, zap-a-doo).

In seventy-two hours and thirty-five minutes, Dad would come down the steps of the big plane, a white smile shining through the California tan. He would wear a Panama hat; no, he would carry it in his right hand; no, his hat would skim behind him across the night sky as he ran toward me.

■ ■ ■

I was afraid I wouldn't recognize him. We stood on tiptoe in the crowd huddled around gate 6.

"There he is!" Theo cried out.

He wore a light-gray hat that I didn't recognize. His blue jacket was wrinkled. The leather briefcase still had *SJB* in gold below the handle. His eyes shone green, startling green, under the tan of his forehead. The smile spread wider and wider: such large white teeth. His hands pulled strong behind my shoulders. The sweet and dank and tang, the cologne, sweat, breath, him—I could barely breathe.

In the taxi going home, everyone talked all at once. Then no one talked and the meter clicked, then everyone talked again. Dad began a story about a parrot in the Los Angeles Airport and Theo asked why planes don't fall out of the sky and Mom asked if he was hungry and Dad kissed her ear until she frowned and said, *"Aber Du! En presence des enfants!"* and he began the story about the parrot again. I sat on the little folding seat facing them, holding Dad's knees when we went around curves. Once he winked at me. Once he said, "I have a pocketful of fancy California matchbooks for your matchbook collection." Sometimes he seemed never to have gone, and sometimes I wasn't sure I recognized him.

He couldn't find his door key, so Mom used hers. In the front hall he stood still and looked around while his fingers tried to find their way into his pockets. He became large. I wanted to take care of his fingers, but the handles of his suitcases held me tight. His deep, dark voice traveled behind him as he visited room after room, deep and dark sounds that didn't settle into place. Gus was chirping. Theo ran ahead, flicking on the lights. Mom walked behind, straightening a pillow on the couch, watching Dad as he poked a finger into Gus's cage, watching as he threw his hat on top of the refrigerator, not smiling at his jokes, watching. I followed them all.

"Is it really you, *Liebchen*?" she asked as he spread coins and keys on his desk.

"Were you expecting Clark Gable?" he replied.

How had he acquired such a German accent while living among Californians? I wondered.

Later, Mom banged pots and dishes in the kitchen. Theo oiled his baseball glove. Dad hummed behind the bathroom door, splashing water all over the place. Everything seemed so normal. I stood in the middle of my room, running a finger through the dust on the radio, scanning the collection, winding the clock. Ten forty-five P.M., almost two hours gone out of how many? Dad had arrived, and already the hourglass had turned over and time was funneling away. Every hour counted. But here we were, banging and humming and splashing carelessly all over the apartment.

"Hey, son, how about knocking? What's on your . . . ? Hey."

It was not exactly a kiss; it was more like a command that I pressed on his cheek. Maybe that's how men kiss each other, I don't know. I don't think he knew, either. He just squeezed the washcloth tighter and tighter and tried like crazy to smile.

"Are you really that tall?" he asked finally.

"Six foot one inch."

"Can't be. That's taller than I am."

We stood back to back and looked sideways into the mirror. We fitted ourselves against each other, shoulders pillowed against shoulders, and I could feel his breaths swelling against my lungs. "Well, what do you know," he said.

We were looking back at ourselves through the mirror's shiny lens. His brown hair spilled to the left and mine toward the right. The collar of his blue shirt and that of my red shirt bunched beneath our chins. Each pair of lips was closed and thoughtful. My father, my replica, except one inch shorter. As close as we had ever come, and already I had passed him.

He nudged his elbow against mine. "Then again," he said, "it's only your curly hair that makes you taller." The bathroom boomed with his laugh.

Our faces looked at each other inside the silver frame of the mirror, like a life-size photograph. His smile began to fade. His eyes wandered.

"Dad?" I turned sideways to see him, the real him. I stood on my side of that narrow space between us, wanting his arms to pull me into the shelter of his chest. "Dad?"

He patted the top of my head. "You need a haircut, son."

He sat on the edge of the tub and began to file his fingernails. "Yankee Doodle Dandy." He always whistled "Yankee Doodle Dandy," the little file purring softly back and forth until the last triumphant stroke, "Macaroni."

"Dad, tomorrow let's talk about those questions I sent you."

"Questions? Oh, those. Sure, Murray, but you know I have the worst memory ever invented." He yawned.

"This is family stuff. You'll remember."

"Mom's the one to ask. She never forgets a name or a birthday. Me, I forget which side of the bed to get out of." He stood up, patted my arm, yawned. "Let's go to sleep, because tomorrow is You-Know-What Day."

"Can't you tell me the surprise?"

"Wouldn't be a surprise, then."

"Dad, I'm glad you're home." But he was already gone.

■ ■ ■

Clopclop, clopclop, the hooves carried us steadily around the park. Warm air swam into my mouth. Mom's gardenia corsage pumped sweetness at me. Sunlight dodged in and out among the tall trees. Clopclop, clopclop. The muscles worked and wove along the horse's back. "She's named Daisy," said the carriage driver, as if we had asked. "Don't ask me why," he said. "Who else but my wife would name a horse Daisy?" Theo waved at everyone, and almost everyone waved back. "Daisy, Daisy, tell me your answer true," Dad sang. "I'm half crazy, da da di da to you."

I should have been feeling ecstatic, or at least happy. After all, a carriage ride around Central Park on a balmy spring afternoon surpassed even a boat ride with a German band around Manhattan. As Mom said with that double-clutch in her voice, laying her head on his shoulder, "You have not forgotten how to romance me, Samuel." That was what I should have felt. But whenever the sun hit my face, I sneezed. And when I closed my eyes, the hoofbeats went erratic and young men rushed from behind trees to grab the reins and pull Daisy to the ground, screaming "Down with the kaiser!" So I kept my eyes open and my head down.

"Murray, why are you so quiet?" Mom asked.

"Just thinking."

"Big thoughts or small ones?"

"Medium-size."

"Well, no doubt even Goethe himself had only medium-size thoughts on Sunday afternoons."

"Not 'Guh-tuh,'" Dad said, wagging his finger at her. "In America they say 'Go-thee.'"

"*Ach, Du.* So long as I pronounce 'Brooklyn Dodgers' you are happy." They giggled and kissed like a couple of teenagers.

"Mom, Dad, cut it out." Theo tugged at their elbows. "Everyone's looking." We exchanged glances over their heads, and for a moment we became parents to our parents. When Theo was fifty years old, his mouth sandwiched in jowls, he would look like Dad. Or maybe it was Dad who had looked like Theo forty years ago.

Clopclop, clopclop. Shortly before the ride ended, I figured out how to begin the interview with Dad.

"Kaiser Wilhelm? What's the big fuss?" he asked in my room that evening. The wheels of the horse squeaked back and forth against his palm.

"You never told me he was a real horse. You never said anything about the revolution and him being shot from under you. Mr. Silberman told me you rode to the Spartacist rally."

"Ah, Franz. The little banker, we called him, because he always counted his money before going to bed at night. What did it get him? Cancer at fifty-five." He tipped the chair and perched his feet on the edge of the wastebasket, a seesaw balance. "Revolution, a dead horse. Why tell such things to happy boys like you and Theo?"

"I'm not a boy anymore."

"Sixteen? Well, perhaps not." He wagged his jaw in a Snerdish smile. "You shave once a week?"

"Twice."

"Twice?" He stroked an invisible beard from his chin to his chest.

"I'm trying to write the history of our family, and I need to know the truth, even bad truth." This wasn't going right. My voice sounded plaintive. I kept worrying that Dad would tip over the wastebasket.

"What does Kaiser Wilhelm have to do with our family?" he asked. The wheels of the horse squeaked against his palm, once, twice, and then stopped. "Son, what do you want of me?"

"Your father, what did he do to you when you told him the horse was dead?"

The silence was unbearably long. He spread the fingers of one hand. "An unhappy business." I said nothing. He set the horse on the desk, set his feet on the floor, cleared his throat, and finally began.

"I stood by his desk. My pants were stiff with dried blood. I told him what had happened, and he said, my father said, 'Come back when you decide how you should be punished.' For a week he said nothing except good morning and good night. My mother begged him. I would hear her begging him in their room. But she had no power over him. No one did."

He stroked the straw mane. "Good morning, good night. Finally I said to myself, '*This* has been my punishment. For a week I've been punished. Enough!' And then I had the idea of asking my friend Willy, who was a fine carpenter—you remember Willy Jacobs?—I asked him to carve a statue of Kaiser Wilhelm."

A young Willy Jacobs sitting on a porch in Berlin, with that same shiny blade slicing a small horse.

"So Willy worked all night, and the next morning I went to my father. 'I'm sorry for what I did, and here is how I make up for it.' My father held the horse with outstretched arms, like so, as if he did not want it to come too close. His black mustache twitched. Then he handed back the horse. 'Thank you, Samuel, but he is dead,' he said. 'Nothing will change that. If you wish to keep this little souvenir, you may have it.' We stood there looking at each other. Then he nodded once, which was how he ended conversations. So *that* was it. *That* was his punishment. We never mentioned it again."

I wanted to say something, but I didn't know what, because I had never had to console my father before. I coughed. "Thank you for giving me the horse," I said.

He cleared his throat. "So, Murray. Enough sadness for your history?" He pulled the Tom Mix Decoder Ring from its cubbyhole and began twisting the dial. "Huh! I had forgotten about this."

I could have ended it there. Another kind of son would have ended it there, as Dad cupped the ring between his hands and said, "Look, it still shines in the dark." A less voracious son would have taken out the Periscope Ring and the Tom Mix Signature Ring so that the evening could wind down through nostalgia and jokes and yawns and good night, son, good night, Dad. A more loving son. But it was because of love that I would not let him go. A kind of love.

"Dad, I read a letter Mom wrote to you. From the Commodore Hotel. She was writing about you and a friend of yours at the camp, about trying to forgive you for something."

A look ran across his eyes, the look of a man who has just received pain from a distant part of his body. "All these ghosts you greet me with, and I am hardly used to moving from orange trees to skyscrapers." He stared out the window into the night and seemed to have forgotten me.

"Mom told me some of it," I said softly. "Her part of it."

He looked at me. "She did, did she? She told you her part, did she?"

"Yes."

"You have to understand, Murray, on certain things your mother has very stubborn ideas." He leaned forward, elbows on knees. "Barbara was a wonderful woman. On Friday nights we played bridge, the four of us. When they had their baby, we felt like one big happy family. 'Seven stuffed cabbages side by side in one pan,' Barbara said once.

"At first I heard merely grumblings, Mom *kvetching*. Barbara should be doing this with the baby, Barbara should say that to Willy. At first I ignored her, thinking it was temporary, the wind blowing wrong for a while. But it didn't stop, and one day I couldn't help myself. 'Stop *kvetching* about Barbara!' I yelled. And Mom yelled back, 'I'm not your maid!' Right away I apologized, but off she went to the hotel, *pschutt*, faster than you can snap your fingers."

So there we were, Dad and Theo and I, in the apartment, with Tante Lotte coming by to cook dinner for us. "It was kind of funny," Dad said. "I brought you sandwiches in my briefcase from the delicatessen because you wouldn't eat Lotte's cooking. How does a woman get so fat when she can't even cook a potato right?" He laughed.

Do you hear, Ferg? Do you hear, Mr. Sklar? It was just a little argument that got out of control. A case of nerves. An innocent misunderstanding. Everyone was innocent, and here we were, laughing to prove it. "Then what?" I asked. "Shortly before we starved to death, Mom took pity and came home?"

"Not yet. She was really mad. Wow. Nothing I said on

the phone made a bit of difference; she stayed mad. So finally I decided, hey, this is no joke. I went to Barricini and bought a five-pound box of chocolates, and to the florist for a dozen roses, and Doubleday's for a book of love poems, and finally to the hotel. I wrote a note saying, 'I promise never to see Barbara and Willy again, if that's what you're waiting for.' The bellboy took it all up to her room."

He stood by the window, looking down at the street. "That was the hardest thing I ever did. Leaving them. Leaving her. Harder than leaving Germany, even." His shoulders lifted and then collapsed. "*Pschiu,* Murray, I'm talking all night here. Enough, yes? Enough for *two* histories."

During the first hour after our good-night hug, I lay happily in darkness. There was my father entering the hotel lobby with roses and poems. There was my mother taxiing homeward with tears and forgiveness. It was like a movie.

Just as I was gliding toward sleep, the voice intervened: Why did he find it so hard to leave Barbara?

Sweat was trickling down my neck. The pillow smelled sour. I wanted to fall asleep.

Why didn't you ask him when he's coming home?

He's already home.

Home for good? Why didn't you ask when he's coming home for good?

He may not have an answer.

Really?

He may not have the right answer.

What's holding him up from coming home for good?

Don't ask.

Is it harder to leave a woman or a son?

When I turned on the desk lamp, it was midnight, and my pajamas were clinging damply to my skin. I sat cross-legged on the bed and surveyed the radio, the desk, the Tom Mix rings beneath the upraised hoof of Kaiser Wilhelm, the seventy-seven cubbyholes of the collection—looking around my room as if I had just returned from a long trip.

I pushed everything off the desk. On the left side I put the scissors, on the right a pen, and between them a blank sheet of paper. I opened the chocolate-brown folder and copied the crucial sentences, Ernst's and Tante Lotte's, Mom's and Barbara's and Dad's, fifteen or twenty sentences in all. I picked up the scissors and began to cut, quickly, roughly, with metallic chewing sounds. I slid the strips into an envelope and slid the photograph in beside them. One step remained. I wrote my own letter to Mr. Sklar, explaining what I had done. *Pages would be a kind of lie. For the moment there are only pieces. Pieces of family secrets. Signed, Murray Baum.*

14

Tuesday. D Day.

Jeep was holding me by the elbow. "Murray, is four pages too short? Did Sklar say six was the minimum or the maximum? I heard last year he tore someone's draft in half right in front of the class. Jesus Christ, I shouldn't have eaten that banana with my cereal." His crew cut bristled like the fur of a scared cat. "Footnotes! Jesus, I have to find those publication dates. Thanks for the help, Mur. Bye."

I leaned over the water fountain, holding the plump white envelope at arm's length, safe from the spray.

"Is that a love letter to some lucky girl, Murray?"

"Ruth!"

"You haven't called me in ten days, and now you're writing love letters to someone else."

"Ten days? Can't be. If today's Tuesday, then—"

"A week ago Friday at eleven-thirty was when we—" She looked left and right and, hugging her books, mouthed a slow kiss. Right there outside my homeroom.

"Ruth!" I stepped back and bumped against the water fountain. "I'll call you tonight."

"You're just saying that."

"No, I'm not saying it. I mean, I *mean* it."

With a shake of her head, she turned and walked off. Did she practice moving her rear end that way, or did it just happen by itself?

Bobby L. clapped me on the shoulder. "Hey, friend, lust is dribbling down your chin."

"Water fountain," I mumbled, rubbing my chin. "You shithead."

"Hey, I'm envious. Ruth's the hottest thing in the eleventh grade."

"Yeah, yeah," I said, trying not to look pleased. "Did you get the JRP done?"

"Two weeks ago. It all depends on planning, Murray. My sister did an essay on Prohibition for her history course at NYU. So I had what you might call a head start doing my JRP on Prohibition."

"That's plagiarism, Bobby."

"Every word is in my own writing." He pulled out his wallet. "Here's something you might need this weekend, Mur. A token of friendship." He pressed a packet into the palm of my hand.

I looked down at the gold-foil envelope and closed my

fingers over it, glancing around to see if anyone had noticed. "Jesus, Bobby! This is a—"

"A rubber. Brand-new. Think of me when you use it."

"Take it back," I said. He dodged around my hand. There was nothing to do but hide the rubber in my pocket. No, Mom would find it there. In the compartment inside my wallet, then.

I bent over the water fountain and rubbed water on my cheeks. I had to cool down before I talked with Miss Moran.

"Greetings." Ferguson was propped on a windowsill, wearing sandals and no socks.

Bare toes don't belong in school, I wanted to tell him. But what I said was, "How's the rabbi feeling on D Day?"

"Splendid. I've just finished proofreading the JRP, and I didn't yawn once. How's yours?"

I waved the envelope. "Here she is."

"A letter?"

"Worse: pieces of letters, plus a photograph."

"Telegrams from the Delphic oracle."

"Great title, but you keep it."

"I've got my title. You will do what you must."

We were silent for a while. I watched his toes wiggling under the leather straps.

"Well, Mur, do you like it?"

"Like what?"

"My title. 'You Will Do What You Must.' It's from Gandhi. He was talking about the disobedience movement in India, but it also fits American COs. West meets East."

"East meets West. One flew over the cuckoo's nest."

Only five minutes left to give Miss Moran my second round of pleas. They had succeeded once, when I had asked for an extra week to write the poetry essay. But twice?

"Murray!" Her face filled with a smile. "My star student." She pointed a pencil toward the empty chair beside her. "Talk with me."

I sat and avoided her eyes. What would she say when her star student confessed his crime? "Well, as things would have it . . . I mean, the fact is . . . It's the Auden essay."

"I've gotten essays in folders and boxes, but never inside an envelope."

"No, no, this is, uh, something else." I tried to flatten the bulge of the envelope but only sent more wrinkles racing across it. "Miss Moran, I'm really sorry, but I haven't written the Auden essay. Again." I looked down at the floor. "My father came home last week, and things got pretty complicated at home. I asked him some questions for the JRP." As I held up the envelope, it crackled between my fingers. "He told me things that were . . . kind of upsetting. All about when he was a boy riding a horse that was killed, and later, about things to do with him and Mom. It's a long story. The point is, I tried working on Auden. I even picked out the poem: 'In Memory of W. B. Yeats.' It's just that—"

"'Now he is scattered among a hundred cities and wholly given over to unfamiliar affections.'"

The papers on her desk stirred in the breeze. The second-period warning bell rang. "Wow," I said. "You quoted that from the poem."

"When I was young I used to memorize a lot of poems."

"That's wonderful."

She shrugged. "Not as wonderful as writing them." She put her elbows on the desk and clasped her fingers under her chin. "Take the time you need, Murray. After things calm down at home, I look forward to reading what you write about the memory of Yeats."

"Thanks for being so understanding, Miss Moran."

The envelope seemed to grow heavier as I carried it from class to class. Heavier and more dangerous hour by hour as seventh period approached, when it was due. Midway through sixth-period study hall I couldn't stand it any longer. "Please, Mr. Sklar, take this," I said.

He lowered the *Wall Street Journal* and peered over his glasses, chewing his pencil—or what was left of it. "What have we here, Baum?" He plucked the pencil from his lips and dropped it beside the others, all deeply chewed. "A handwritten excuse from Mama that Murray was throwing up last night and couldn't do his JRP?"

"No, sir. It's my JRP draft. My only excuse is the one I wrote for myself."

He took out my letter and read it and then read it again. "You don't make things easy, do you, Baum?"

"I'm sorry. The reason I—"

"I wasn't reprimanding you. 'Pages would be a kind of lie.' Hunh!" He scowled out the window. "Can you imagine what it's like up here? After years of working with these poky pubescent puppies, you're tempted to lower your standards. Out of misplaced pity. Or sheer fatigue. And then someone comes along who tempts you to hold out for another few years."

A deep line curved down from his nostril to the corner of his mouth. A fan of tiny wrinkles twitched beneath his left eye. It was a weary face.

"You look pale, Baum. Are you all right?"

"Yes, sir."

"Good." He bit the pencil with what might have been a smile. Carefully, he folded the letter into the envelope and slid the envelope into the pocket of his jacket. "Very good."

All afternoon I felt as if I were riding buoyantly inside that pocket.

■ ■ ■

Somewhere between dessert and the second cup of coffee, he announced he was leaving. I wasn't surprised. The signals had been building for several days: those silences during meals, when we heard our forks scraping against our plates; the slipperiness between her eyes and his as they met across the table and zoomed away; and finally his quick cough as he set his spoon in the saucer and launched the after-dinner speech. It was a short speech, and no one asked any questions. Theo washed the dishes, Mom and Dad listened to Edward R. Murrow's news analysis, and I tried to do my homework.

A Sunday flight, three-fifteen in the afternoon: three and a half days away. Thursday and Friday and Saturday. Then the Xs would resume their familiar march across the calendar. I wished he would leave sooner than Sunday. It was so painful to hold him as if he weren't about to disappear. So tempting to believe I could hold on to him.

"What did Mr. Sklar say about your family history paper?" He stood in my doorway, wearing the orange and green Hawaiian shirt he had bought the year before over our embarrassed protests. "Is your dad going to get a mark of A?"

"No way to know."

"Can I come in, Murray?" His body displaced huge amounts of air. The room turned small as he sat on my bed.

"You're crushing my poetry book."

He lifted one thigh and pulled out the book. "W. H. Auden. When I was in school, they only let us read dead authors. And I mean dead."

"Dad, I have a lot of homework to do."

"I'll only be a minute. Mom thinks you're angry about something. Is she right?"

"What do you think?"

"Why do Jews always answer with a question? Murray, please."

"When are you coming back? Coming home?"

"*Na ja,* that depends on what I do to establish the text market, and of course decisions also must be made at the home office. I wish I knew exactly when, believe me, but . . ."

He rubbed his palms down his shirt, leaving moist streaks among the orange and green trees. "I have the idea of you and Theo visiting me in California when your school ends. How do you like that?"

"I don't want to visit you, Dad. I want you here."

"I wish I had the magic to do that, abracadabra."

I didn't smile.

He stood up. "I'm sorry, son." He stood above me, puzzled, as if trying to remember the sequence of moves in a hug, but I didn't help him. "I love you," he said.

"Goodbye," I whispered.

Thursday and then Friday.

Mr. Sklar gave back my JRP draft with a note attached.

> Good work, Baum, and now what? Are you going to make a tidy truth out of messy reality, or are you going to acknowledge the true messiness of reality?

The scribbled note joined the other pieces in the JRP envelope. There was nothing else—no grade, no corrections, nothing but more wrinkles softening the envelope where it had been carried in Mr. Sklar's pocket, against his chest.

Thursday and Friday, Friday and Saturday.

I kissed Ruth after the Gregory Peck double feature, inside her mouth where our tongues pushed and slid hungrily. When we paused for breath, she said, "You look sad."

I shrugged.

"Is it about me?" she asked.

"No." He was my father. He was my problem. How could she understand? Going home, I felt lonely.

Late-night radio stations blurted and hissed as I rolled the dial. The Philadelphia A's sputtered in my ear for an inning or two, during which Gus Zernial blasted a record-making seventh homer in four days, but then static rolled in and the A's disappeared. Messy reality.

Dad took us out to eat pizza, and tomato burned the roofs of our mouths. Dad said he would certainly, almost certainly, be home by July, but we shouldn't ask for impossible promises. Mom toyed with the uneaten crusts on her plate and didn't say anything to any of us.

"What madness," she exclaimed that night in the living room when the radio announced that Chinese and North Korean armies were moving south, leaping over their comrades' corpses, hundreds of thousands of men pushing American armies back toward the Thirty-eighth Parallel, where the war had started a year before.

Friday and Saturday, Saturday and Sunday, three-fifteen, TWA flight 56.

The roar of engines made it difficult for me to think of anything else. The propellers blurred into faint gray circles. The huge silver body trembled and then rolled on its tiny wheels down the runway. Faster. Runway. Straining upward. Desperate roar. And when it disappeared, it left nothing behind. Almost nothing. He had kissed me on the cheek. I remembered the sweet smell of his cologne but not what he had whispered, if he had really whispered anything at all.

In the taxicab going home, the three of us had nothing to say.

Mom lay on her bed with a damp washcloth over her eyes. Theo crouched in front of the living-room radio, doing his homework.

"He disappeared in the dead of winter": I read and reread Auden's poem and thought of nothing but the hunger in my stomach. I made a sandwich and wasn't hungry and wrapped it in wax paper and put it into the refrigerator. I brushed my teeth until my gums burned.

In that last moment before I turned off the lamp beside my bed, I felt a terrifying wrench of homesickness. But it must have been something else, because I was home, wasn't I?

15

The following Saturday I laid W. B. Yeats to rest shortly before lunch.

> In the variety of his meter and rhyme scheme, and of course his imagery, Auden shows us the variety of the poet he admired. His eulogy is sad, but joyful, too. Auden does not let us forget how much there was to Yeats. He covers him not under black cloth, but in a coat of many colors.

I was sure that last paragraph would send Miss Moran into ecstasy. I read it aloud to myself, and then I read it to Ferg over the phone. "Bravo," he said. "Would you write my eulogy when the time comes?" At that very instant the sirens began to sound, climbing from a long growl to a frantic warble as the city tested its civil-defense warning system. "I was only joking," Ferg shouted.

I read my paragraph to Mom, too—twice, because the first time she didn't listen. "*Ach*, those sirens will be in my nightmares again. Aren't two wars enough for one life?"

I phoned Sol and read him the paragraph. "Nice," he said, "really nice, Mur." For the next hour he described Lianne's face and Lianne's family and Lianne's ideas about school and life, and asked me to reassure him again that a guy wasn't crazy to fall for a girl, even have dreams about her, after only two dates.

Before I could think about it too long, I phoned Arlie and said whatever happened to tumble out of my mouth, which was, "I still know your number by heart."

"Murray?" she asked, muffled, as if emerging from a long sleep.

"Is it too early? Because believe me, I didn't plan to phone you, and actually I don't know why I am, except I did. Oh God."

She was laughing by then. "I don't have the slightest idea what you're talking about, Murray, but welcome back."

It went more easily after that. I read her my Yeats paragraph. We talked about school, and my father, and her daydreams of visiting Paris that summer. When it began to go uneasily, when my throat tightened around unspoken questions such as "Where are we going?" I hastily said goodbye.

Finally there was no denying it any longer: Yeats was

dead, and my essay was done. The time had come, no denying it, to face the JRP.

I emptied the envelope onto my desk and stared at the pieces of paper. They moved away from my breath, curling against the pencil sharpener. It was Yeats's last afternoon as himself, said Auden. But where was Willy himself or Dad himself or anyone else among these white strips I had cut out of years of silence? Stubborn silence. As stubborn as Mr. Sklar tipped back in his chair.

Furiously I mixed the papers, under and over, sideways and upside down. All right, Mr. Sklar: you asked for untidy truth, and you'll get it.

Nothing happened. Barbara and Willy remained in Connecticut, and Mom in the kitchen, and Dad in California, and I hadn't written a word.

Two o'clock.

A dozen sentences and one photograph: dumb stuff. They refused to tell me what Willy did because, and what Tante Lotte meant when, and how Dad really felt about, and what Mom expected but was afraid to.

I needed messy reality, whatever that meant. A handful of Barricini candy wrappers? A billy club stained with a patch of dried blood? Should I dump those on Mr. Sklar's desk?

Three o'clock.

I crossed the room and stared Duke Snider in the eye. He stared back, as unwavering as the Louisville Slugger above his shoulder, unquestionably himself. Good old Duke, batting cleanup on the reality team.

That was when I had the idea. Whether it came from Duke or me I've never understood, but it undeniably came and wouldn't go away. I dug in the bedroom closet among

Dad's empty sleeves and scratchy woolen collars and silky linings, inhaling the aroma of his sweat.

There it was, the brown suede jacket, the one he wore to Ebbets Field on cool evenings early in the spring and late in the fall, when the season was very young and everything was still possible or the season was almost over, the Dodgers had been mathematically eliminated, and we cheered anything because on opening day the following year every team would be in first place again. Peanut shells chattered in the pocket.

With the jacket draped over my shoulders, I sat at my desk and stared at the wall of cubbyholes. A film of perspiration spread over the places where the suede sleeves slept upon my arms.

The slow shush of passing cars rose and fell like ocean waves against the windowsill. A piano played a muted sonata many apartments away. The city was breathing evenly, forgetting the panic of sirens. I shrugged off the jacket. I was ready. The words came quickly.

Truth and Consequences: A History of My Parents
by Murray Baum

When Samuel Baum and Annelise Nadelman were growing up in Berlin during the early 1900s, they did not know each other. When she emigrated to New York City in February of 1933 and he in March, they did not suspect that they would meet in April. But meet they did, at a photography show of a friend of hers, Ernst Meyerowitz. Within days she was writing, "You shall never be sorry about being in love with me."[1] He in turn wrote of his "fatalistic optimism" for their future together.[2] Six months later they married. Seven months after that, he told her, "I don't know how to think in terms of three of us."[3] I was the third, arriving on September 16, 1934. A fourth, Theo, arrived three years later.

In this essay I hope to explain why my parents' lives have taken the directions they have. Why, first of all, did my father go to California on December 27, 1950?

It took me three pages to explain, almost two hours of writing and erasing and writing again before I had the pieces laid out in some kind of order. His bosses had assigned him to a new market, but actually he was fighting with Jacob Silver, and most of all there was that loyalty oath he wouldn't sign, a stubbornness for which his bosses had banished him to California, "a sunny Siberia." (That was such a great phrase, I almost underlined it.)

As my mother once said, my father's refusal to sign was heroic but also dangerously naive.[4] What if the company had not arranged a compromise but had fired him, the way schools and movie studios and so forth are firing people who will not sign loyalty oaths.[5] To be true to one's conscience is admirable, but truth can hurt people.

My father knows this and regrets it, but he can't help it. He is a man of principle, a man who must tell or do the truth, even if it causes pain to his family or himself. Back in Berlin after World War I, for example . . .

I stopped writing when I heard the shuffle of Mom's slippers along the hallway floor. Slow and wary steps. Then she was in the doorway, shielding her eyes with an arm against the light. "Murray, have you gone crazy? It's one in the morning."

"I'm fine. Working on the JRP, that's all."

"At one o'clock, working? Only burglars work so late."

She stood behind me, rubbing my shoulders. "May I read it?" she asked.

I laid my hand over the page. "When I'm done."

"Darling, you must get some sleep. Teenagers need—but what's this?" The sleeve of the jacket hung limp between her hands.

"I borrowed Dad's jacket."

"Next you walk around in his shoes and play his magic tricks on us."

"Mom, please."

It took me two whole evenings and part of an afternoon to write the rest of it. One paragraph notched into the next and then the next. I was writing the way Preacher Roe was pitching, seven and then eight and finally nine wins before he lost a game.

> Back in Berlin after World War I, for example, he supported the revolutionaries—secretly, because his father supported the kaiser. One day, Samuel rode his father's favorite horse . . .

The Kaiser Wilhelm episode came quickly. The next night after dinner—Spartacists, gunfire, and the dreaded Herr Baum—while the wooden horse kicked its hoof in the cubbyhole above my head.

> Although my father is a man of principles, he hasn't given up everything for them, the way his lifelong friend Willy Jacobs did.

The story of Willy and the clubbing on Schermerhorn Street was easy—I had written it often enough already in my head. The next part, the part about Barbara, was quite another matter. I put down a sentence and crossed it out, another sentence and crossed that one out.

> A family friend.
> My father's friend.
> A woman my father knew.
> Used to know.
> Loved.

Each phrase seemed like a different kind of accusation. My shoulders ached, as if I had been carrying a heavy suitcase up a steep mountain, but I couldn't stop. Not now. "They won't hand you their secrets," Mr. Sklar had said.

> Unfortunately, Willy and my father broke off their friendship because of a terrible misunderstanding between my parents. My mother accused Dad of carrying his friendship with Barbara Jacobs "across the line." He denied it. She didn't believe him. Anger and suspicion pulled them further and further apart, like a tide carrying a child out to sea while his parents' backs are turned.[14] When my mother went to a hotel and refused to return home, tension climbed to the danger point. A tragedy of truly Shakespearean proportions seemed to be in the making. Just in time, my father promised to stop seeing Willy and Barbara. It was, he says, the hardest decision of his life.[15] He made it because of his commitment to his wife. If there must be pain, then let it be to himself rather than to her.
>
> The crisis was over, but it stays alive in people's minds, and no one seems to agree on what it meant. My mother calls it "an unpleasant story,"[16] while my father calls it "no joke."[17] My mother's sister, Lotte, believes my father took a turn toward silence and sadness.[18] Ernst Meyerowitz refuses to say anything at all.[19] Of course the Jacobses

> have vanished, which is a statement of some sort or other.
>
> Personally, I think that the crisis, although deeply upsetting, did not mark a "turning point" in my parents' history together. Before as well as since, they have remained true to each other as husband and wife, and also true to their individual personalities: the "*Luftmensch*" ("the man who floats in air") and the woman at home.

As I ran my fingers along the warm silk lining of his jacket, I found a little pocket, inside which were three ticket stubs that read "Unreserved Grandstand, June 17, 1950." Carefully I returned them to their resting place. Without taking off my clothes, I climbed into bed and fell asleep.

The last section, in which I told my mother's history, gave me no trouble. The Weimar days as nurse and "flapper," the escape from Hitler's Germany, romance and marriage and motherhood: each episode settled neatly upon the white page, paragraph by paragraph, in colorful detail. It was as if I were describing a photograph in front of my eyes.

> My parents became American citizens in 1938, but I think she has been more reluctant about it. No baseball or "loud" Hawaiian shirts for her. A part of my mother, one might say, still lives in the old homeland.

I went to the kitchen and ate a chocolate-chip cookie. "How goes your book, Mr. Historian?" Mom called from the bedroom.

"Almost done."

I took a glass of milk and another cookie back to my desk. The story had come back around to the present and was waiting for me to finish it.

This history of my parents ends in the present, but of course their lives will go on into the future for at least another twenty years. In other words, it ends at the halfway point, so we will have to wait and see what consequences come after these truths.

I put down the pen, took a deep breath, and raised both hands high. It was the longest essay I had ever written, fifteen notebook pages, plus nineteen footnotes, ready for Mom to type up over the weekend.

The JRP was finished.

16

What did Thomas Hardy do after writing the last page of *Jude the Obscure*, or what's-his-name at the end of the *Decline and Fall of the Roman Empire*? Surely they didn't put on their pajamas and go to sleep.

I found the ice cream sandwich in the far left corner of the freezer compartment, behind the green beans, where I had hidden it the week before from Theo, who was still too short to see that far back. After the last bite melted in my mouth, I phoned Ferg.

"I wish I were heading in your direction," he said.

"What does that mean?"

"I've been *un*doing my JRP—shrinking it and shrinking it until there's almost nothing left."

"But last week you showed me that first draft."

"Every time I reread a sentence I found a flaw, or it seemed trivial, and I cut it. And then another sentence. And another."

I heard a long sigh, as if the phone were leaking air. "Ferg? You still there?"

"Murray, listen to this. 'A man's conscience says yes by saying no. As Gandhi's life suggests, few words are good enough, and deeds are best. As Gandhi's death suggests, the only success is that every failure has been perfectly spoken.'"

"Ferg, I . . . Maybe I need to read the rest of it to understand."

"There *is* no rest of it."

"That's it? Your whole JRP is those three sentences? Jesus God, Ferg."

"Three sentences. The essence. Pure."

"But that's like saying a one-inning ball game is purer than a nine-inning game."

He laughed. "Isn't it?"

"That's crazy, Ferg. Who wants to go to Ebbets Field for a twelve-minute ball game? You want to spend the whole goddamn afternoon there, let the thing develop, have time to worry about who's coming up for the Cardinals in the top of the ninth. You want to know that it could go into extra innings, Ferg. A one-inning game is . . . nonsense. Sometimes you—"

"I'm sorry I made you mad."

"Ferg, you worry me."

"You sound like my mother."

"I mean it. You're whittling everything smaller and smaller. At this rate—"

"At this rate I'll grow so small that I'll come to school and you won't see me. Stuart Little."

"Ferg."

"A mouse driving an invisible car around his doctor's office, careening into chair legs."

"Ferg, you've got to stop this. It's not funny."

"It certainly isn't."

I heard wet noises, as if he were blowing his nose. "How about you and me getting together for an ice cream cone?"

The noises subsided. A long pause. "Ice cream?"

"Ice cream. Chocolate, vanilla, strawberry. Remember?"

Another pause. "This one may be too much even for Dr. Turds Mole."

■ ■ ■

Is their life after the JRP? someone had written in red crayon above the sink in the school bathroom. Dutifully I took out a pencil and changed *their* to *there.*

Red Crayon couldn't spell, but he was smarter than I gave him credit for. After the JRP, I felt paralyzed. I sat at home waiting for something to happen. All afternoon.

All evening. Mom and Theo went to see *South Pacific* because Mary Martin was about to quit after two years of washing her hair every matinee and evening, and Theo had begged to see her one last time. I said I had heard enough "Bali Ha'i" coming from his room, so they went without me.

I cleared the scrap paper off my desk and spread my fingers across the empty surface.

Few words are good enough.

I sat and listened to the silence during which, again and again, the phone didn't ring and no one said, "I know your number by heart."

Every failure perfectly spoken.

I arranged the mail from Dad in chronological order. Nine cards and four letters. Thirteen into 156 days equals exactly twelve, but of course that included the week he was visiting.

Visiting his own home?

■ ■ ■

All through Saturday afternoon, Mom typed the JRP with a comforting clickclack. Then the sound stopped and she was standing in my room. "What do you think you write here?" She held the typed pages straight out from her shoulder, like a dirty towel. "A Shakespeare tragedy! I suppose your father is Hamlet." She sat down heavily on the bed, while the pages fluttered to the floor. "How dare you?"

"You gave me the letters."

"Not for you to make up this . . . soap opera."

"I have the evidence. Nineteen footnotes."

"Don't you get smart with me. 'Giving up his dear friends caused him pain. All for the love of his wife.' What about my pain?"

"Mom!"

"You want the truth? I tell you the truth." She lit a cigarette and shook the match roughly. "Giving up the Jacobses wasn't his idea. It was my idea. Mine. 'For six months I don't want you to see her,' I said. He argued and argued until finally I went to the hotel. There I waited for two days, two whole days, before he promised." She exhaled a dirty-gray stream of smoke. "But that wasn't the end of it."

Smoke was clouding my room. I wanted her out of here.

"Last summer I opened his desk drawer and found a color photograph. Barbara. The beauty queen, somewhat plump now. Barbara is looking at me from my husband's desk drawer. 'It's nothing,' he says. 'One day she phoned up and we talked awhile, and she sent me the photo.'"

"Mom, stop."

"'If it's nothing,' I said, 'promise me never to speak to her again.' But of course he refused. The same old argument." She ground the cigarette against the side of my wastebasket. "The same old argument except this time he's in California." She stood up and gestured toward the pages between her shoes. "Now write what really happened."

"But now—I mean—it's due tomorrow, and . . ."

"Plenty of time. Change a few sentences, and I type them tonight. I need to make the stuffed cabbage."

When would it ever be finished?

No one told me the same story.

Dad would never promise.

Late that night, after Mom had typed up the rest of the JRP, she offered to type the revisions. I said I had already written them in pen. That was a lie. I hadn't changed a single word.

17

With final exams only two weeks off, I Scotch-taped a day-by-day study schedule on the wall beside Duke Snider. *Review French on Sat; Math on Sun; Engl. on Mon. . . .* I needn't have bothered. I might as well have written *Ruth, Arlie, Ferg, and Sklar. And Ruth and Arlie.*

■ ■ ■

When Ruth asked me to go out, I promised myself I would tell her I was in touch with Arlie again. But I never got around to it. Instead, by way of a hundred hand-in-hand circles around the Central Park skating rink, and an arm-in-arm stroll among the Rockefeller Center flowers, and an hour of hard kisses on her living-room couch, I arrived at Ruth's right breast. She allowed my hand. She greeted my hand with wriggling pleasure as it explored the nylon slope of blouse and, nervously, bra and then, incredulously, flesh. Her nipple grew. Her fingers scraped my back. My face felt hot and cold and very hot. "God!" I exclaimed, and I heaved myself free.

"Don't you like it?"

"Too much. I like it too much."

She was buttoning her blouse. "I'm glad you're not the kind who takes advantage of a girl."

"I'm sorry, Ruth."

"For what?"

What was I sorry for? "Forget it."

"Oh, I can't. This night was too special to forget."

As she took my hand and looked up at me, her dark eyes brimming with all my virtues, I realized just how much advantage I had taken. "You deserve something special," I said.

I kept saying it under my breath for fifteen blocks as I walked home, until at my doorstep I promised myself I would invite her to the Junior-Senior Prom.

■ ■ ■

The phone rang early the next morning, bringing Arlie's throaty voice. "Asleep? Come on, Rip Van Winkle Baum, it's spring."

"Arlie."

"You don't sound very glad."

"I called you all week and you weren't home."

"Oh, Murray, must you hold grudges?"

Did she propose our going out together, or did I, or we?

There was no time for questions. Only time to take a shower, eat some toast, and catch a bus to Fifty-ninth Street at eleven o'clock sharp.

There she was, with her back to me, standing beside the fountain in that familiar white dress with one strap off the shoulder. I wished I could dance up to her like Gene Kelly and take her hand, and then the two of us would swing gracefully around the fountain.

She turned as if she had felt me watching, and I ran toward her with open arms.

"There you are at last," she said, hugging me. "I'm starving."

We found big jelly doughnuts in a tiny grocery store whose mustachioed owner made jokes in Italian, to which Arlie responded in French. We walked through the jewelry district, looking at the diamonds in the windows as we licked our fingers and debated the Sinatras' divorce.

"Fickle Frank," I said.

"Dumb Nancy, to let herself be fickled," Arlie replied.

We rode down Fifth Avenue on the upper level of a double-decker bus, holding hands, too contented to talk.

Beside the arch of Washington Square, a saxophonist with one gold earring played jazz—cool, difficult jazz—to a semicircle of people who nodded and swayed and tossed coins into the open sax case.

Finally we were standing on the crest of the Brooklyn Bridge, where the wind blew her hair like a blond flag toward the Atlantic Ocean.

For four months I had renounced her, and now suddenly we had resumed where we had broken off.

"Strange how things happen," I said. "You want my theory? We're part of a great design. Up there behind that white cloud, Thomas Hardy is writing like crazy, writing out our lives."

"No thanks. You be Jude the Obscure if you want. But I'm Arlie, and I'm in nobody's novel." Holding the handrail, she tipped back stiff-legged on her heels. "At night you can hear the wind playing the cables like harp strings. In the key of F sharp."

"F sharp? Who told you that?"

"I made it up." She laughed and kissed my mouth. "Welcome back, Murray."

But what about Ruth? I had promised her. No, I hadn't promised her. But something had been promised last night on her couch. I should talk with her soon.

■ ■ ■

I found a message from Mom on the kitchen table: *Call Ferg.* But I forgot to call, in the panic of four hundred French vocabulary words plus quadratic equations. And because Ferg wasn't in school on Monday, I continued to forget.

On Tuesday he seemed strangely altered, as if he had lost weight. "What did Sklar say about your JRP?" I asked.

Ferg smiled. "'Three sentences are too many for the Delphic oracle and too few for the JRP.' Quote unquote. He wants to talk with me tomorrow."

Then I recognized the strangeness. "Your glasses. What happened to your glasses, Ferg?" He moved like a subterranean creature, his head following the sounds of things, his hands feeling out a path for his body.

"I forgot them at home."

"Forgot them? You couldn't have got four steps out of bed before walking into a wall."

He smiled, a blind smile that aimed a yard away from my face. "Okay, I didn't forget them. Do we really need to see twenty-twenty? After all, perception simply gets in the way of vision."

"Ferg! Goddamn it. Put your glasses on like everybody else."

He pawed in his lunch bag and pulled out his glasses. "I was just experimenting."

"Well, cut it out. A JRP that's three sentences long. No glasses. These weird tricks are driving me crazy."

"You're not the only one," he said softly.

I pulled off a crust of bread that was dangling from one of his lenses. "After exams, let's talk."

■ ■ ■

Miss Moran gave me what I had expected: *If Auden has wrapped Yeats in a coat of glorious colors, so does your essay. Make the most of your gift of words. Grade: A.*

Mr. Sklar gave me trouble. *You've moved from pieces to pages,* he wrote at the top of the JRP.

> Beautiful pages. You certainly know how to turn a phrase. Still, you could have pushed further. Although you've read your sources meticulously and asked good questions, at times you shy from disagreeable answers. In my view, these key questions remain:
>
> 1. Did Samuel get into trouble simply because of bad luck and naïveté? Dead horse; loyalty oath; sunny Siberia. Step back and think about how to explain this history. As accident or choice?
>
> 2. You have heard a lot from two sides of the emotional rectangle, but only a polite note from Mrs. Jacobs and nothing at all from Mr. Jacobs. What does reality look like from their half of the rectangle?
>
> 3. You're the author of this history. But aren't you also an actor in it?
>
> Grade: B+.
>
> Sklar

Key questions remained. After all this, the JRP was once again undone. A tiny pain fluttered behind my left eye. I crossed my arms on the desk and rubbed my forehead along one wrist. How could I ever put an end to this history?

I dropped the paper into a drawer. B+. I'd settle for that.

■ ■ ■

What should I say to Ruth? Between Yeats poems, I drafted different apologies without ever pinpointing what it was I was apologizing for. Things hardly became clearer when I met her at three o'clock and dropped all my books.

"I can't hear you down there," she said as I muttered on hands and knees.

"I'm sorry but I can't take you to the prom I'm really sorry," I said in one desperate breath.

"But you never asked me."

"Of course I didn't. But I can't."

"Bye." "So long." "Break a leg." Friends brushed past us on their way home while I stood there watching her unforgiving face.

"I enjoyed Saturday night," I said at last.

"Don't change the subject."

"I didn't. I mean, I want to see you again."

"You just said you don't want to take me to the prom."

"Yes. No."

"I'm the kind of girl who feels very strongly. Right now I feel very hurt. And angry."

"I'm sorry." I reached toward her. "What can I do?"

"You might try jumping in the nearest lake."

■ ■ ■

On prom night, Arlie and I whirled without pause. We waltzed and fox-trotted at the school gym, and then we drank ice-cold champagne at Sol's parents' midnight brunch, and then we laid two white roses on the doorstep of what Arlie insisted was e. e. cummings's skinny house, and as dawn began bleaching away the night, we boarded the Staten Island ferry.

"'We were very tired, we were very merry. We went back and forth all night on the ferry,'" I recited. "You be Edna and I'll be St. Vincent."

We waved at Miss Liberty, and on the return trip we waved again, standing in the bow where the cool air rushed against our faces. The skyline of Manhattan was cutting a zigzag horizon across the pink sky.

"I love you," I said.

"I love you, too."

"What I mean is, I'm in love with you, Arlie."

This time she didn't reply. I pulled her to me.

"When you hold me so close," she said, "you can't see me."

"I'm seeing you. I'm kissing you with my eyes wide open. Look, Ma, no hands." I flapped my arms and made a cackling laugh.

"We've been through this argument too often, Murray. And you always end up hurt."

"Why don't *you* ever end up hurt, Arlie?"

We stared at each other across that unexpected question. Who knows where it might have led us if the ferry whistle hadn't blared and we hadn't run belowdecks?

SUMMER

18

The "Hail, Seniors" meeting of King Arthur's Round Table should have been a gala occasion. Foxx's invitations, written on silver foil in what looked like blood, promised *Wine, Women, Song, quantities limited, so come early.* Sol brought silly green party hats with feathers. Jeep flashed a ten-dollar bill—his parents' reward for his having made it safely through eleventh grade—and promised to pay for all the hot dogs we could eat. It should have been grand.

Maybe we were expecting too much. Or maybe in those green hats we didn't look like ourselves. In any case, we were full of jumpy questions and didn't listen for answers. "Didya get your report card?" "Whatcha doin' this summer?" "Wanna go to a ball game?"

Foxx picked us up with a rendition of *The Thing,* a movie in which vegetables from Venus come to Earth to devour dogs and sheep, but Bobby L. dropped us again with a joke about a blind Japanese waitress in a kosher deli. Ferguson turned a pencil end over end. Foxx was humming scales up and down. Jeep built little columns of nickels that he toppled with one finger and then rebuilt.

I tried a toast. "To the brothers of the Round Table," I said, raising my glass. "May we have a summer full of lovely maidens and timid dragons." But after we drank and Bobby L. belched and Sol said "Excuse you," Ferguson went back to his pencil and Jeep to his nickels and Foxx to his humming.

"Hey, Bobby," Jeep said, "I bet my mother you'd eat seven bucks' worth of hot dogs, and you're still on your first. You got ulcers, or what?"

"Yeah," added Sol, "what's happened to the love affair between you and food?"

"Maybe he's found a girl to eat," Jeep said.

"Maybe he's turned vegetarian like Rabbi Ferg."

We were all watching Bobby L. to see which prod would be one too many.

"What do you say, Mr. Big?" I asked.

He smiled and patted his stomach. "Are you assholes ready for a surprise? A big surprise. I've lost twelve pounds this month."

As our hoots subsided, Bobby L. raised a hand. "But that's not the surprise. You know why I'm getting in shape? Because next week I'm signing up with the marines."

"Jesus Christ!" someone said.

"Jesus H. Christ!"

The marines!

He leaned back, his hands clasped across his chest, and gave us a little smile.

"You mean you're not going back to school?" I asked.

"It's called boot camp, pal. Eight weeks of boot camp and then off to Korea to tear up a few Commies."

"Korea," Sol said softly. "What did your mother say?"

"She cried for a while, and then she said, 'It's your life.'"

"Or your death," Ferguson mumbled.

Bobby L. turned toward him. "The marines sure don't write you a fucking money-back guarantee. But you know something, Mahatma Ferg? That's what I like about them. It's *real* out there. Not like all those multiple-choice French tests and JRPs that ask you to jerk off inside your head."

"Life or death is certainly a real multiple-choice test," Ferguson replied. He took off his glasses and blinked blindly at Bobby L.

Nobody said anything. Bobby suddenly seemed older than the rest of us. He had unrolled a future ahead of himself, straight into the barbed wire of Korea. For a month he had been losing weight, talking to marine recruiters, preparing to wrap a belt of grenades around his waist, and none of us had noticed until this afternoon, when all at once he had outgrown us.

My stomach went tight against my belt. We were going to fall away. No matter how hard we held on to the Round Table.

Foxx was on his feet, and then we all were. "Lots of luck, Lieutenant," he said.

"An hour after you hit that beachhead," Jeep said, "the Commies will surrender."

"Bobby L. Kirk Douglas."

"Hey, before you go," Sol said, "why is it Bobby L. instead of just Bobby?"

"'Cause my father was called Bobby. He was Robert L. Brown, and I'm Robert L. Brown, Junior. They didn't want to call me Junior, thank God, so they gave me the L. After he died, the habit just kept on going." He squared his shoulders and coughed. "He would have made colonel. That's what everybody said. Bobby L. Brown was going to make colonel faster than anyone since Douglas fuckin' A. MacArthur."

Bobby L. looked over our heads. Jeep and Sol were watching him with puzzled frowns. Foxx was smiling toward the floor. Ferg, without his glasses, was blinking at nothing in particular. I couldn't meet anyone's eye.

"Should auld acquaintance be forgot . . ." As we began to sing, I closed my eyes for fear my friends would see how lost we all were becoming.

19

All morning I killed time. It wasn't easy, killing time, especially at the start of a vacation, when you were out of practice. I spent an hour and a half throwing away old algebra quizzes, filing essays, and, especially, reading Ferg's cryptograms.

As things would have it, we do not know what comes next. Believe me when I say, "Do not believe me." It became a hide-and-seek game, leafing through notebooks for those little yellow squares of paper, each inscribed with his minute script. *The only success is every failure perfectly spoken.* I hadn't realized how many he had sent across our classrooms. *Turds Mole Forever!* That was the last one; it had slid into my hand just as the three-fifteen bell rang on the last day of class and we all broke into cheers. I snapped a rubber band around the yellow squares and filed them under GREAT SAYINGS.

I cut out the week's baseball stats, underlining the names of all the Dodgers. Robinson was at the top, of course, with .385, followed by Stan the Man at .367. "Now you stay good but not too good, Stan My Man," Dad would have been saying as we studied the list. "Dem Bums come first, am I right, Murray?" He loved to say "bums," as if it were a dirty word. Two months into the season, Dem Bums were very much in first, five and a half ahead of the Cards and the Reds, their largest lead since 1947.

I called Arlie, but no one answered.

I listened to the WQXR news at the top of the hour, and then all over again at the top of the next hour, meanwhile racing from room to room synchronizing clocks. I hadn't realized how many clocks our family owned: one on Dad's desk and one next to their bed; one next to my bed; Theo's cuckoo clock with the lead weights, and his electric clock; the stove clock, which had died at 3:03 sometime before I was born, and the square red one on the kitchen wall; plus the old grandfather clock in the hall, which had stopped at four-thirty on some day at the end of December because only Dad knew how to wind it. Eight clocks, five of which worked but every one of which—I discovered as the WQXR hour beeped and I ran, counting seconds loudly over the news—every one of which told a different time.

I poured a glass of milk, sat down at the kitchen table, and opened the *Times*. As I studied the map of the Korean War zone, I tried to imagine Bobby L. shooting at Oriental soldiers, wading through mud, somewhere among these little black arrows.

I called Arlie and no one answered. All week I had been calling. Once I had left my name with her mother; the second time I had told her I was Gus Zernial.

Mom wasn't coming home until at least nine o'clock, after the Planned Parenthood board meeting and dinner with Ernst. Theo was out somewhere with his friend Jay. Hours to kill.

I started reading the first chapter on *From Here to Eternity* and stopped just where I had stopped the day before.

At twelve-thirty the front door slammed as I was standing in the middle of my room, and I realized I had been standing there for quite some time.

"It's me," Theo shouted. "Anybody home?"

"Nobody's home."

"Hi, Murray." Theo's pants were caked brown with mud. "Jay and I saved this girl's sailboat. The wind had blown it over, way out in the middle of the pond where she couldn't get it. So we waded in and saved it."

"Get a reward? Your picture in the *Daily News*?"

He pulled off his sneakers without untying the laces, then pulled off his pants like a pair of banana skins. "Jay says there are alligators in that pond."

"Alligators? Get off it."

"No joke. Kids who visit Florida on vacations bring back these tiny alligators, and their disgusted parents flush them down the toilet. So these little alligators end up in the sewers, Jay says, where they grow bigger and bigger, until some of them crawl into the Central Park pond. Hey, why does the grandfather clock say it's four-thirty?"

"Because it stopped, and Dad's the only one who knows how to wind it. It's been four-thirty for months."

"No kidding. Hey, are there any ice cream sandwiches left?"

"Tell you what," I said. "Let's go out for ice cream cones—my treat."

"You must be feeling rich."

"Bored."

"Then why won't you go to camp with me this summer?" He was flexing his biceps, first one and then the other, prodding them with a thumb.

"I'm too old for camp."

"Sixteen isn't so old."

"Old enough."

"For what?"

I looked past him, stared over the skyscrapers into the pale-blue sky. Somewhere an assignment hovered in waiting for me, although I couldn't define it—could barely imagine it. A man's shadow . . . a voice . . . a blurred landscape . . . and then it evaporated, whatever it was, and I was left with simply a vague sense of an appointment for which I must stay home, in readiness.

"Old enough for what?" Theo repeated.

"It's hard to explain. This summer I just . . . I want . . . I don't know. C'mon, it's ice cream time."

▪ ▪ ▪

A pile of mail was waiting inside the front door when we returned. On top, a bill from Bloomingdale's. Next, for Dad, the New York Chess Club's newsletter. A couple of airmail letters for Mom with fancy stamps from Israel and England. The *Reader's Digest*, which Theo subscribed to for the jokes. At the bottom, a letter to me from Dad.

Something about the envelope made me nervous—perhaps its thickness or the typed address. His other letters had been thin and scribbled.

> This letter will be no fun, I'm sorry. I have just read your JRP again. First I congratulate you on the good grade and compliments by Mr. Sklar.
>
> Also you write some beautiful paragraphs. For example, the part about Mom back in Berlin makes a fine "portrait." You have always been talented with words.
>
> Nevertheless, some things I must argue with you. For many hours I sit here asking myself why not let it go past in silence. Why make "a federal case"? But I decided, Murray, you should know you are mistaken. A son

should know what to think about his father and mother. (This is one of my "principles," you might say.)

You make a strange and wrong story of why I am here in California. It is as I always tell you: a special bussiness assignment. Nothing else. I don't know why you wish to get so smart about my almost losing my job and being sent to "sunny Siberia." (Also I don't like you reading my mail—how did you read Mr. Hersey's letter?) Only *Mom* was worried I lose my job. *I* knew it would be alright in the end. She is the worryer in the family, you remember. Yes, I do not always agree with Silver. But people don't always get along on the job. Look at Dixie Walker and Jackie Robinson!!!

But seriously. Always you ask me "when do you come home?" and you never hear what I answer, and now you get further mixed up by what Mom tells you. So I ask you: *Please Listen For Once!*

~~This business with Barbara and Willy is~~ I wish you would stop fussing about the Jacobses. Mom thinks *she* asked me not to see them for six months, but that is not the way it went. It was *my* idea, I already told you. A difficult idea, because they were our good friends. But also necessary because otherwise it seemed Mom would never get over her ~~craziness~~ alarm. She should not have told you about this fight between us—this isn't children's knowledge. Please understand, Murray, about certain things Mom is not the sensible person she is the rest of the time. Things like feet on the couch, and turning the hall light off. And Barbara! I don't know why, because Barbara is a good loving person.

I don't want to keep fighting with you about Barbara. Nevertheless: *listen to me, once and for all*—there is nothing to promise before I go home. I made only one promise, which is the day we married, and that is promise enough in my book. Why is it not enough in your book? Why must you cry "promise, promise!"? Believe me, I don't enjoy living among strangers out here. But who knows, these months apart may be for the best. (My "fatalistic optimism," *natürlich*!) Because in the end you may finally agree that the truest love is given, not commanded.

I love you.

~~Samuel~~
Dad

Secrets. More secrets. Don't tell me any more.

"Promise," she said. "Why must you cry 'promise, promise!'?" he replied. Dragging me into the middle of their argument.

What am I supposed to do with all your secrets?

"Listen to me, once and for all," you shout over my head.

What do you want of me? Me, damn it! Your son!

I licked my fingers and pressed them against my burning eyes.

I shoved the letter into its envelope and shoved the envelope deep under the woolen sweaters in the bureau. Then I closed my door and turned on the radio so I wouldn't hear Theo giggling at *Reader's Digest*.

▪ ▪ ▪

This time Rabbi Ferg couldn't save Turds Mole from drowning.

"I'm sorry," the woman's voice said over the phone, "he's not here. Who's calling, please?"

"Murray, a friend of his. Do you know when he'll be back?"

"Oh, Murray. It's Allen's mother. How sweet of you to call. No, I'm afraid we just can't predict when Allen will be back."

"Before dinner?"

Her silence went on and on. At last she said, "I gather you haven't spoken with him this week."

"No, but what . . . ?"

"Allen has gone off to the countryside for a rest. His father and I decided it would be a good idea, at least for a few weeks." She said it in a firm, flat tone, as if reading a statement she and her husband had written for reporters.

"What countryside? What's happened?" I shook the receiver.

"Yes, dear, we're all upset."

"What's happening?"

"He was under pressure. A lot of pressure, too much for a young boy, even one as mature as Allen. That project for Mr. Sklar, it went badly, no doubt you know that. I suppose Arthur—Allen's father—shouldn't have become involved. They had never argued before. I shouldn't burden you with this, Murray, but Allen always spoke so warmly of you. He doesn't have many friends his own age. The doctors assure us—"

"Thank you," I said to stop her. "I understand," I said, to keep Ferg from being further garbled. Address, phone number—just give me simple facts, please.

She told me facts. Haven House, Peekskill, New York. Actually just outside Peekskill, on a country estate. No phone calls except from immediate family, but letters were encouraged. Visitors on weekends. Two hours by train. Not a hospital and not exactly a mental hospital. A place to rest, with good food and genial recreation (croquet, a pond). Staff people who knew how to listen helpfully.

I wrote it all down meticulously, gravely, like a message you take from someone who is calling from a phone booth to report a highway accident. "Thank you, Mrs. Ferguson.

Yes, I will call you in a few days. Yes, I will write him immediately. No, I won't worry. Yes, I understand."

After I hung up, I couldn't read the address because I had written everything meticulously on the same line, over and over.

I gave the paper a shake. Goddamn him, why had he done this to me? I crumpled the paper. What right did he have to play his stupid game until it wasn't a game and he left me? I threw the paper against the wall and threw the pencil after it and the ashtray and the coffee cup and the Manhattan and Bronx and Queens phone books. Why, Ferg? Why couldn't you be like everybody else in the goddamn world? I was tearing the *Times*, page after page, a wonderful ripping sound, white and black ribbons of newspaper curling all over the table, the rug, my shoes. Did you travel two hours by train without your glasses, Ferg, blinking like a blind man? How can you play croquet, Ferg, if you can't see the wickets? I walked around the room, kicking chairs.

No one was home when you wanted them.

Suppose Mrs. Ferguson let me live in his room. Under his black cosmic ceiling. There I'd be when he came home tanned and happy from a month among helpful listeners.

Wrong. All wrong. No one in Peekskill would help Turds Mole, whose every failure was too perfectly spoken to be heard.

20

Dear Murray,

My mother told you of my hasty exit to this place. I could have called before I left but there already was too much noise. On the train, the suitcases chattered in the overhead rack while Dad and I rode without a word.

Haven House is no country for young me. The old in one another's arms, hammocks in the trees—those dying generations at their song. Yes, Mur, I brought Yeats with me—not a welcomed guest, however, because the counselors (who call themselves staff and ask me to call them Bill and Roger and Peg) think I need less poetry, more prose. They sound like Mr. Sklar rebuking my Delphic JRP. At least he called himself Mister and permitted a fair fight.

Work crews hammer "One Way Only"
To each bridge and tunnel jutting
From this shrunken island.
With nothing in his pocket
but *Collected Yeats*,
Youth pleads in vain
With tollbooth attendants,
And leaps at last into that dolphin-torn,
That gong-tormented sea.

I'm lonely out here among the crickets and staff. Write.

Turds Mole Forever

PS. I am wearing my glasses.

Dear Ferg. That was as far as I got. I was used to yellow squares of paper across a classroom, not letters from upstate. I didn't know him up there in Haven House. As I held my pen over the blank page, I became a little afraid of him, or of what they might find inside him.

I'll write tomorrow, I promised.

Meanwhile the front hall narrowed between heaps of camp supplies. Mom pedaled the sewing machine far into the night, naming every sock and shirt and bathing suit and

Dodgers cap "Theo Baum." She made Campbell's soup and ham sandwiches for dinner and had no time to talk. Theo Baum. Theo Baum.

■ ■ ■

"Paris! I'm going to Paris! Oh Murray, I can hardly believe it. A present from my French aunt." Arlie practically sang her news over the phone, and I tried to echo her joy.

"Espresso at cafés every morning!"

"Among bearded artists."

"Chatting in French."

"*Mais bien sur*. Oh, isn't it terrific, Murray?"

"Terrific."

"Well, I'll miss you, *mon ami*!"

"Write me."

When I hung up, I was exhausted. I looked at the phone and couldn't believe what it had just told me. A whole ocean away? I wanted to call her back. My fingers closed around the metal receiver and squeezed until my arm was trembling, but the phone was too heavy to lift.

Dear Ferg,

As you can see from the newspaper clippings, things are looking up in this world of ours. The Dodgers are rolling toward the Series, led by Boomboom Hodges and In-the-Dust Robinson and Pitch-'Em-by-'Em Roe. I'm hoping to get to Ebbets Field soon to cheer them on.

The Korean talks sound like the best antiwar news in a long time, don't you think? Poor old Bobby L. may arrive too late for "the action." Well, he can always join the French foreign legion.

And the good old Central Park merry-go-round is moving again. Fifty-seven new horses. But no brass ring, the Parks Department says, in case a kid kills himself reaching.

We miss you. Arlie and Sol and Lianne and Foxx send you greetings and kisses and well-wishes and hellos (you figure out which from whom).

As for me, I say: come home soon. The crickets can get along without you, but Manhattan can't.

Mazel tov,
Murray

PS. Arlie is going to Paris for a month. Lucky her.

I wrote it in a rush, before I could think about it and get stalled. Rereading the letter, it seemed unbearably cheery. But what was a guy supposed to write to his friend in Haven House? Not little yellow cryptograms. Was he even allowed to read newspapers up there? Maybe Haven House was like my dentist's office, full of fat couches and wildlife magazines. Maybe Ferg ambled all day across the lawns, his hands folded behind his back, reciting Yeats to himself. And behind him ambled heavyset, white-coated, balding counselors.

But even unbearably cheery news was better than none.

Dear Dad.

That was as far as I got. Nothing else came to mind. Nothing at all. Across several time zones I shouted absolutely nothing at him. How did Mom manage to keep on typing those letters, clickclack, during however many days he had been gone?

That's when I realized I had stopped counting.

■ ■ ■

Each week the summer settled more heavily upon the city. Each noon the businessmen walked to lunch a bit more slowly, with their jackets slung over one shoulder, a hemisphere of sweat in each armpit. Secretaries sat on benches with their heads tipped back, earning lunch-hour tans. High-speed fans shuddered in windows. Each week more people departed the city for vacations.

Bobby L. went to Camp Lejeune in North Carolina. "Keep your nose clean," we said. "Don't let them cut your hair too short," we said. None of us knew how to say goodbye to a marine, so at Grand Central Station we shouted a lot and avoided looking at his mother, and when the gate opened, each of us shook his hand without a word. Walking down the ramp, he looked straight ahead, his back stiff, marching in one-man formation.

The next week thirteen thousand boys and girls filled Grand Central with suitcases, duffel bags, tennis rackets, and tears as they went off to camp. "Use suntan lotion," Mom shouted over the noise, "and write me on those postcards I gave you." Theo submitted to her hug, then dropped his baseball glove and gave her a quick hug of his own. "See ya later, alligator," I said, and then I heard myself saying, "Call me if you feel homesick." My fingers cupped his neck, the way a grown-up would say goodbye.

He looked at me in surprise. "You were always the homesick one, remember?"

Riding home on the bus, I remembered those nights on a top bunk among eighteen slow-breathing, snoring bodies, with moths flinging themselves against the screen beside my face. I was glad I wasn't going to camp. I turned to Mom to tell her about the moths, but she was staring out the window with a handkerchief against her lips. "You okay, Mom?"

She shook her head once, still staring. "Okay," she said finally.

I tried harder. "I bet that when we walk in the door you're going to sit down and type your first letter to Theo."

This time she turned. "Such a smarty-pants son," she said, "but you lose the bet. I wrote him last night."

"You're kidding! Before he left? What could you write about before he even went away?"

"The thought, not the news, is what counts." She rearranged her dress under her thighs. "It is the two of us now."

After that we didn't say anything. The bus swerved around double-parked cars and lurched through yellow lights. Our shoulders bumped against each other. My leg perspired where it was squeezed against hers. Just the two of us going back to that apartment.

■ ■ ■

A few days later it looked like the beginning of a clothing store, or the end of one. Lumpy mountains of shirts, shoes, coats, and hats sprouted up everywhere, leaving narrow aisles between. To travel from room to room, I had to put one foot delicately in front of the other.

"Why can't you be like every other mother in the world and do your spring cleaning in the spring?"

"Do you want a mother like every other mother?" She was on her knees in the dining room, folding tablecloths.

My finger began to throb from serving as the temporary bookmark squeezed inside the eight-hundred-plus pages of *From Here to Eternity*. I hadn't meant to have a long conversation when I paused en route to the kitchen. But now that there were only the two of us among all these rooms, I couldn't walk by without a word.

"I did," she said.

"You did what?"

"I wanted my mother to be like all the others. With that long red hair of hers, she was too beautiful. 'Throughout Berlin, men dream of your mother's red hair,' my father said once, so proudly. I was seven or eight. The next morning I walked to school looking at every man and wondering: Did you dream of my mother? And you? And you?"

She winced as she got to her feet. "Oof, these knees are rusty." She pushed the hair from her forehead. "It's funny. When I was a girl, she was too close for me to judge if she was as beautiful as they said. And when I grew older and got some distance, then she was already old and not beautiful. That is a—*wie heisst das?* it begins with a *p*."

"Paradox."

She laughed. "You read my mind. And what else? What are you reading there that is so big?"

"Just a book." I tried to step back, but a pile of blankets blockaded me.

"*War and Peace*?" We had a quick tug of war, which I lost. "Ah, not Tolstoy but Jones." She raised one eyebrow. "Do you read forward, or do you read only where the book falls open by itself to the sex scenes?"

"Mom, this is an important piece of literature. A novel about the peacetime army, men's values, and . . ." I couldn't remember the third phrase on the back cover.

"And sex. And dirty words. *Ja,* get out of here before I spring-clean *you*."

Down through the afternoon the vacuum cleaner whined and the iron hissed, the mop clattered against the pail, soft music and voices trickled out of the radio. I pretended the apartment was crowded with tenants. I watched the dust float through the white-hot stripes of sunlight and imagined people in every room talking, playing cards, drinking espresso. The heat thickened on my face. The dust floated.

"Murray!" I woke up with a start. "Murray." She was still knocking on the door as she pushed it open. "I just heard on the radio that Bob Fellow hit a no-hitter."

"What did you say?"

She repeated it and, between yawns, I deciphered the news that Bob Feller had just pitched a no-hitter—the third of his career. "That's big news, Mom. And by the way, pitchers pitch and hitters hit."

"*Ach*, I'm such a *Dummkopf*. Promise me this summer we sit down for three days and you teach me baseball, okay?"

Hit a no-hitter! It seemed amusing at first. But gradually it began to irk me, and by the end of the evening I was thinking, How am I supposed to talk with someone who can't tell a pitch from a hit?

In bed I let *From Here to Eternity* open to the page that Foxx, and Jeep before him, and Bobby L. before Jeep had discovered, where Karen unzips her shorts, drops them along with the halter, and leads Warden to the bedroom. She shuts the door and turns toward him, both arms lifting to reveal the roundness of her breasts, while the long scar on her belly points down to that mysterious triangle. She whispers, "Now. Here. Now. Now," in the hot darkness closing between them. Closer. Closer. Until at last with a single cry they spill over the edge of desire.

I lay under the damp sheet, hugging my knees, trying to comfort myself.

21

With nothing in the day ahead to summon me from the breakfast table, I ate an extra bowl of Rice Krispies and an extra piece of toast with marmalade, and read the newspaper from front to back, all the way from the war headlines and city politics, through pressure-cooker recipes, weddings, editorials, book reviews, and radio listings, to the New York Stock Exchange—every column and paragraph of the history of yesterday. That's how I discovered the want ads.

Boys—Young Men
with or without bicycles
deliver telegrams
$30 to start 40-hour week
Western Union
60 Hudson St. (near Chambers)

Young Man. Under 24, free to travel, California,
return. Must be neat-appearing, single, ambitious.
Permanent work, circ. sales, with excellent future.
See Mr. Joe Martin 10 A.M. to 12 Noon,
Hotel Woodward, 55th & Bwy. DO NOT PHONE.

Stonehand, line-up in position,
$125, SMITH'S AGENCY, 251 W. 42 St.

Silkscreen Squeegee Men, $1.20 / hour,
Active Agency, 80 Warren St., Room 408

I read each ad intently, as if it were one of those tenement windows you glimpsed from the elevated train while you rumbled past. You saw a cat, a torn pink curtain, a woman's arm upon the windowsill, and made each the clue to the lives inside that room.

When I turned the page, I discovered the rest of the plot: those "Boys—Men" who "wanted situations," the applicants who would inhabit those rooms.

> Salesman, personable, aggressive, desires future with reputable outfit. A sales interview will be profitable to you and I. AL6-1096.
>
> Vet, 29, 6′ 3″, 235, personable, seeks interesting position. Box 133, NYT.
>
> Young Man, 30, married, some knowledge uphol., wants future. 196 W. 127th St.
>
> College graduate, accounting, 26, married, car, draft-exempt, diversified experience, anything with future. ME5-6110.

Personable salesman vied with personable vet. Young Man and six-foot three-inch Vet and Married College Grad jostled shoulder-to-shoulder through the narrow doorway of the future. "Anything with future," the last one said. That "anything" made me unreasonably sad.

■ ■ ■

At first there were just the two of us. Sol and I sat in the little park behind the Public Library, sipping Nedick's orange drinks and propping our hands like visors over our eyes. After an hour inside the darkness of the Grand Central Newsreel Theater, the sunlight hurt.

"Woody Woodpecker was pretty funny."

"Lousy sports, though."

Pigeons hustled up for handouts. A bearded man in a torn shirt slept on the bench across from us, one shoe dangling from his toes. I yawned, and yawned again, groggy in the afternoon heat.

". . . but the way she said it, I knew she didn't really—Mur, are you listening to me?"

I nodded. He was talking about Lianne. Every day he talked in detail about Lianne—her hair, her clothes, her opinions, the magazines she read—like some tourist who had returned from an exotic country.

". . . the other night, for example, I just about—" He interrupted himself with a sigh. "I mean, I love her so much that I go crazy wanting it. But she'd never respect me if—you know."

"Yeah," I said, and I realized it was the first time I had ever heard a boy say he loved someone. "Yeah, I know."

We hunched forward, elbows on knees. The pigeons gurgled and strutted in the dirt. "Yeah," Sol said.

A red-cheeked cop strolled up, twirling his nightstick, and contemplated the man on the bench. The shoe swayed in the breeze. "Hey, gramps," the cop said. "Naptime's over." Winking at us, he held the stick at arm's length, wiggled it once, and swung. The shoe tumbled twenty yards into the hedge. Pigeons flapped in panic. The bearded man sat up and rubbed his eyes.

"Go back home to the Bowery," the cop said, prodding him in the shoulder.

"Let's get out of here," I said to Sol.

At the hedge, I went down on one knee and, way back

there, found the shoe. The leather was scabbed and twisted; a smell of decay spilled out. I caught up with the man at the Forty-first Street gate.

"God bless you, kid," he said. Tucking the shoe under his arm, he limped onward.

Then there were three of us, Sol and Lianne and I, eating the meat loaf that Sol's mother had prepared before she and Mr. Cammer went out to see a play.

"We'd love to have you go to the movies with us, Murray," said Lianne. "Wouldn't we, Sol?"

"Sure. Or phone somebody, Mur, and we can double-date."

No, you couldn't ask a girl for a date an hour and twenty minutes before showtime, not a self-respecting girl. But neither did I want to tag along with Sol and Lianne, the third wheel to their bicycle built for two. So I phoned Foxx.

"Perfect timing, Baum," he said. "Zoe and I—you remember Zoe, don't you? the one with the lovely fanny? ouch, just kidding, Zo—we've been rehearsing my new song, and it's marvelous, if I do say so myself. Tell you what, we'll taxi on over and perform the world premiere in Sol's living room."

Then there were five of us. Zoe sat cross-legged on the floor playing a flute while Foxx pounded on the piano and sang "Sexual Overtures" in a nasal voice. "Now this overture for mammals is my favorite," he said. "Keep an ear out for the mother whale on the flute." Zoe swayed. Her silver earrings shimmered in the light. At the end we shouted "Encore!" and he sang the ostrich aria, which Lianne said brought tears to her eyes. "Encore, encore," Sol said, and we each drank a second glass of wine borrowed from his parents' liquor cabinet. When he finished writing the insects' overture, Foxx explained, he would start on the opera itself, which was titled *The Origin of Species*. Sol pointed out that insects were subphyla, but Foxx said that was ridiculous, no one would listen to an opera titled *Origin of Subphyla*. By this time Zoe was playing the mother whale's song again while I accompanied her on spoons, and Sol was refilling our glasses, and then Lianne announced she wanted to go out on the town. "Follow me," said Foxx.

I was humming the ostrich aria when we arrived via hodgepodge streets at the San Remo Café. Inside were sandals, bare feet, desert boots, white satin slippers, toenails painted red, toenails painted black. I didn't dare look up from the sawdust-covered floor until we were safely seated at our table. A black beret, a greet beret, a gleaming bald head above a bushy beard, two earrings in one ear and one in the other, a purple flower blooming out of blond curls, and more. I squinted through the smoke until my eyes teared.

"Everybody looks at everybody because that's part of the show," Foxx was saying. "But don't stare at the faggots, kids, that's not cool. And of course, act as if you see Negro-white couples every day of the week."

Zoe grabbed Foxx's mop of hair and gave it a little shake. "If you weren't so cute, you'd be really obnoxious."

The waitress set down glasses of red wine. "Two bucks and a quarter, folks," she said. "And let's pretend you're over eighteen, shall we?"

And how old was she? Her face was young, her scratchy voice was old. The name tag on her chest said *Maria*.

Candlelight shimmered in Lianne's eyes. "Look at that man's hands," she said. "Silver rings on long black fingers. Sexy!" She pushed her fingers under her thick hair and let it billow down, shaking the flame. Lianne seemed new tonight. We all seemed new. I wondered about unlacing my sneakers and wiggling my toes in the sawdust.

A deeply tanned man wearing a blue stocking cap waved at us. "That's Gene—Gene Gardner," Foxx explained. "He's a sailor, or used to be before they laid him off. He ran guns to Spain in the civil war back in the thirties or whenever that was. Later he ran guns to the Free French in Africa, just like Humphrey Bogart, and on the return trip smuggled Jews to Cuba. After the war he said too many nice things about Russia. So here he is, blacklisted, in dry dock, a fantastically nice guy except when he gets soused."

"What a story," I murmured. As I wiggled my toes in the sawdust and smiled back into Lianne's pearly white smile, I realized her braces were gone. When had her teeth shed their metal skin? "What a wonderful story!"

"Well, half of it may be lies, but they're damn good lies."

Half lies or half truths—either way, Foxx had sat at these marble tables listening to real sailors the same nights I had been finishing my algebra homework. "You know something, Dan, and Zoe and Sol and Lianne?" I had their attention now. "I'm going to write a story about Gene Gardner." My four friends nodded in agreement. "A novel!" I said, and they nodded with fervor. I wanted to say something else that would pronounce the great emotions boiling inside me, but I couldn't get beyond "Furthermore." I paused, and repeated it, louder: "Furthermore." When everybody nodded, I decided anything else would be redundant. Finding that I was on my feet, I sat down and drank more wine. Beneath the sawdust, furry and ticklish, my bare toes felt a tremor taking place underneath the city. The summer was gathering speed.

■ ■ ■

In the morning my brain was swollen into a pumpkin by the first hangover of my life. I had forgotten how the ostrich tune went. I had forgotten what Zoe had said so sweetly on her doorstep when either Foxx or I—or both of us—kissed her good night. All I could remember was "Furthermore."

Mom snuffed out her cigarette when I entered the kitchen. "Good morning. Or should I say good afternoon?"

"'Good morning' is fine." I poured orange juice. "Mom, would you rather have a son who smuggled guns to Spain or one who wrote the great American novel?"

"I'd rather have a son who came home at some decent hour."

"It wasn't so late."

"At one-thirty you were still not home and I was half crazy thinking of everything that could have happened to you. Finally at two-fifteen I hear you come in and when I check to be sure you're all right, I smell cigarettes and wine."

I could have stopped it there with "I'm sorry," or at least deflected it by asking for aspirin. I could have spread it thin and harmless in the course of a long, rueful narrative of my night on the town. Or I could have promised that my first hangover would be my last. But what I said was "I don't tell you when to come home, so why should you tell me?"

Her eyes narrowed. "Take that back. Right now." Her fingers turned white around the coffee cup. "You hear me?"

"I'm almost seventeen years old."

"I am your mother, Murray. You will not talk to me like this."

My head was throbbing terribly. "What kind of mother?" I shouted. "What kind of mother goes out with Ernst till midnight?"

"You shut up." She grabbed my wrist and jerked it. The cup wobbled, tipped. Coffee gushed across the table.

"Let go of me."

We stood facing each other, breathing hard. A thin stream of coffee was splashing onto the floor.

"Ernst is an old friend," she said.

Four streaks of blood surfaced inside my wrist.

"An old friend of the family. Do you hear me?"

I held the arm to my mouth. The blood tasted sour. The coffee was dripping into a brown puddle at our feet.

"Oh, darling, are you hurt?"

"Mom, let's go to California."

"California!"

"We'll fly out there and talk with Dad."

"California? What *Unsinn*!"

"It can't be that expensive."

"I don't mean money. I mean why should we go when he is coming?"

"He is? When?"

"Any week now."

"Which week?"

"How should I know exactly which week? He comes when he comes." She looked down at the floor and shook her head. "What a mess."

That was the day I went for my first run.

22

I had no design, not even a direction. I simply wanted to run; my legs wanted to run. All through breakfast they flexed and churned beneath the kitchen table.

I put on sweatpants and a white T-shirt, pattered down the back stairs, and emerged on the street. I raised my head, testing the air. A thin salt aroma floated over from beyond the Hudson. Far downtown a clock gonged, joined by another and then a third. It was time to move. Other people walked fast, but I felt the need to run.

One block at a time, one corner at a time, plunging through green lights, swerving from reds. Pedestrians turned to stare. "Hey, kid," a cabdriver shouted, "where's the fire?" My sneakers scuffed against the sidewalk; my hands scooped the air. Scoop-ah, scoop-ah, I built my rhythm along the asphalt of the city, block after block, until each breath scorched my lungs and I staggered to a halt.

I had run as far as Forty-third and Lexington—the Chrysler Building. Behind the rounded showroom windows, the automobiles circled slowly under brilliant spotlights. A fat-fendered blue Plymouth nosed behind a sleek white Chrysler, which pursued a tawny DeSoto, which pursued a jet-black Chrysler, which pursued the blue Plymouth. Around and around, the driverless cars trailed each other soundlessly. I saw my miniature reflection sliding along their chromium ribs.

I began running uptown. Scoop-ah, scoop-ah. Green and green. I moved with smooth strides, left leg, right leg, left and right, scoop-ah, scoop-ah.

"You can run for hours but can't buy bread when I ask?" Mom greeted me. "Are you training for the Olympics?"

I shrugged and laughed. I didn't yet know why I had run that morning. Or why I ran the next. And the next. Into the heat of the summer.

Soon I discovered how to synchronize with the intervals of traffic lights. First and Second avenues were the most dependable, now that they had one-way traffic and staggered lights. Park Avenue was dependable in contrary fashion: its lights changed along ten blocks at a time, so whether I ran downtown or up, by the third corner I would hit a red. Lexington's rhythm I never diagnosed, so it was always a gamble. Third I ruled out: running under the El train was no fun. Those were the avenues to the east. To the west lay Madison, an obstacle course of poodles, and Fifth, broad-shouldered and airy but thronged by sluggish tourists. So I ran eastward, ignoring the stares and wisecracks of New Yorkers seeing a boy running like crazy.

One night when my fingers scooped the air with exceptional ease, I found myself along the East River, racing reflections on the water. Ahead of me waited the Brooklyn Bridge, sewn in two silver loops to the black sky. But of course the bridge was beyond my reach. Midtown was where I belonged. Between Madison and First, Seventy-ninth and Thirty-fourth, I ran my rounds.

In the second week my breath and heart and legs finally understood each other. My feet bounced back from the pavement with the ping of fresh spaldeen balls. When I no longer had to think about my body, random messages came jaywalking across my mind. Jokes, phone numbers, birthdays, nicknames. I became the mailman of midtown. Running down Seventy-seventh Street, I bounced a cryptogram off Ferguson's ceiling. On Sixty-sixth I sang a greeting through Foxx's window. On Forty-seventh I blew a kiss toward Arlie's room. And one morning on Sixtieth I passed Ruth's brownstone and slid an apology under the locked front door.

■ ■ ■

Ruth. She returned to my thoughts as if she had been away on a long trip. Which in a way she had: she had been wherever it was that I stashed my shame until it was, maybe, safe to touch.

Shortly after Mom went out—"See you later, darling, after dinner with Ernst"—I stood in the kitchen beside the phone and rehearsed for Ruth. "Hello": that would be easy enough. "Hello, this is Murray"—or should I be safe and say "Murray Baum"? Ridiculous. How many Murrays did she know? But then what? Should I leapfrog her angry question and say I hadn't called because of laryngitis? A month of laryngitis? I slammed down the phone after the first ring. The healthiest idea would be not to call at all. But damn it, I missed her.

"Damn it, Ruth, I've missed you," I said.

"Thanks, but who is this?"

"Oh, Jesus. This is Murray. Murray Baum."

"Ah, *that* Murray." She laughed. "Well, this is Ruth's mother." She laughed harder during my paralyzed silence. "No, it's me. I was just kidding."

"Well, you certainly made a fool out of me." The score was even, which might make things easier. "I'll start over. Hi, this is Murray, and I'd like to get together with you. Maybe see a movie or go roller-skating."

"Like we used to in the old days. Is that what you mean?"

"Yeah."

"Pick right up where we left off."

"Yeah, sort of." Things were *not* going to be easy.

"After a month of nothing. Is that what you mean?"

"Look, Ruth, I know I should . . . well, you deserve . . ." The silence went on miserably.

"Okay, Murray, I'm really very mad at you, but it's too early for a nasty fight. Come on over and let's do something fun."

"Gee, I'm glad you understand what I was—"

"I *don't* understand. I told you: I'm mad. And I don't want to talk about it right now. Come over quick, before I change my mind."

"You mean now?"

"Well, what do you think I mean?"

"Wow. Thanks, Ruth."

She hung up.

A half hour later I was standing six inches from her shiny black door, wondering whether to push the buzzer a second time. Suddenly the door swung open and there she stood, hands on hips. "Well," she said. "You don't look any different."

"Different from what?"

"From how you looked when I last saw you."

"A hundred years ago, you mean?" I laughed a little. "Can I come in?"

"No."

"Oh, come on, Ruth. I thought you said—"

"Because we're going out." She brushed past me and stepped onto the sidewalk. "Follow me, Murray."

"Where?"

"Put yourself in my hands."

For an hour we walked around Central Park, talking about this and that in careful tones of voice, laughing nervously, like on a first date. We bought some Cracker Jacks and fed a small mob of squirrels. She let me hold her hand as we walked along the pond and watched kids shouting at their sailboats when they drifted beyond reach.

"Would you rather have a boy or a girl for your first child?" she asked.

"I don't know," I replied, in case there was a wrong answer.

"Well, personally, being the sister of my whiny little sister, I want a boy. Named Richard." She squeezed my hand. "Not Dick or Richie."

"Richard," I said emphatically. For a moment, as one of the sailboat boys looked at me over his shoulder, I thought Richard was already with us.

Then we came to the carousel, where the fifty-seven freshly painted ponies rose and fell in hurdy-gurdy glee. We stood on line like two giants among the eight-year-olds waiting to board. "A treat for children of all ages," said the ticket man. I mounted a green horse and slapped the reins against its wooden neck. I waved at Ruth on her palomino. I leaned back and sang along with the pipe organ—"Daisy, Daisy, give me your answer true"—while the park whirled round and round.

"What next?" I asked as we walked in dizzy spirals.

"I'm hungry."

"A picnic. How about a picnic in my apartment?"

"A cookout on the living-room lawn with your family?"

"With frozen food we buy at the grocery store and with just ourselves because my Mom's eating dinner out with a friend."

Ruth tightened her fingers among mine as we crossed the avenue. Or perhaps I tightened mine among hers. All the way home I wondered who was doing what, and what difference it made.

"Do not remove foil," I read out loud from the package. "Heat forty-five minutes. Eat immediately."

"I'm not eating tin foil."

"It might taste better than the Salisbury steak underneath."

"Depends how hungry you are," she said.

"Very hungry." I pulled her toward me and pursed my lips.

"Hold it." She twisted free. "It's time for us to talk. About Arlie. What does she mean to you?"

"Ruth." I reached out, and she stepped back. "Listen, Ruth, it's kind of hard to say. She's gone now. She went to Paris, you know. The Junior-Senior Prom got all mixed up. I shouldn't have—"

"Cut the crap, Murray. Tell me what you feel for her."

The heat of the oven swept in waves against my legs.

"It's over," I muttered.

"What?"

"It's over. She and I are friends, that's all."

"Platonic friends?"

"Platonic friends." I coughed. What else did she need? Should I sign in blood?

"Come on," she said, taking my hand. "Give me a tour of the apartment while dinner's cooking."

Room by room she nodded and touched furniture and whistled to Gus, following the trail of my anecdotes, not noticing that Dad's desk was cleared and his side of the bed unwrinkled. The collection was the highlight of the tour. "Such cute boxes! All the way from A to Z." She ran her fingers along the labels, reciting the names in a singsong voice.

Then she lay back on the bed, her hands folded on her stomach. "I feel like I'm getting to know you," she said. She patted the pillow beside her. "Why are you standing over there so far away, like a museum guard or something?"

As we fitted chins and arms and hips together, the muscles tightened in my stomach, and heat filled my face.

Her tongue probed between my lips. I tasted her slippery mouth as her hands pulled my shoulders and my hands went down her back and onto that soft rise of her behind, where I felt her go tense. She licked my ear as she rubbed, slowly, against my thighs and chest, making high-pitched noises while I stroked the naked flesh beneath her skirt, but she didn't say no, as if I had the right to touch down there, her naked thighs.

"Mmm," she said.

"Mmm," I replied, kissing her neck.

"You smell different now. Like you're burning up."

I stopped moving. Lifted my head. "Oh, my God." I scrambled to my feet. "The dinner!"

I skidded down the hallway in my socks, trailed by her laughter. I snatched the two packages from the oven. I peeled back the tin foil and exposed the shriveled sphere of steak.

■ ■ ■

Dear M & M. Dear Family. Theo's letters arrived in wacky rhythms, sometimes two or three at a time, then none for a week. The insides were wackier: a bird feather; the names of his fourteen best friends; "knock knock" jokes; little stick figures with balloons rising from their mouths exclaiming "Howdy doody!" Occasionally he wrote a full sentence: *I have gained 4 1/2 pounds but still hate peenut butter,* or *My sunburn is not bad anymore.* His handwriting looked like

Dad's, ambling above and below the line, sometimes sprinting up the margin for no apparent reason.

Cher Murray. Mon ami. Arlie sent a large card of the Eiffel Tower and small ones of Paris street scenes, scribbling excited phrases. How did a Frenchman pronounce "Arlie"?

Dear Turds Mole. I sent clippings and cheerful gossip to Ferg at Haven House, and he sent back cheerful anecdotes and little drawings of flowers. I waited for him to ask me to visit, but he didn't.

■ ■ ■

One morning out of the blue, Foxx phoned. "Hey, friend and countryman, lend me your ear. I've got a job for you, a big job out there in the real world, stopping the witch-hunters. But you have to act fast. Toot sweet."

It was the first time Foxx had ever phoned me. I was flattered, although I hadn't the slightest idea what he was talking about.

"Don't worry, Mur, I'll explain when I see you. Are you with me or not?"

Twenty minutes later I was with him on Bleecker Street. "Where'd you get that hat, Foxx?" I asked. It was a green felt hat, swollen into the shape of two lumpy hills, with a red feather jutting from the side.

"Somebody walked by and gave it to me." He took it off. "You want to wear it?"

I jammed the hideous thing on top of his curls. "What's this job you were talking about? What witch-hunters?"

He pulled a thick sheet of paper from his back pocket and unfolded it. *Speak Out for Freedom! Stop the Witch-hunters!* The big black letters marched across the top of the page. Beneath them, in red and blue: *Why Is Dashiell Hammett in Jail?* "We're going to a meeting with my brother and the guys who wrote this poster," Foxx said, "and we're going to be late unless we hustle."

As we trotted through the narrow Greenwich Village streets, Foxx explained that someone named Jasper had brought this poster to the printshop where his brother worked. Jasper was a playwright, a young, very talented, and very experimental playwright whom of course I hadn't heard of, but I would, you bet I would, as soon as some producer was willing to take a chance on *Outrage Onstage*, his musical starring two tape recorders and three sopranos. In any case, Jasper was part of a group that was organizing a rally in support of Dashiell Hammett, the famous writer, who had just gone to jail for not giving names to the House Un-American Activities Committee. Speak out for freedom, in Union Square, at two o'clock, a week from Sunday. The rally organizers needed help from bright young men like myself. "You're a natural for this one, Mur, because of all that Communist business with your father, which Arlie told me about. Murray Baum's my man, I thought. Am I right, or am I right?"

He swooped the hat toward my head, and I ducked. Arlie had told him! She had been talking with Foxx about me and my secrets. I felt as if I had been stripped while lying asleep. Betrayed. "What did she tell you?"

"Your dad wouldn't sign a loyalty oath, so they shipped him to California until he shapes up. It's not exactly the Alger Hiss story, but it's something."

I didn't like hearing things about my father coming out of Foxx's mouth. And yet I also liked it. I felt proud. My father, who refused to sign. Arlie and Foxx had been talking about my heroic father, and now I, his son, had been chosen to fight the witch-hunters. Foxx and I would join forces to rally the people and get Dashiell Hammett out of jail.

I punched Foxx on the shoulder. "Okay, comrade, let's go get 'em."

"Here we are." It looked much like the San Remo Café but, under the glare of daylight, more serious. People conferred in low, businesslike voices, studied newspapers, smoked. The radio played flute music. A skinny dog beat its tail on the dusty floor.

"Hey, Danny, over here." Foxx's brother seemed to belong to another family; he was squat, round-shouldered, with strips of black hair over the dome of his head. But the Foxxy rush of words was the same.

"So who's your friend? Murray, is it? Okay, Murray, meet Palko over here, him with the sleepy look on his face. Johnny Remarque on my right. Mr. Frank Goldfarb, who's a lawyer with the ACLU—our pleasure, Mr. Goldfarb. And of course Dean Jasper, only nobody calls him Dean. This is my kid brother, Danny, and his friend—Murray, is it? You kids want anything, like Cokes, for instance? Okay, Jasper, tell us some good news."

Two hours later the meeting was done. Jasper's yellow pad swarmed with penciled notations:

Speakers: L. Hellman? (Ask Miller)
  Congressman Marcantonio; which Negro?
Publicity; press—
  ask Johnson for funds: $4,776
  Parade permit, NYPD. Rain???
Harrington? Howe?
Beware the Trots!

The names belonged to strangers, the topics were obscure, the controversies were bewildering ("You gotta stay clear of the guild, otherwise they'll red-bait you to hell and back''; ''That sounds like Trotsky talk''; ''Bullshit—what the libs want to hear is . . .''). But the general thrust was clear, thrillingly clear. The six of us in this dusty café were going to bring together a thousand—maybe ten thousand—people to defend the civil liberties of the famous author Dashiell Hammett.

I was going to help it happen by putting a thousand posters on a thousand fences, doors, and walls. *Speak Out for Freedom! Stop the Witch-hunters!* Five hundred by next Saturday. A week later, five hundred new ones with the names of the star speakers. I would have to move fast because cops and landlords didn't like ''leftie'' posters decorating the bourgeois walls of their city. Move fast and under cover of darkness, with a roll of posters in one arm, a big sponge and a pail of water in the other. Swab the back of the poster, slap it up against the wall, and move on.

As Foxx and I left the café, I wiggled my toes inside my sneakers. So this was why I had been running every day since June. Without knowing it, I had been in training for the cause. And who knows, maybe after a thousand posters went up and ten thousand people came together, a man named Dashiell Hammett might be let out of jail. This wasn't gunrunner stories. This was the real thing.

''Thanks, Foxx. Thanks for asking me along,'' I said.

''Stay cool, pardner. It ain't over yet.''

''Those were fascinating guys.''

''Yeah, it was quite a morning, all right. Not that it's going to shorten old Dashiell's jail term by more than a minute, because he's one of those dogmatic Fifth types, and these days you might as well throw away the key for them. But I'm hoping Jasper remembers me after all this, 'cause when he gets famous in the theater world, he'll be a good friend to have. Get this: *Outrage of Species: An Opera for Soprano Mammals*. He'd love it."

"For Chrissake, Foxx."

"Uh-oh, did I offend you again, Baum? Was it the mammals?"

I grabbed his arm and forced him to look at me. "Hammett isn't a joke. And neither is jail."

He looked at me until I began to feel foolish. "You really hate for people to be in jail, don't you?" he said. He started walking again, and I hustled to keep up. "So your dad wouldn't sign. If HUAC calls him, I suppose he'll take the Fifth. Well, Mur, you got a hell of a dad, not like mine, who knows only one kind of fifth and drinks it every night until he passes out. That can be a bit frustrating if you're a little kid wanting to hear a bedtime story." He laughed and swerved down the subway stairs. "Hey, have you heard from Arlie?"

"What?" I pattered after him. "Damn you."

"All I said was, have you heard from Arlie?" He put a hand on my shoulder as we stood on line at the change booth.

"Yeah, a few postcards. How about you?"

"She sent me a picture postcard of Notre Dame because she knows how I hate everything to do with Catholicism. And she wrote on the back completely in French, which she knows I can't read a word of. She must have been laughing all the way to the post office. God, I miss her." As we pushed through the turnstiles, he glanced at me. "Hey, relax. All I'm saying is I like the girl. You can love her all your life if you want, no sweat off my behind."

I was going to tell him about Ferg up at Haven House, but the train roared into the station, and by the time we were on board, he had begun another story. I wished I had taken the green hat when he offered it. Maybe next week, when we met with Jasper again.

Four nights in a row I exited stealthily from the apartment, armed with posters and sponge and a red plastic beach pail. It wasn't as easy as it sounded. The paper bunched up with too much water and fell down with too little. When I finally got a poster to stay flat on the wall, I stepped back and saw that it was tilting steeply to the right. And how in hell was I supposed to watch out for cops and doormen while fending off panhandlers and drunks, not to mention a hundred nosy dogs? At the end of the first night, exactly ten walls of the Upper East Side told New Yorkers to speak out for freedom, and my shoulders ached. During the second night I got the hang of it: swab, swab, right corner, left corner, rub down, rub across. By Thursday midnight, five hundred black and white posters were blooming on the East Side, West Side, all around the town, including my masterpiece, the front door of the federal courthouse where Hammett had been sentenced.

On Friday morning, as soon as Mom went out shopping, I called Foxx to announce my triumph, and woke him up. "Murray? Jesus H. Christ, man, it's before noon. My tongue feels broken. All right, all right, what is it? Oh, shit, I meant to call you yesterday. The whole thing's off. It's just off, I don't know why. My brother left me a message, something about the police permit. Hey, I'm sorry, really truly, pal. It was fun goofing around with you, let's get together again next week, but please make it after noon, okay?"

I slammed down the phone. Goddamn him. Why hadn't he told me? Here I'd been running around the city pasting "Freedom" on the walls, believing it would add up to something, and he'd been fast asleep with the news. One minute Union Square was thronged with ten thousand people chanting "Hammett, Hammett," and the next minute it was wiped empty. Silent.

I leaned on the kitchen windowsill and looked across the narrow, sunless air shaft to the brick wall of the next apartment house.

He should have called me.

I dialed his number, but no one answered after ten rings. "Fuck you, Foxx," I screamed into the receiver. "Fuck yourself to hell," I screamed at the refrigerator. "You'll never fuck me again," I shouted, slamming the kitchen door and the living-room door and the front door as I went out to run.

For days I passed my posters with grateful surprise, as if I were seeing a friend waving from across the street. They aged rapidly, buckling with rain and summer heat, tearing in strips from fingernails and knives, disappearing under posters of smiling city councilmen and rye bread. When I thought of Jasper and Palko and Foxx's brother, they seemed like part of a movie I had seen long ago. I thought of borrowing Hammett's books from the library, but I never did. It was bad enough reading his name on the front page of the *Times*.

▪ ▪ ▪

What I did was run, every day, through a different neighborhood. As I laced my sneakers tight and rolled the socks over the rims, I mapped out my tour. Feeling rich? Run past the uniformed, shiny-shoed, Gilbert-and-Sullivanish doormen blowing their whistles at taxicabs in Sutton Place. Feeling sad? Run under the dark, thunderous roar of the Third Avenue El. Feeling grand? Run down the marble steps of Grand Central Station, swerve among the porters, and circle the four-faced clock. Feeling hungry? Run through the gravy-thick air of Yorkville, inhaling Wiener schnitzel, red cabbage, and beer.

On the Lower East Side I slowed to a walk. There were simply too many pushcarts and bearded men and dogs and clothing stalls and fruit stands and boys pitching baseball cards. These were not really "my people." A generation ago they had lived in shtetls where, unlike Berlin, there were no coachmen, no cafés, no operas or flappers or even photo albums. Still, like other Jews, they had made their exodus. Now I walked among them in my sneakers listening to Yiddish that sounded almost like German, and to Russian and Polish and Hebrew that sounded nothing like German, and I felt strangely at home. Leaning her fleshy arms on a second-floor windowsill, a woman chewed a pickle and looked down at the open-air market. A white cat sat beside her, licking its paw. She caught me staring and blew me a kiss, a pickled kiss: "Shalom, darlink."

"Shalom," I called back, imagining myself climbing the steps two at a time, entering her fleshy hug, and finding my place at the table beside the gruff, bearded man and the five pale children, to eat our borscht and dark bread. "Eat, eat more, darlink, you must be famished"—she would pronounce it fa-*mischt*—"from all this American running." Soon I would grow too fat to run, I would be fat enough to join the men down in the dairy restaurant, who muttered intensely to each other between slurps of soup, argued fine points of the Talmud, reminisced about the breeze that moved like a cool stream through the streets of the faraway shtetl, and by late afternoon were belching and dozing and waiting to be summoned home by our children.

Early one Sunday morning I ran as far as the Brooklyn Bridge, gave one glance over my shoulder, and entered the pedestrian path. At first it felt no different from any land-rooted sidewalk. Then the cables soared in unison at the corners of my eyes, and the river unfurled beneath me, and the wind began to sing. At the crest I looked back and shouted something, in no language I had ever heard, to the skyscrapers of the island. Again I shouted, and thrust my arms straight into the sky.

What I did was run, every day, rain or shine, deep into the heat of July, so that events seemed to spread evenly, safely, across a plateau. The Dodgers were up by eight and then nine games, entrenched in first place. "Oh the monotony of it all," Dick Young wrote in the *News*, "when you're covering a club like the 1951 Dodgers. Nothing but win . . . win . . . win." Ten times a day on the radio the Four Aces sang "Tell Me Why." Mom and I sat at the kitchen table, finishing dinner quickly because there were only two, not three or four, parts to the conversation. After dinner Ruth and I would double-date with Lianne and Sol, and after I took Ruth back to her apartment we would kiss in the doorway until perspiration was trickling down my chest.

Day by day the city slowed down, emptied a bit more, turned quiet a few minutes earlier at night. Many mornings I awoke and couldn't remember what I had done the day before, except run.

It felt comfortable, safe, to be living on a plateau so wide that the edges were beyond reach. You couldn't fall off even if you tried, I said to myself one day. And why would you try? I asked myself the next day. And a day later: Why, why would you try to fall? And then one morning: Why are you asking these questions?

Suddenly I wanted to run fast and far and in a straight line.

23

I pulled open the desk drawer and reread Mr. Sklar's comments on the JRP.

> 2. You have heard a lot from two sides of the emotional rectangle, but only a polite note from Mrs. Jacobs and nothing at all from Mr. Jacobs. What does reality look like from their half of the rectangle?
>
> 3. You're the author of this history. But aren't you also an actor in it?

I found Mom's address book beside her typewriter. J & K Plumbers; Jackson, Arnold and Eve; Jonas, Fritz; Julia (Redmonds, the cleaning lady). Nothing in between. Not even a name angrily crossed out with sharp pen strokes. In her book, Jacobs, Willy and Barbara, had never even existed.

I wanted to agree. Why not forget the Jacobses, put on my sneakers, and continue my neighborhood tours? Because that was an evasion. I must find two people who had packed up and fled to Connecticut with the secrets of 1946. I had to complete the JRP—not for Mr. Sklar but for me.

Four months ago at the Public Library, I had trailed Willy in vain through the pages of the *Times*. This time I would begin at the Bell Telephone office in Grand Central Station, with its rows of phone books for every major city across the country. How many different Connecticut directories could there be, after all?

There were more than twenty, from Bridgeport to Windham, and there were dozens of Jacobses—whole tribes of Jacobses—living cheek by jowl in every Connecticut community. In Bridgeport and Danbury and Darien and East Hartford there were thirty-six William middle-initial Jacobses, and four W. Jacobses, but no Willy. Had he turned into a William? Surely the "vurrker" wouldn't dress up as a button-down Arrow-shirt William. Possibly he was a terse W., underground man, although that was usually the choice of single ladies afraid of obscene phone calls, and I couldn't imagine Willy's being afraid of anything.

In East Haven and Fairfield, I only found W.'s and Williams, making thirty-eight names altogether that I had copied into my notebook. And I hadn't even reached Hartford, which was populated at least three inches thick. At this rate . . . But he showed up in Greenwich: Jacobs, Willy, 45 Oak Ave., Circle 6–9087, out-in-the-open Willy, with no bourgeois middle initial, simply and defiantly himself.

I had found him. Now what? I could send a list of questions, enclose a copy of the JRP, write a persuasive, mature letter explaining that in the interest of historical truth, etc., etc., and wait a week, a month, forever.

I had to phone. Even though I was terrified by the thought of their voices coming alive in my ear, I had to phone. Anything was better than the silence of 1946. I could hardly hear the clink of falling quarters and dimes through the pounding of my pulse. "Hallo. Villy Yacobs here." That was all I needed to know for now: he existed, in Greenwich. I sucked one deep breath of triumph and hung up.

The next morning, Mom asked, "Where do you and your friends go so expensive that you need next week's allowance?"

"Palisades Amusement Park," I said with all the casualness I had rehearsed. "I won't be back until late, so don't make dinner for me."

An hour later the Greyhound bus heaved backward from its berth, grated into first gear, and rumbled north along the cobblestoned avenue. The buildings shrank from thirty and forty stories to five or six in the Bronx. Green trees multiplied and thickened. After White Plains the traffic lights disappeared and the bus cruised in high gear while the driver whistled tunelessly through his teeth. There were only five passengers: an elderly couple with many shopping bags, a Negro man asleep with a toothpick between his lips, a thin woman leafing through magazine after magazine, and myself. "Hello," I wanted to say to someone, "where are you going?" But the space between us was too wide. I watched the countryside bounce past, and wondered what I was going to say when Willy and Barbara opened the door. "Hello, you may not remember me, but . . ." "Hello, I'm sorry to trouble you, but . . ." I looked down at the fourteen questions I had written neatly in the notebook, but the swaying of the bus made me nauseous.

From the bus station it was a ten-minute walk along quiet, tree-shaded streets. Children were playing on the lawns. I waved and they looked at me without waving.

The lawn in front of 45 Oak Avenue was empty. I took a breath. Rang the bell. Soft footsteps approached from the other side of the door.

"Hello?" The word rolled from her throat, carrying the same flat Kansas accent I had overheard on those hot nights at the camp. I had grown so tall that she had to look up to see me, shading her eyes with one hand.

"Barbara Jacobs?"

"Yes?"

"My name is Murray Baum."

I watched the name take hold in her blue eyes. "Murray!" She gave a little laugh. "Sam's boy." Her eyes moved around my face as she tried to recognize me. "What are you doing here?"

"I came to talk with you."

She stood on tiptoe and looked over my shoulder. "By yourself? I don't understand."

"I took the bus."

"From New York? After all these years?"

I held up my notebook. "I'm writing a history research paper about my family, and so I've been collecting stories from relatives and friends."

"History paper? I don't understand, but come in."

As she opened the door, white sunlight spilled over her into the hall beyond. I followed her inside, closing the door behind me and pausing as my eyes tried to make out shapes in the sudden dimness.

"This way," she said. "Willy took Lizzie to the pool, so we'll have a quiet hour or so."

The living room was bluish-gray, with narrow windows framed by white curtains that let in strips of yellow light. I sat on the edge of a chair. She sat on the blue semicircular couch across from me, tucking her shirt into her shorts. "How long has it been?" she said. "Six or seven years?"

"Almost five. Since the summer at the camp."

"Of course. I was still nursing Lizzie, and you were just a barefoot boy in a red bathing suit. Not even a teenager. Now you're doing historical research."

"I was going on twelve."

"You read a lot of books. And played Ping-Pong with

your brother, until he lost and cried and stepped on the ball."

"We stopped playing after a while because the grown-ups wouldn't buy any more balls. Anyway, it got too hot."

"God, it was hot that summer. The creek felt like matzo ball soup, that's what your father said."

With a rough movement, she tucked some loose hair behind one ear. Blond hair that was almost silver. "Do you want a Coke?" When she jumped up, her thighs trembled below the edge of her shorts.

"Yes, please." She had grown plump (Mom was right), but she seemed light, as if she carried her body from the center of her spine.

I looked around the room. A stormy seascape hung between the windows. Two color photos of a smiling blond girl—Lizzie—stood side by side on the mantel over the fireplace. In the corner beside a bookshelf was a radio-phonograph console. A blue book lay on the floor beside the couch, open and facedown—the only thing out of place.

I unscrewed my pen and opened my notebook. *I found them!* I wrote. *At last I'm going to*

"So, Murray, what's this research paper of yours?"

I took a sip from the cold green bottle. As long as the Coke lasted, I would last.

"The Junior Research Paper. The JRP." She was here, she was real—wiggling her toes on the carpet, playing with a button of her pink shirt, Barbara Jacobs, six feet away. "Like I told you, I'm writing a history of my family, starting from when my parents were born and explaining how they came to America and got married. Mr. Sklar, my teacher, is really tough. He made me revise the paper because I didn't go far enough with my interpretations. School's over, but I want to do another draft and get it right."

"Homework during summer vacation." She glanced at the photographs. "I'll have to tell Lizzie about that. But where do I fit in?"

"I've been interviewing people who knew my parents."

"Willy has known your father practically his entire life, starting back in Germany. I'd rather you left him out of this, though."

"All right."

"I came into the picture only ten years ago."

"Great. That's the period I'm working on."

"Oh, really?"

I made some doodles in the notebook. "As I recall, you and Willy spent a lot of time with my parents."

"Almost every weekend, plus summer vacations."

"You must know a lot about them, then."

"We took care of each other's babies, played bridge, went on picnics."

"It sounds really happy."

"I guess it does." She bent down and pulled at a toenail.

"But not entirely, I suppose."

She shrugged. "Nothing's a 'lived happily ever after' fairy tale. That's how the stories ended which I used to read to Lizzie. Willy would got so mad. 'Don't teach her those fairy tales. The truth is capitalist oppression.'" She pointed toward my notebook. "Are you a Marxist historian?"

I shook my head.

"Ah. Just a son writing the history of his parents."

"Yes." I turned the page. "Can you tell me some more?"

"What do you want to know?"

"Let's start with 1946."

"You could write a whole book about 1946."

"I gather there was some kind of trouble."

"Murray, that's years ago now."

"Whatever you can remember will help."

"Okay, while he's not here. Just a few questions."

"What was the trouble?"

"That's a polite word for it. Disaster is more like it."

I wrote *disaster* in my notebook.

"One night Willy was down at union headquarters in Brooklyn," she said. "Back then he was a labor organizer, you know. When he left the meeting, he got into an argument with a cop. Who knows who started it, but in the end Willy was lying on the sidewalk, his head split open by the cop's nightstick."

"God, that sounds awful."

"Scary as hell, let me tell you. Two inches deeper, the doctor said to us, and Willy would never have talked again. But at least that put a stop to his labor organizing. Two months later we moved out here."

"This is a really pretty house."

"Thanks." She looked at her watch. "What time does your bus leave?"

"Not for a while." I sipped the Coke. "I have a couple more questions. Can you tell me about the camp?"

"Oh, yes. The camp."

"I read in the letters how Willy and Dad first got the idea for the camp, but what happened after that?"

"What letters?"

"My mother let me read a collection of family letters."

"She did, did she?"

"They go back to the time when she and Dad met."

"Strange that she let you read private letters."

"Yes, she did. There was a long one she wrote to my father at the end of the summer of 'forty-six."

Barbara said nothing.

"She mentioned you," I said.

She laughed sharply. "Oh, let me imagine how she put it. 'That Barbara woman tried to snare all the men, but what can you expect, she comes from Kansas and dyes her hair.' I heard it so often I've memorized it, down to the German accent. Did I get it right, Murray?"

I said nothing. Now I knew she would give me what I had come for. All I had to do was sip my Coke and not succumb to shame over what I was doing to her.

"The camp," she said. "Whatever your mother thought about it, the rest of us had a grand time. Dancing under those lanterns. A scavenger hunt. And of course you kids loved swimming down in the creek."

"In one of my mother's letters to Dad, she mentioned something that happened one night."

"I told you, Murray. Many things happened."

"She was walking by a cabin. Through a window she saw you and Dad."

"You dug up everything, didn't you?"

"I'm sorry, I shouldn't—"

"Listen to me, Murray. It was stupid of us, but it meant nothing. Just a kiss. Not what she thought it meant."

I nodded.

"Everyone loved Samuel Baum. While Willy was off at those meetings of his, coming home for an hour to eat a sandwich and change his shirt and talk on the phone, Sam helped me cry or laugh. Sam kept me from leaving my husband. Do you understand that?"

"I think so."

"He was our best friend. He loved us both."

"I understand."

"But Lise didn't, and Willy didn't. I could have talked until I was dead and they still wouldn't have believed me."

She made a sound in her throat. "And here I am, talking to you. Sam's boy."

I looked away, embarrassed by the pain in her face.

There was a silence. My lips were sticky with the film of Coke. When I looked up, she was gazing somewhere beyond me.

"But even he turned away. Willy was so low, so desperately sad, I thought that maybe if Sam talked with him . . . If his oldest friend came over for a couple of beers . . . I phoned, and we talked like the old days. We joked about whether we would recognize each other, and he promised to call back. That afternoon I sent him a photo of me and Willy and Lizzie on the front steps." She looked over at the phone. "He never called back."

A family snapshot on the front steps. That was the "beauty-queen" photograph Mom had found in Dad's desk—the damning piece of evidence before he left home. I had pictured a portrait of Barbara alone, bare-shouldered, red-lipped, smiling ravishingly. How much else had I misunderstood? How much had Mom gotten wrong?

I cleared my throat and closed the notebook. "It's time for me to go."

Neither of us moved. She looked at my forehead, at my chin, and into my eyes.

"You look like your father," she said. "You have his mouth."

"Thank you."

"Tell me, how is he?"

"Fine. Dad's fine." Enough pain. I wouldn't tell her that Dad had given her up but kept her photograph in his desk.

"What did he say about me?"

"You were a good friend. That's what he said." The man who made no promises.

A vase swayed on an end table as she abruptly got to her feet. Her eyes were shiny with tears. "I guess you should go."

I stood up.

"Tell them . . . I don't know. Nothing." The hug startled me. It ended before I could respond. "Don't think badly of me."

I understand why Dad loved you in whatever way he loved you, I pondered saying as we walked toward the front door. *Still, I can't help liking you,* I prepared to say. Vehemently, *I like you,* I was about to say when the door opened on us, and in a gush of sunlight we froze.

"Who have we here, darling?" He was a rectangular silhouette blockading the exit. Lizzie, wrapped in a pink towel, peeked at us under his arm.

"Back so soon?" Barbara said gaily. "Darling, you'll never guess who this is. A hundred guesses and you'll never—"

"Hallo. Villy Yacobs here." I flinched as he shook my hand, but the bone-cracking squeeze didn't come.

"Hello, sir, I'm Murray Baum." Still the hand lay slack inside mine.

"Murray Baum." Gradually the fingers tightened. "Well, well." Tighter. Pain shot up my arm. Finally he let go and smiled broadly. "Quite some surprise, Murray Baum. Have you come alone?" His eyes jumped from my face to Barbara's and then to the hall behind me and back to my face as he smiled still more broadly.

"Yes, I'm alone. Actually, I'm on my way out."

We stood wedged in the doorway. Pleats of flesh hung beneath his chin. The green polo shirt rose over his belly and disappeared under the belt of his khaki shorts, out of which poked two sleek, tanned legs. The more he came into view, the less I recognized him.

"Leaving. Oh, what a pity. No time for a cold drink, at least?"

"I don't think so."

"He has to catch a bus," Barbara said.

"Come, come," he said. "After all these years you don't have five minutes to chat?" He took hold of my elbow and steered me down the hall past Barbara, with Lizzie hopping behind us. "Murray Baum. Well, well."

As Lizzie jumped knees-first onto the couch, he looked me up and down. "You have become such a *grosser Mann,* I would not have known you to be little Murray with his nose in a book. Do you remember me?" I nodded too quickly. "*Ja, ja,* sometimes I hardly remember myself," he said, smiling. "Now then, a drink, yes? Barbara, be an angel and bring us two beers, the coldest you can find."

"I don't drink beer," I said.

"Nonsense. You don't want me to drink alone, do you?"

"Me, too," said Lizzie. "I want beer."

"Go upstairs and change into dry clothes," Barbara said over her shoulder on her way to the kitchen, but Lizzie stayed where she was, watching me.

Willy took a chair and pointed me toward the other one. "You come from the city. Months go by since I've been there. The hardware store keeps me busy, you know. If you had more time, I'd show you it. Six thousand square feet in the center of town. 'Everything a handy man needs,' so goes our motto."

"Sounds wonderful."

"Hard work. Six days a week is no picnic, but I'm used to it. All my life I work hard, and you see what I get for it." He leaned back and swept his hand in a wide, low arc. "Not bad, you agree? But my daughter here, she says she needs a television like her rich friend June."

"Jane, Daddy."

"Do you have television at home, young man?" he asked me.

"Just a radio," I said as Barbara entered.

"Isn't it funny, darling," she said, putting down the drinks and potato chips, "how Murray dropped in to say hello?" She sat on the couch and put her arm around her daughter. "How was your swimming lesson?"

"I breast-stroked for one and a half whole laps." Lizzie took a handful of chips.

"*Prosit*," Willy said, raising his bottle toward me. He tipped back his head and took a long swallow. "Tell me, Murray, how goes your family these days? In good health, I hope."

I nodded.

"We don't get any younger, you know. Which is why my wife has twisted my arm to play tennis, didn't you, darling?" He laughed and took another swallow. "Who would have believed Villy Yacobs on a tennis court?"

That was how it went. Willy talked about tennis, the hardware business, and the cucumbers in his garden, interspersing questions about what grade was I in and how old was Theo, until the potato chips were gone and Lizzie, yawning, shuffled out of the room, and I was bewildered. Where was Ya Ya Yacobs, whose silver knife had skinned wood to ribbons at his feet? It wasn't a trick of the beer, because I drank nothing from the bottle in my hand. It was Willy himself who was tricking me. Instead of going underground, he had gone overground, among swimming pools and hardware stores and bulging khaki shorts, hiding openly in front of my eyes. Clever Willy. How could I unmask him?

"Willy, darling," Barbara said, "we don't want Murray to miss his bus."

I leaned toward Willy. "Dad says you and he have been best friends all your lives, since before the 1918 revolution."

"*Ja, ja,* Samuel was my longest and best friend."

"Comrades?"

He looked at me from under his eyebrows. "A funny word for an American boy to use. No, Samuel and I were not exactly comrades. Once maybe so, during the Depression. We walked picket lines together, and listened in Union Square to the May Day speeches. And *ja,* come to think of it, he and I planned to go to Washington in 1941 with the Negroes. How was that called, Barbara?"

"The March on Washington. But we've had enough nostalgia for one afternoon. Did you have a good afternoon with Lizzie?"

"Fine. The March on Washington. Why was I telling that?"

"Because you and Dad used to be comrades, you said, before—"

"Ah yes, comrades, back in the good old days. However, after the war, 'forty-five, 'forty-six, the red-baiters and the union-busters set to work. I saw that we on the Left would soon be fighting for our lives. Do or die, I warned." He was talking faster now, his fingers thrumming on his bare knee. "I was in the electrical workers' union, and I warned them. The goons and scabs are coming, I said. And of course I was right. *Ja ja,* dead right. Two years later that shithead Carey and his Committee for so-called Democratic Action took over. What I didn't know was that the goons would get me first." He bent his head and divided the gray hair with his fingers. "See that?" A wide white scar angled from his forehead toward his left ear. "I bet you never saw anything like that." He sat up again, his face flushed.

"Enough, Willy," said Barbara.

"He's interested in history, isn't he?" He held up his bottle. "Bring me another, my sweet, and I promise no more beer today."

I wouldn't meet her eyes as she left the room.

"How did you get that scar?" I asked.

He told me then about that icy night on Schermerhorn Street, the four comrades, the cry of "Fuck you, scab," the fistfight, the cops hustling over, "Gestapo swine!" and the stunning sidewalk against his face—everything exactly as I had imagined it in the Public Library. Two months after peeling back the brittle skin of newspaper, I saw the bones at last.

"Where was Dad during all this?"

"At some fancy midtown restaurant with your mother to celebrate her birthday. The baby-sitter gave him the message when he got home, and straightaway he came to the hospital to sit by my bed. For hours he sang German boy-scout songs to me. So Barbara told me later, when I had left the coma. Boy-scout songs! *Typisch* Samuel. Always a boy. Yes, he was my friend. But comrade? Songs are not politics. 'I have a wife and children at home,' he said when I asked him to labor meetings."

"Willy!" Barbara slammed the bottle on the table. "You agreed to leave all that business behind."

"*Aber Du—hör auf*. There are things this boy should know."

"Why? For God's sake, why?"

"Because Samuel is his father," Willy growled. "Because he was our friend."

Both of them were looking at me. My heart was pounding fast and loud. I took a sip of beer. "What should I know, Willy?" I said.

She sat on the couch and shook her finger at him. "Just the union story, and then he goes home."

"No doubt your father meant to be good. But a good heart isn't good enough. Action is what counts in the final analysis. In the end he betrayed his comrades by letting others fight the battles."

"But he wouldn't sign the loyalty oath for his boss. Did you know that?"

"He wouldn't sign. *Wunderbar*. Did he organize a collective protest against the oath? Personal purity is the easy part."

"How did he betray you? Did he have to be on Schermerhorn Street and get clubbed to—"

"Hold it, boy. Now you sound like the rest of them—Lise, Samuel, my wife—all of them, everyone mixing up what is personal into what is political. I don't want Samuel's head broken open. Nor do I blame him for my head broken open. I never said he betrayed Villy Yacobs. I said he betrayed the cause, the larger cause, when he stayed home to play with his family and enjoy the purity of his silence. Did I ever say he betrayed Villy Yacobs? Why should I say that? We must remember that the only important betrayal is when a man . . . We must remember that a man must . . . How shall I say . . . ?"

His voice died. As he scanned the room, a strange expression crossed his face. "How was Villy Yacobs betrayed? I used to know. Betrayed. I used to know the name. But now . . ." He looked at Barbara. His chest heaved. "*Ach, meine Süsse,* you were right. Better not to look back."

His hand reached toward the radio and then fell into his lap.

I stood up and slowly backed away from that smile which was not a smile. "Look, I shouldn't have dropped in. I'm sorry. Thanks for the drinks." The smile hung on his lips. "Goodbye," I said.

He shook my hand with a sleepy motion.

For the second time that day she walked me down the hall. "I warned you, damn it. I told you not to ask him." She held the doorknob without turning it. In the dimness I could see only her silver-blond hair. She sighed. "Oh well, I suppose it's done now. It's over, isn't it, Murray?"

She opened the door, and the sunlight rushed in. She looked young as she gave me a wistful smile. She looked like the beauty queen she once had been.

Beyond her shoulder I heard him calling, "Tell him we are happy out here."

■ ■ ■

When I arrived home, Mom was reading while some piano concerto played on the radio. "So how were the Palisades, darling?"

I stood in the center of the room, grimy, wearied by the bus trip, and hungry. I looked down at the white seam cutting crookedly through her gray hair.

"Mom, I want Dad to come home."

"I know, darling."

"I want you to bring him home."

"*Na ja,* I wish. But he has his job, you know."

"Stop asking him for promises, and he'll come home."

She laid the book facedown in her lap. "Murray, we have already discussed all this."

"I went to see the Jacobses today."

"You what?"

"I visited Willy and Barbara today."

I began with the discovery of their phone number, and then the phone call and the bus ride, setting down each piece of the story like groceries out of a shopping bag. Barbara, the disaster, the kiss. One at a time. She closed her book and turned off the radio and fixed her eyes on me. Willy, the cops, the friend who was no comrade, and "tell them we are happy." She listened without a word.

"Dad made a mistake," I said. "And so did she. Everybody made mistakes, Mom, but it's done now." I tightened my fists until they hurt. "It's time to let him come home."

"All I ever asked is—"

"Coming home will be the promise. For God's sake, Mom, don't ask for more than that."

My voice cracked. My fists fell open. Exhaustion poured through my shoulders.

"Leave me alone," she said.

As I walked away, I heard the crackle of cellophane and the quick hiss of a match.

24

Three days later, when Mom laid the telephone receiver on the table, softly, as if it would break, and her eyes widened with unsaid news, I prepared for someone's death. "It's Samuel. Your father. He wants to talk with you."

Not dead, then. "Hello." Try again, louder, through the clot in my throat. "Hello."

"Murray! Your voice sounds so deep. Have you grown to seven foot?"

"It's just that you're so far away."

"That's why I called, to tell you I'm coming home next week. I start driving east on Wednesday morning, and . . ."

Next week? But I wasn't prepared for him.

Next week? Seven days of looking for a blue DeSoto, listening for footsteps weighted by suitcases coming down the hall.

"Murray, are you there?"

"I'm here."

"Can you believe it? One hour ago I talked with the home office, and presto! Bye-bye, California."

He sounded giggly and strange. A strange voice around which would grow a man who would be my father again. After seven months. Next week.

"We'll go to Ebbets Field and cheer for them Bums. We'll go out to a restaurant and eat all the spaghetti you can eat. What do you say?"

"You bet" was all I could manage to say before my throat tightened with tears. I thrust the phone into Mom's hand and turned toward the window and closed my eyes.

"*Ja,*" I heard her say behind me. After a long silence, again: "*Ja.*" And following a longer silence, "We'll see, darling."

The receiver clacked into place. Then her hands were on my shoulders, turning me toward her radiant smile. "If I could whistle, I would whistle," she said. "You whistle for me, Murray. Come, let's celebrate." She bent down and pulled a gleaming green bottle from the cupboard. "Champagne. Of course I'm already a little drunk with the news. Can you believe it? I must call Lotte. No, she talks too long. First Ernst. No, Theo—call Theo to leave camp early." Her thumbs were pushing at the neck of the bottle. "Watch out."

The cork popped, hit the wall, and bounced along the rug while champagne gushed.

"Oy gevalt," she squealed, licking her upstretched arm.

I drank one glass and then a second. We popped popcorn. She phoned everybody. I put on Theo's *Oklahoma* album and she hummed "Oh What a Beautiful Morning" while Gus chirped in the background. We drank champagne and told jokes that Dad used to tell and planned the menu for his first dinner at home, and through it all I postponed my question.

"Did he say why he was coming home?" I asked the next day, as she washed and I dried the champagne glasses.

"Because the job out there is finished, that's why. Please be careful, that glass is very easily broken."

"Everything is all right, then?"

"How should it not be? He is home soon, and that's that. Really, darling, the glass is from my grandmother and mustn't be chipped."

"I heard you. But what about the promise?"

"Better I dry it myself. Promise? Oh, no!"

The silvery glass seemed to hesitate en route from my fingers to hers, and then it dove toward the checkered linoleum and, with one boom, disappeared.

"Ach, du lieber Gott," she said.

For the next half hour we absolved each other on hands and knees, gathering up the fragments. "It was an accident," we repeated. "Accidents happen."

After that I invented ways to get through the week without asking questions. In the afternoon I ran and in the evening saw a double feature with Ruth. In the morning I ran and then I vacuumed half the afternoon and ran again, looking for blue cars, and all evening I wrote letters to Arlie and Ferg and Theo. In the morning I ran through the rain while people pointed and dogs barked at me. After lunch I read magazines beside the window in case a blue car drove up, and later I played three rounds of Scrabble with Mom while we kept the music low enough to hear the elevator possibly rumble open. For three days in a row I listened to the Dodgers play the Reds, including one doubleheader, inning after inning of the roar of crowds and the crack of bats, while I scored each play in my Spauldeen official major-league score book and, between innings, went to the window just in case. By Thursday morning Robinson was hitting .356, Campanella and Reese .324, the team as a whole .290—fat numbers that I chewed like Double Bubble gum as I ran for miles past cars of various shades of blue before coming back to shower and eat lunch and head to my room to read, to sit, to read some more and listen to the Four Aces singing so loudly I almost didn't hear the front door open.

"Halloo-oo!"

The voice was so much clearer than on the phone. It moved from room to room, like a large animal searching.

She laughed, they shouted each other's names, they said nothing for a long time, and then she called, "Murray. He's here."

I kept staring at the blurred words in the book, not wanting to let go of this moment, savoring the bittersweetness of this last moment into which so many months had finally shrunk.

He came upon me. His hand took charge of my elbow. The smell of coffee and his red shirt touched me. His mouth found funny ways to say my name against my neck. His cheek scraped my cheek. There was so much more of him than I had remembered.

"Bravo," he said, putting one fist above the other and

swinging an imaginary Louisville Slugger along a smooth horizontal arc. "Oh, my friends, this one is *out* of here."

"The Duke?"

"Nosirree. Hodges."

"*Ach,* you boys. One minute home, and already you talk baseball talk. Come, Samuel, the Dodgers will wait till tomorrow."

With one arm stiff around her waist, he swung her through the doorway. "Everything can wait until tomorrow, *Liebchen*, except one thing."

"Unpacking the car, you mean?"

His laughter boomed like a bowling ball down the hallway.

He was home.

Dad had come home.

My hands couldn't decide what to do with themselves, so I gave them the wooden horse to roll back and forth, quietly, along my leg.

"Murray, where are you?"

They were still enwrapped arm in arm when I entered the living room. Dad's other arm rose shoulder-high to outline a place beside him, one plus one plus one. "Look at us," he said, kicking one leg high. "A regular Rockettes."

"You're impossible," she said with a laugh. "Why don't you and Murray unpack the car?"

There were sober brown cardboard boxes and bright-red shopping bags, suitcases and crumpled magazines and a long cardboard tube marked *Fragile,* a stack of art books tied with rope, three tubes of suntan oil, plus bottle caps, cupcake wrappers, wooden spoons, Texaco maps, and one shriveled apple core. It was like a table of contents to Dad's life in California, all the stories I wanted to hear until I understood where he had been for seven months.

We both were sweating hard as we trudged between car and lobby. "Glad to have you back, Mr. Baum," said the elevator man.

"You bet, Frank."

"California must be some kind of place, huh. Didja see any movie stars?"

"Every day I had lunch with Rita Hayworth. It got boring after a while."

"Rita Hayworth, huh?" Frank's belly bounced in delight. "Boring, huh? That's a good one, Mr. Baum. Glad to have you back, yessir."

"Back in time to put some bricks on my son's head before he grows too tall."

Gradually his belongings clambered and heaved and wedged their way into the apartment. It was a mess, but Mom didn't seem bothered by it. She propped her feet up on a box and read a magazine, touching his hand or leg when he passed. Humming a tune, she set out roast-beef sandwiches and deviled eggs.

"Samuel," she said, "is the corn in Oklahoma as high as an elephant's eye?"

"*Oklahoma,* is it now? Where is my former wife who listened to Verdi?"

I couldn't see why that was so funny, but they laughed together like a pair of crazy people, flapping their sandwiches.

"You have a brand-new wife now, made in America," she said. And they were off into giggles again, while I chewed another deviled egg.

They kept on doing that. In Café Geiger it was the worst, because everybody stared at us when the violinist stood beside our table to play. "We're on our honeymoon," Dad told him loudly, "and this is our son Murray."

Sunday was more of the same. "*Aber Du*, Samuel, I barely recognize you under that tan!" Tante Lotte exclaimed. "Like a regular Indian you look." She circled him with tiny steps, patting his cheeks, his shoulders, his hands. "I am so happy I could cry, but I won't. So happy you must be, Murray, to have your father home, yes? I can hardly believe it. What do they say in the movies? 'Am I dreaming? Pinch me.' Oh, Samuel!" she shrieked as he pinched her behind. "If Max were here, God bless him, you wouldn't dare."

"But what man could resist trying?"

"So happy," she said. "You must tell us all about California, positively every detail. What time did you arrive yesterday? No flat tires, I hope. Such a long trip. I remember when my father—"

The doorbell rang. "It's open," Dad shouted.

Ernst paused on the threshold with a champagne bottle in his hand, studying our faces. In three long strides he crossed the room to shake Dad's hand. "*Gruss Gott*," he greeted him.

The noise mounted through two helpings of pot roast and several glasses of champagne and several portions of *Apfelstreuselkuchen*, followed by brandy and then, "by popular demand," Dad's Mortimer Snerd imitation, "duh, duh," his eyes rolling like pinwheels. "Duhh, Mr. Bergen, how many feet in a yard, you ask? Well, that depends on how many people are standing there. Yup, yup."

I propped my hand between his shoulder blades, asking Bergenish questions and feeling his voice vibrating under my fingers until I couldn't hold back any longer and broke into wheezing, hiccuping laughter that made my stomach hurt. "Excuse me," I said, and I rushed toward the bathroom.

The door was closed. I knocked once, and again. "One

moment,'' Ernst's voice called out. The handle rattled a few times, and the door slowly opened.

''Hi,'' I said with a hiccup.

''Ah, you, too, Murray?''

''Me what?''

He smiled and adjusted his bow tie, making it more crooked. ''We have even more in common than I realized.'' He stood in the doorway, staring intently at me. ''Sixteen. I can't remember me at the age of sixteen. Thank God.'' He reached down and tugged at the zipper of his pants. ''The only advice my father ever gave me was 'A gentleman should keep his mouth as closed as his fly.''' He lurched sideways and grabbed my arm. ''Stupid advice.''

''Are you feeling bad, Ernst?''

''You ask hard questions, Murray. How should I feel today? Good, better, best? How does a best man feel?'' He began to chuckle deep in his throat. ''The best man never feels as good as the groom. That's my advice.'' The sounds kept rolling from his throat, not like laughter at all now. He pulled me closer. ''But you have him to yourself again, so who cares about anyone else, right?''

I pushed past him before I heard more—before I smelled his breath again. I locked the door, filled a glass with water, and then realized that my hiccups were gone. ''Here's to you,'' I whispered, raising the glass to my pale face in the mirror, and I poured the water into the sink.

It was almost four o'clock, time to pick up Theo at Grand Central Station. Ernst and Lotte waved from the curb as we roared off in Rosie. Dad insisted that we push every button and slide every lever, until with headlights beaming into the sunshine and an opera spilling from the radio, we cruised into a No Parking zone, where Mom promised to charm every policeman while Dad and I ran down the ramp to find Theo.

We saw him before he saw us. He stood serenely among suitcases and a baseball glove and a box marked *Careful! Turtle,* wearing a Dodger cap low on his forehead. Tall, lean, even more tanned than Dad, this unperturbed person seemed to have outgrown the Theo I had known. Who was this older brother of Theo? But Dad didn't hesitate, swooping in for a hug that sent Theo's cap flying. Did I look as changed as Theo, I wondered? That was something for me to ask Dad. There was so much to ask Dad.

"You can look at her through this hole," Theo was saying. I stooped and looked, and the turtle's unblinking eye looked back. Theo nudged me. "Say 'Hello, Lulu.' She knows her name."

It seemed too stupid, saying hello to a turtle in the middle of Grand Central Station. "Come on, Theo. You gotta see Dad's new car. With a push-button radio."

"Still tuned to California stations, of course," Dad said.

"You mean," Theo asked, "we're going to hear California? Wow."

In the car everyone talked at once while Theo pushed the buttons and the radio blurted Toscanini and the Four Aces and the Giants and Ajax the Foaming Cleanser and Toscanini, and Mom pinched everyone's cheek, repeating "Can you believe it?" until I wasn't sure what it was that I should believe.

Theo's baggage joined Dad's baggage along the hallway and in corners and behind the sofa—too many pieces to fit into the narrow rectangles of closets and drawers. "Hello in there," I said to Lulu. For several minutes we looked at each other, longer than I had ever before looked into the eyes of a turtle.

■ ■ ■

That was Sunday. By Friday the boxes and bags were gone, the hallway was clear, and the closets and drawers were full. Theo was in the second day of a Monopoly game with Jay, with paper money and little green houses all over his room. Dad ate his Rice Krispies behind the sports page while Mom poured the coffee. "Happy trails," he called after he gave himself a last look in the mirror, tilting his straw hat and leaning down to Mom's lips. In the evening the hat lay again on top of the refrigerator. Theo read comic books. Mom knitted. Dad moved his finger down the columns of numbers in a company report, whistling under his breath.

Hello, we said; goodbye, we said; hello, we said again, in perfectly normal tones of voice, as if we had never had to shout into black telephones. Pick me up a carton of Pall Malls at the drug store, *Liebchen*, she said. How about tomorrow we go to Jones Beach, he said. As if he and she had never stood beside separate oceans. On Sunday night Theo sat beside the radio, stirring his chocolate ice cream into soup, and said, "Shh, here he comes."

"Tell the people your name, Mortimer."

There we all were, so firmly in place that one could almost believe he and Theo had never been away.

"Hey, Theo," I asked as we oiled our gloves, "any big adventures up at Camp Whatchamohawk?"

"Just a couple of kids who broke their legs, and a raccoon one night in Randy Mossman's bunk. Hey, did you hear Dad's taking us to a ball game on Saturday?"

"Dad," I said, as we played gin rummy, "I'm glad you're home."

"Me, too," he replied, picking up the eight of hearts.

"Dad," I said, after he won by twenty points, "why did you come home?"

"What a question! To be with my one and only wife and boys, of course. This time I deal." He shuffled the cards and then spread them wide like a peacock's tail between his hands.

"I went to see the Jacobses, Dad."

"So Mom told me. If you want to know the truth, I think that was a kind of crazy thing to do." He shuffled again and began to deal. "One, two, three . . ."

She had told him! All week he had known, while I hadn't known that he knew!

". . . nine, ten. So Willy showed you his scar, did he? Poor Willy, still playing revolution. And how is Barbara?"

"Fine." I pushed the cards across the table and stood up. "Everyone's just fine," I said as I walked away.

I said it quietly, but I wanted to scream. Scream until the windowpanes shook. Theo had been living in a log cabin with twelve boys and a raccoon and a turtle, Dad had been living among palm trees four time zones away, and I had been living here in this apartment every day and every night. So why was I the one who felt out of place?

25

People were coming back in droves. One morning Ferg appeared as suddenly as he had disappeared. "The staff pronounced me fit as a fiddle," he was saying on the phone as I tried to swallow a mouthful of toast. "Come on over and see for yourself."

He was fit, all right. He had a tan that shone like polished leather; a crew cut; a brown and white striped shirt with matching shorts, ironed smooth; muscled legs that ended in shiny brown loafers. Ferg looked too healthy to be Ferg. Was I in the right house? I looked toward the ceiling for the canopy of stars.

"Yes, it's me," he said. "Or at least an updated, rehabilitated version of me. Do you want an apple?"

"No, thanks. I'll just sit on this chair and listen to you eat."

"An apple a day keeps the counselors at bay. That's what Metcalf—one of our group up there—used to say at lunch."

It helped to hear him talk about "up there." Maybe it had been just a kind of camp, after all. Maybe underneath that buff-colored skin he was still the old Ferg. "Was the food as good as at Buddy's Grill?"

"I think the word is *wholesome.* Or square. Or balanced. Take your pick. A lot of eggs, juice, fruit, green vegetables. And at dinner two kinds of meat, which I didn't eat. That's the one thing I held out on. Anyhow, now I'm ready to take on Joe Louis." He flexed a bicep.

"Did you get that by playing croquet?"

"Croquet and softball and swimming and morning exercises. *Mens sana in corpore sano*, which roughly translates as 'healthy inside and out.' I'm a regular jock by now."

"A Latin jock."

"Wednesday and Saturday nights at eight o'clock was movie time, if you like Doris Day and Jerry Lewis. Believe it or not, after a few weeks they grow on you. Like poison ivy. Besides movies there was lots of talk. Every morning, talk talk talk with the staff one to one, afternoon talk talk talk in group. I bet they could teach an elephant to talk about his feelings."

I smiled broadly as I tried to get used to this fit and chattering Ferguson.

"Don't do that," he said. "I know how I'm acting, and I don't like it. I'm feeling nervous because you're the first person I've seen in the real world except for my parents. And you're nervous, too."

"Not really."

"Yes, you are." Holding the apple core by the stem, he placed it on a napkin on the desk. "But the worst part is that I'm afraid I've forgotten how to stop talking." His eyes peered at me through his lenses in a steady melancholy. "All day and all night I'll dribble away in stupid little words. Like a faucet. Talking endlessly, like Foxx. God, how often I thought of motor-mouth Foxx this summer as I talked myself inside out every day, starting with—"

I squeezed his hand with all my strength. "Ferg! Stop it!" The small bones slid and ground inside my fingers.

"Ow!" He jerked free and pulled back to the corner. There he nursed the hand against his chest. "Thanks, Mur."

"God, I'm sorry."

"No, I mean it. Thanks." He took a pack of gum from his pocket. "Want some?" I shook my head. "This summer I discovered the wonderful rhythm of gum. You can't stay glum if you're chewing gum. But enough about me. Tell me about you."

"Well, Dad came home, and Theo's back from camp, and I don't know, I'm running five miles a day."

He chewed busily, waiting for more. I gave him more: a rousing rendition of the San Remo Café. He smiled and nodded in all the right places, and at the end he was still waiting. This time I gave him the posters for the Hammett rally that never happened. "Foxx did it again," I concluded. "The bastard."

He nodded and chewed and eventually said, "Didn't you write me about finding those friends of your parents', the Jacobsons?"

"Jacobses. Oh, yeah." How could I have forgotten? It was here in this very room that I had first recalled that last tumultuous night at the camp: "No man lays my wife" and "Slut!" Now it was time for the sequel.

I began slowly, with the bus ride to Greenwich, but then I sped up, skipping over details, impatient. I was tired of telling stories. Talk, talk, talk. "So there they are, the Communist street-fighter and his beauty queen, living in the suburbs with Lizzie's swimming lessons and a cucumber garden. Pathetic, isn't it?"

"Not if that's what they want."

"Do they really want it, though?"

He shrugged.

"You could feel it the minute you walked into their house, Ferg. Everyone was afraid."

"Why shouldn't they be? You spelled trouble."

We scanned each other's faces. "'Every failure perfectly spoken,'" I said. "Don't you remember? 'As Gandhi's death tells us, the only success is every failure perfectly spoken.'"

"I don't know, Mur."

Why was he doing this? Contradicting me. Contradicting himself.

"You sure you don't want a piece of gum?" he asked.

"Damn it, Ferg, what's the matter with you? Don't you see? They're all lying. She's still half in love with Dad, but she sits there next to her half-cracked husband, saying, 'We're happy.' Mom and Dad dance around the apartment as if they'd never had a fight in their whole life." I grabbed his arm and shook it. "I hate it. I hate them."

He was jerking back and forth.

"Nobody asks *me* if I'm happy," I shouted.

"Murray, stop!"

I let go. His glasses hung slanted across his face. He straightened them, tucked them behind his ears. "Hey, friend, I feel for you. I really do," he said.

I nodded.

"It'll be okay," he said.

"It's not okay."

"Your father's home."

"Why? He can't just suddenly show up and—"

"Does it matter why? Maybe you're better off not knowing. What the hell: he's back. Enjoy him." He took off his glasses and rubbed them against his shirt. "Actually, I'd love to go with you and your dad to a ball game, if you wouldn't mind my tagging along."

He smiled shyly and looked down at his loafers. I looked up at the stars. In daylight they were bare and dull.

"Ferg, do you remember when Turds Mole was born?"

"On a Thursday afternoon in April on the third floor of the New York Public Library. Look, I know lots of things have changed this summer. But I'm still your friend, even in this stupid haircut. Okay?"

I gave a little nod.

"Okay, Turds Mole?" he persisted.

"Yeah. Okay."

■ ■ ■

Foxx sent me a photograph he had cut out of the *Daily News*. The caption described the scene:

> Passersby and cop aid Harry Shanahan, 40, of 131 East 45th St., while his Chihuahua lies dead near curb. Shana-

han, attacked by muggers while walking his dog yesterday, was knocked to the ground, falling on his pup and killing it. The dog had yelped fiercely until help came.

Murray, comrade, Foxx had scribbled along the side, *don't forget me. In this world a man needs all the yelp he can get.*

I didn't reply.

■ ■ ■

Mom and Dad were getting dressed up to see *The King and I.* At breakfast a week before, he had slipped the tickets under her English muffin. "Orchestra seats, center aisle, big date," he bragged while she hugged him.

Theo and I were drying the dinner dishes when they appeared in the doorway. "Golly," Theo said, "you look like out of the movies."

Dad's hair shone, and his tuxedo jacket gleamed. One hand jingled coins in his pocket, and the other buoyed Mom's elbow. Her dark eyes sparkled behind her veil. In high heels, with the pleats of her black dress swooping down her body, she seemed like a beautiful woman who was nobody's mother.

"Bye-bye, darlings. Don't stay up for us."

"Happy trails."

A whiff of perfume lingered where they had stood.

"Come on," Theo said, "let's take the popcorn to the living room and listen to 'Space Patrol.' If we sweep up the crumbs, Mom won't know."

"I'm not hungry."

"What's wrong, you on a diet?"

"Hardeeharhar."

"Or is it tired blood? Or coffee nerves?"

"Just leave me alone, wouldya?"

"Sometimes you make me sick." He went down the hall, pushing his feet with slow, scraping strides. When he reached his door, he shouted, "Why don't you go to school to learn how to act like a brother?" The door slammed, Gus chirped in panic, and I couldn't hear whether Theo was crying.

"I'm sorry. I'm sorry," I said, not loudly enough.

An hour later he found me on the fire escape outside Mom and Dad's bedroom window. "What are you doing out here?" he asked, boosting himself onto the sill and sitting cross-legged beside me.

"Killing time."

An ambulance siren raced by below our feet. Frank Sinatra sang from a radio in a nearby apartment.

"How much time have you killed?" he asked.

"Not enough."

Above the dirty clouds an airplane rumbled westward. Sinatra stopped singing, and the D.J. promised thunderstorms with highs around eighty, and humid, very humid. Through the twilight I couldn't see Theo's face clearly.

"Do you want to play Monopoly?" I offered.

"I want you to stop being mean to me."

As Rosemary Clooney sang, the thunder began.

Over the noise he said, "Answer me."

"Theo, no matter what I do, I'll think of you as my brother. Okay?"

"Okay. But what else could you think of me as?"

The rain began ringing on the metal bars of the fire escape. Soon I smelled that musky smell of wet summer asphalt. Side by side, Theo and I sat there, our drenched pants and shirts pulling heavy on us.

■ ■ ■

I ran a daily forty-minute route south, east, north, and west, up Seventy-ninth Street and into the lobby, the elevator, and the shower. I ran it without thinking. My body knew the way.

Ernst visited with his bow tie and white wine. From the chair he chatted with Mom and Dad on the couch. "You're better than best man," I wanted to say to him, but I didn't.

Foxx sent another photograph of accidents.

Six Red leaders were rounded up and put in jail.

The Giants were on a win streak—eight, nine, ten, eleven in a row—but the Dodgers stayed ahead by ten or nine, nine and a half or nine, eight and a half.

Allied and North Korean negotiators deferred replies on truce talks, expressed hope for renewed talks, renewed their talks, became stalled in talks, averted a break in talks, and talked "unproductively."

26

I was home alone, about to crack open a soft-boiled egg for breakfast, when I heard myself saying, "I can't stand this." The sound hovered for a moment in the middle of the kitchen. "I can't stand this," I shouted. Even with everyone gone, the rooms were filled up with their happiness. Filled to bursting. They were so busy being happy. No one but Theo listened to me. After everything I had done for them!

I flicked the knife through the egg and pulled off the crown. Yolk trickled down the side of the egg cup.

Get out: I had to get out of here. Stop running in circles and really go somewhere. Out West. Anywhere.

I looked down at the tiny yellow puddle on the table. Shouldn't I think about this? What exactly was I trying to accomplish? Where?

Don't think! Go, quick, before they come back from Tante Lotte's.

In the hall closet I found a Macy's shopping bag.

Was I really going to do this?

In my room, I dropped a T-shirt and khaki pants into the bag. On top of them went socks, comb, toothbrush, and *From Here to Eternity*. Too heavy. I pulled out the book and put in a magazine. I grabbed the pink china pig, plucked the cork from its belly, and shook it. Nine quarters, six dimes, and some pennies. Plus twenty-three dollar bills from the desk drawer. They made a thick lump in my pocket.

I put on my Dodgers cap and jacket and looked around once: the plaid bedspread, the radio, Duke Snider, the cubbyholes.

Go! Quick! Wherever I was going.

The bag flapped against my leg as I raced to the kitchen. *Dear Mom, Dad, Theo,* I wrote on the pad. No time for an explanation, even if I wanted to write one, and I didn't want to. They had had their chance. But a simple *goodbye* would send them into a panic. What, then? Something to give me time.

I'm spending the night at Ferguson's. Will call tomorrow. Love, Murray.

Three sentences, and I had set myself free. A whole day and night with no one in the world knowing where I was.

Free to do anything I wanted.

At the front door I felt I had left something behind. I looked over my shoulder into the sun-filled living room, and for a moment it seemed to become very small, as if I were looking through the wrong end of a pair of binoculars. The chair and the couch sat empty around the coffee table. A magazine lay open on the couch. The radio stood silent. I wanted someone to say goodbye to me.

If I had thought about what I did next, I wouldn't have dared do it. I opened the Manhattan phone book, found Moran, J., and dialed. One ring, two rings. Be home, Miss Moran! You're the only one who understands.

"Hello?" She spread the word long, tilting it up at the end.

"Hello. This is Murray."

"Murray?"

"You know, from English class."

"Well, hello."

"Yes." I shifted the phone to my other hand and stared at the bag. "Miss Moran, I was wondering if I could talk to you."

"Is there something wrong?"

"No. I don't know. I thought maybe we could have a talk."

"Of course."

"How about if I come over now?"

"Come over?" She waited the slightest beat. "All right. The downstairs buzzer's broken, so stand on the sidewalk and shout 'hello' toward the top floor."

I hung up the phone and grabbed the cord handles of the bag. I pattered down the stairs so as to avoid any questions from Frank the elevator man, broke into the brilliant summer heat, and headed downtown.

"Hello-oo." I squinted toward the bright sky, and she waved from the window. After the front door buzzed open, I climbed the stairs and there she was in the doorway, wearing white and blue, smiling.

"Come on in."

I set the shopping bag in a corner, between a pair of red boots and some smudged tennis shoes.

"I'm making some lemonade," she said over her shoulder. "Have a seat, if you can find a space."

Her apartment was three sunny rooms patrolled by two cats. Flowerpots lined the windowsills. A poetry book lay open on the kitchen table. A curtain of green glass beads divided the front room from the back, tinkling when I touched them. Behind them I glimpsed a double bed covered with pink sheets.

"How are you?" she called from the kitchen.

"Okay."

Books were everywhere—in shelves, stacked behind a chair, spread open on the floor with scribbled red comments like the ones she had scribbled on my papers. Maybe it was on this very couch that she had read my Auden essay.

I sat on the couch and watched her set a pitcher and glasses on the narrow table between us. Her hair was loose around her face, catching flashes of sunlight as she poured the lemonade. Blue and green swimmers dove in zigzag patterns across her white shirt.

"Ice cubes?"

"Yes, please."

She dropped two in my glass and settled back into her chair. It was like being in the teachers' room again, only now, with one leg folded beneath her, she didn't look like a teacher.

"How has your summer gone, Murray?"

"So-so."

"Just so-so?"

"With ups and downs."

She sipped lemonade, looking at me over the rim of the glass. Her eyes were a lighter brown than I had remembered, almost golden. "It's been so muggy the past few weeks, sometimes I find myself wishing for fall," she said. "Then I tell myself, this is your vacation, enjoy it." She pulled her blue skirt down, over her knees. "What have you been reading, Murray?"

I pushed away thoughts of *From Here to Eternity.* "Mostly newspapers and magazines. I know I should be reading books." The couch was so soft I felt I was sinking.

She stirred the ice cubes with her pinkie. A cat jumped into her lap and began purring as she rubbed its ears. "Well, Murray, what brings you here?"

I'm leaving home. Going west. But if I said that, she would turn solemn and raise difficult questions. Safer to begin with the past.

"Do you remember about my father in California?" I asked. She nodded. "Well, three weeks ago he came home—for good, this time. He's back in his old job." I shifted my weight, trying to get comfortable. "My brother came back early from camp. So everyone's home together again, the way it used to be."

She smiled. "Great."

"Yes." The second cat sat beside the bead curtain, glaring at me.

"What's the problem, then?" she said.

"I feel worse than when he was gone. I don't want to do much of anything, except run, and even that's no fun anymore. But when I try talking to them, they don't understand. Even Ferguson doesn't understand." I scratched at a mosquito bite on my wrist. "This sounds stupid, doesn't it?"

"No, it doesn't."

"What, then? What's wrong with me?"

She leaned toward me, spilling the cat to the floor. "Things at home can't jump right back to normal. Not after all that's happened."

I nodded.

"How could anyone simply put painful memories out of his mind? It takes time. And meanwhile, you're going to feel confused. Hurt."

I nodded again, wanting her to keep talking. Her voice was tender.

"It's hard, isn't it?" she said.

"I want to leave them."

"Of course you do."

"I know, it sounds crazy."

She shrugged. "Anyone would feel like leaving."

I tightened my shoelace. "Well, I did."

"Did?"

"Leave." There, I had said it out loud. I kept my head down. Clenched my jaw. She said nothing. "I wrote them a note saying that I was going to Ferg's tonight. That was a lie." Still she said nothing. I looked up at her. "I'm leaving home. Going west."

She nodded solemnly.

"I don't know where or how long yet," I said.

"Of course not."

Suddenly I felt as if I were pushing on a door that someone on the other side was pulling on. She wasn't going to try and stop me. "What do you think?" I said. "Is this a mistake?"

"It all depends, Murray."

"On what?"

She shifted in her chair, folded her arms under her breasts. "When I was fourteen I won the Saratoga County poetry-reading contest, which meant I would go to Ithaca for the statewide finals. My father wouldn't hear of it. Train fare, hotel bill, just to recite some verses and, at best, come home with a wooden plaque. Even Mama's tears didn't work."

She reached back and lifted her hair off her neck, then let it fall. She took a slow breath. "Two nights before the finals, I pulled a twenty-dollar bill from his wallet. I pinned a note to my pillow saying goodbye, I'm going to Ithaca. I crawled out of my window, got on my bike and rode five miles to my grandmother's farm, and slept in the barn. I woke up the next morning to see her standing over me. 'Your mama telephoned, Jeanie,' she said. 'Do you want me to pack you a lunch for the train to Ithaca?' I thought I was dreaming. 'Won't Daddy kill me?' I said. 'You leave Perry to me,' she said. I went, read my Keats sonnet, didn't win anything, not even a ribbon. When I got home my father was mad at me for a month." She rested her chin on her hand and sighed. "So, Murray, I do understand."

"But do you think I should go?"

"You're the one who has to answer that."

"Isn't that the point of your story, to take a risk?"

"If you want to pay the price."

"But you did. You went to Ithaca."

"I had a grandmother."

She leaned forward and drank some lemonade. I dug at the mosquito bite until it bled.

She wouldn't give me the answer. It wasn't fair. She had told me that story, but I had to decide what she meant.

A cat strolled up to her chair and meowed. "Hungry, Cleo?" she murmured, bending to scratch its head.

"What time is it?" I asked.

She went to the kitchen with cats at her ankles. "Half past

twelve. Keep talking," she said over her shoulder, "while I feed these monsters." The cats purred, flicking their tails like whips, as she opened cans and scooped brown meat into bowls.

"Talk, talk, talk," I said. "What's the use?"

"What?"

"I'm going to the bathroom."

It was a pink room filled with fragrances. The medicine cabinet brimmed with objects. A pink powder puff and an orange one; eyelash brushes; frothy orange shampoo; tubes of lipstick named Mandarin and Passion Rose; a jar of almond-scented lotion. I pictured her standing where I was standing, amid these fragrances, rubbing lotion along her arms and her legs.

My face went hot. I shut the cabinet door. At night she looked into this mirror and brushed her hair, swiveling to see herself over one naked shoulder, then the other. I turned and bumped my hip against the sink, dizzy from all this fragrance. A green toothbrush dangled in the slot beside the water glass; the other slot was vacant, and I thought of the red toothbrush in my shopping bag.

All right—if she was waiting for my answer, I'd give it to her. I splashed handfuls of cold water on my face. Leaving the faucet on to cover my noise, I peed. I combed my hair with stiff fingers and opened the door.

"Welcome back," she said. She was wearing a red apron over her skirt. Bacon was crackling in the pan. "I'm famished. How about a BLT sandwich?"

"I've been thinking, and I've decided not to go west right now. I want to stay."

"That makes sense. I'm sure you'll work things out at home."

"Here. I want to stay here."

"Oh, Murray, no." She wiggled the spatula in midair.

"Why not? For a night or two?"

"You can't stay here. I'm sorry."

"A little time to figure things out."

"This isn't the way."

Inside my chest I felt something cave in. I turned away and looked at the room crowded with books. She didn't care. She was telling me to go. Miss Moran. All she cared about was my words on a page.

I'd show her. I'd show them all.

I straightened my shirt at the waist. "I'll be on my way, then," I said. "Thanks for everything."

"Where are you going?"

"Ferg's. Where else?"

She put down the spatula and smoothed her palms along her apron. "I'm glad you came." She smiled, but there was a sad expression in her eyes. "Good luck, Murray." She stepped forward and hugged me, quickly, her hair brushing my cheek.

I thought I was going to cry. I bit down on my lip, and the feeling passed.

"Will you be all right?"

"I'm fine, Miss Moran." I picked up the shopping bag.

We stood in the doorway, with the cats purring and coiling around our legs. The smell of bacon drifted from behind her. "Just think," she said. "In four weeks we'll be seeing each other at school."

■ ■ ■

"Ferg? Listen, I don't have much time because I'm calling from a phone booth." A perspiring fat man stood outside, staring at me. "Did you call me today?"

"No."

"Good. Because if you had, my parents would've wondered where the hell I was. I told them I'm staying with you tonight."

"Come on over. I'm not doing anything."

"No, listen to me. In case they call, I want you to tell them I'm staying with you. But I'm going on a little trip."

"Where to? What's the big secret?"

"I can't explain now."

"Are you all right, Murray?"

"Of course I am. Look, Ferg, I've got to run."

The dime fell away with a distant clink-a-clink. I pushed open the glass door. "Hey, kid," the fat man said. "You talkin' to your psychiatrist in there, or what?"

The bag flapped against my leg. Every few blocks I shifted it to my other hand. A crosstown bus would have been easier, but soon enough I would have more than my share of bus riding. Might as well get the most out of this last look at the city. This last slow-motion tour before I reached the Greyhound terminal.

"Where will I go for ten dollars?" I asked the ticket seller.

He peered at me through the bars of the window, rolling a cigar across his mouth. "You want me to guess where you're going?"

"What I mean is, how far west will ten dollars take me?"

"You want recommendations? Personally I say forget New Jersey." The cigar rolled back.

"Seriously. How much to, I don't know, Cleveland?"

"Cleveland will cost you eleven ninety-five."

"Is there anything closer?"

"There's all of Pennsylvania closer, kid. You're doing a quiz-show stunt, aren't you?"

"I'm trying to figure out how far I can go for ten bucks."

"Well, Philly's five bucks, so you can go there twice." The cigar wagged up and down. "Only that would be twice as boring as once."

"Look, if Cleveland is eleven ninety-five, what's almost that far?"

He licked his thumb and ran it across a map on the wall beside him. "Twinsburg. Cuyahoga Falls. Ever heard of them?"

I shook my head.

"Neither have I. Hey, fella, it ain't none of my business, but do your parents know where you are?"

"My parents? Sure. I mean, that's where I'm going, out west to see my parents, except right now I've only got ten dollars for the first part of the trip."

He looked me up and down. "Okay, kid. Youngstown, ten seventy-five. Pittsburgh, nine-fifty. That's one way. What's your pleasure?"

"Pittsburgh, one way."

"Next bus leaves at two-ten. Bon voyage." He pushed my ticket under the window-cage.

Pittsburgh. Had I heard a telepathic message from Chuck Dressen that the Dodgers would be playing in Forbes Field tomorrow? I bought the *Times* and opened to the sports page. Dodgers versus Pirates at Brooklyn. Chuck Dressen and I had scrambled our telepathy. When he said "Home game," I heard "Away game." Well, then, I would go to Pittsburgh for no reason. Except that it was west. The route ran westward, just as clocks ran clockwise.

Forty minutes to go. Hurry up! This was beginning to feel tedious, or dreary, or in any case not like an ecstatic adventure.

I counted my money: $15.74. I bought two Hershey bars and put them in the bag for later.

Twenty minutes to go.

I turned the page and found myself looking at the want ads. *Acct desires per diem work, write-ups. Painter wishes work from landlord anywhere.* What had happened to all those personable young men?

I leaned back and closed my eyes.

"Express bus for Pittsburgh now loading at gate three."

As I stepped up into the shadowed interior of the bus, I thought I heard someone call my name. *Murreee.* High and fading, like a faraway bird. When I turned, I was looking into the yawn of a fat woman with a baby in her arms, and behind her stood a line of strangers.

"You in or out, buddy?" the driver asked in a bored voice. But he had already punched the ticket, and I was already committed to whatever it was I had begun this morning, or whenever I had begun it.

The motor grumbled into life, the bus lurched, and the city rolled under my feet. Ninth Avenue, Tenth, Eleventh, west, west, into the sunless tube of the Lincoln Tunnel with a ton of river over my head, west, west.

I awoke somewhere in New Jersey, my neck stiff from its strange angle of sleep. Fifty miles from home? A hundred? It didn't matter. I was free and on the move, speeding into new territory; that was all that mattered. Out here no one knew my name. Free.

I took a deep breath and watched the landscape skimming past. Brownish swamps. Huge gas cylinders, with filigree ladders spiraling up their sides. In the distance a freight train inched across a bridge, its red and yellow cars like matchboxes. I should remember this.

When I reached into the shopping bag, I realized I hadn't brought paper or even a pen. There was only a small heap of clothes, a comb, and a wrinkled *Life* magazine, plus two

Hershey bars. I ate some of the half-melted chocolate and read the magazine.

DeSoto. You can stretch out more . . . but you bounce less in a shiny new 1952 DeSoto.

In Pittsburgh I would buy pen and paper.

Marine Air-Devils in Hot Pursuit! Blood-Red Trails Streak the Sky! . . . Howard Hughes presents John Wayne and Robert Ryan in The Flying Leathernecks. . . . *Bares the Hearts of the Women Who Wait.*

Ruth wouldn't like this movie. Ruth? It seemed weeks since Ruth.

Model Commie girl, Traude Eisenkolb, defects to West—with smiling photographs to prove it.

In Pittsburgh I would phone Mom and Dad.

Something Nice to Come Home To: The Cold Cut Dinner. Ingenious wives are finding ways to build glamorous and well-balanced meals around the all-meat economy of cold cuts.

But what exactly would I say after those quarters and nickels stopped clinking? "Sorry, Mom, I can't come home tonight because I'm putting up posters in Pittsburgh"?

Crackpots Hit Jackpot. Dean Martin and Jerry Lewis enjoy their best-paying personal appearance tour.

"No, Dad, I'm fine. I'll explain everything later."

A trailer truck passed us, honking its horn madly. "Go to hell," our driver growled, beating his palm against the horn.

Suddenly I tasted something sour, a bubble of anxiety.

Where am I going?

West.

How far West can you go on one pair of socks?

As far as the ocean.

Until the wrong ocean holds me up?

Too many questions.

Where am I going? Where am I going?

"Harrisburg." My neck hurt more than before as the bus driver's voice dragged me from sleep. "We'll be here for a twenty-minute layover. Bathrooms are to the right, snack bar to the left."

I yawned a mouthful of gasoline fumes. Harrisburg, Pennsylvania. In my sleep I had crossed a second state line. If this were Europe, I would have to change my dollars into francs or drachmas, find the right words in French or Hungarian for doughnuts and milk. Emigrating was easier in America.

Five-thirty P.M. In five hours I would arrive in Pittsburgh and buy pen and paper. And call home. And then what? Keep going west, that was what. Until I found what I was looking for.

The doughnut was too sweet. The milk was warm.

It was hard to be excited all by myself.

Harrisburg's bus station looked like everywhere's bus station. The same gray lockers, the same butter-yellow snack bar, the same gray-faced men asleep on the benches, their heads tossed back.

Twenty minutes left too much time to think. Twenty minutes left too little time to think.

I went into the men's room and tried not to smell the urine of an afternoon of men. I got back on the bus and tried to fall asleep. The bus sped deeper into the sun, which burned like a red coal on the horizon, and I couldn't stop thinking that in Pittsburgh there would be a bus station with gray lockers and sweet doughnuts and men with their heads tossed back. And after Pittsburgh, Youngstown. And then Cleveland, and then Chicago. Until the ocean put a stop to it.

Somewhere in the middle of Pennsylvania I became

frightened. A sour taste filled my mouth. I needed to talk to someone besides myself.

I sounded the names of everyone I knew. I wrote them invisibly with my finger on the window. All I could see out there was the white reflection of my face with a finger pointing at it.

There were millions of people out there who spoke my language, but I might as well have been a refugee from Poland. Whom did I know west of Manhattan? All I knew in Pittsburgh was the names of Pirates, and in Cleveland that fella named Feller, and in Chicago Minnie Minoso herself. Oh, I was tired of laughing at my own jokes. I was so tired.

Mr. Silberman! In Cleveland! So I wasn't alone out here, after all. The door would open gladly to my knock, Mrs. Silberman would fuss over me with hot meals and hot showers, and then Mr. Silberman would usher me into his special room lined ceiling-to-floor with silver safe-deposit boxes. "Do you remember when we talked about horses?" he would ask in that paper-thin voice. "You were much younger then." Yes, I would sleep safely with the Silbermans while I figured out where I was going.

I watched the coal-black darkness chip away bit by bit with the lights of houses, all-night gas stations, used-car lots, steel-mill furnaces, and street lamps, until finally downtown Pittsburgh was honking outside my window.

"Last stop. Bathrooms to the left, snack bar to the right."

At first, as I stood in the phone booth to call Information, I couldn't understand what was wrong with the dial, and then I realized that my tears were in the way. As I squinted to find the 0, there were more tears, until I knew that even if my finger blindly found the hole, my voice would fail me.

Why couldn't I make this simple phone call to reach Mr. Silberman?

Because you'll wake him up.

Eleven P.M. It's not too late.

It's too late; you can't wake the dead.

But he isn't dead. We would have gotten a call.

All right, then, *you* explain the tears.

I don't know.

Yes, you do.

All I know is, two wrongs don't make a right. One runaway Baum is enough.

There was no air left inside the phone booth. I banged open the door and nearly bumped into a woman.

"Watch out!" she shouted.

I swerved. The shopping bag snagged on my heel and tore free from the handle. Socks and comb and chocolate spilled out on the dirty green linoleum floor of Pittsburgh's bus station.

A terrible feeling rose into my throat, like nausea, but it wasn't nausea. Homesickness! I wanted to go home. Whatever I had been trying to accomplish since I folded my clothes into this bag on East Seventy-ninth Street however many time zones ago, it was over. I wasn't sure what it was. And I didn't care. For the moment, the homesickness said enough.

"Thanks," I said to the little girl who helped me gather up by belongings. "You want a chocolate bar?"

She looked longingly at it. "My mother'd kill me taking candy from a stranger."

The Pittsburgh bus station. A peculiar place to discover I wanted to go home. I could have saved myself a lot of trouble by figuring that out in Miss Moran's apartment, or even in my own room. On the other hand, you can't return home without leaving.

They were going to be so happy to hear my voice.

"Next bus to New York departs at two-twenty, gets you there at eleven A.M. in the morning."

East. East. Gathering the bag in my arms, I crossed the waiting room with long strides. In the phone booth I hummed along with the little concerto of nickels and quarters.

"Where in hell are you? *Mein Gott!* Such tricks! You are shameless! Cruel! We're worried sick. Kidnappers." They were on both extensions, two phones versus my one. I held one arm against the glass wall to fend them off.

"After Mrs. Ferguson called us, we called everybody," Mom said. "Absolutely everybody," Dad said. "Even the Jacobses," she said. "Where in hell have you been?" he said. "Your time is up," the operator said.

I pushed coin after coin into the slots until they finally quieted down enough to hear that I would return from Pittsburgh in the morning.

"Pittsburgh!" Mom shouted. "Why Pittsburgh?"

I slammed down the receiver. No one had screamed at Dad when he called long-distance. We hadn't cried "shameless" and "kidnapper." How had he gotten away scot-free?

27

The apartment was ominously quiet. "Helloo-oo," I called, bracing for a fusillade of accusations.

When they appeared—Mom and Dad out of their room,

Theo out of his—they surprised me with their soft hellos. Mom gave me a hug, Dad a handshake, each wearing the stiffened face of someone who's heard some bad news. Theo stared at me as if I had been away for years. Everyone was on tiptoe. No one mentioned my torn paper bag. I felt ambushed by politeness.

"Well," I said, "now what?"

"We have all day to talk," Mom said, taking hold of Dad's hand.

"Wash up, eat something first," he chimed in.

"I saved some waffles and blueberry syrup for you," Theo said, rocking on his heels.

"Thanks," I said. The accusations would be postponed.

The hot shower massaged my weary shoulders and rinsed off layers of grime.

In fresh clothing, I sat by myself in the kitchen, eating waffles and reading about yesterday's doubleheader win by the Giants.

An hour of postponement.

"Feeling better now, darling?"

They sat in a line on the couch while an opera poured quietly out of the radio. Dad looked up from the crossword puzzle, pencil hovering. Mom slowed her knitting needles. Theo wriggled his rear end, getting ready for a show.

"I guess you're waiting for true-confession time." I stood there in the center of the room, licking the syrup off my lips. How much did they already know? I tried to read their eyes, but their eyes told me nothing.

"Well," I said, taking a deep breath, "I didn't go to Ferg's. I went to the bus terminal and got on a bus thinking I would go cross-country. But in Pittsburgh I realized I wanted to come home. That's when I called you." They sat silent, motionless. "I know I should have called earlier. I'm sorry you got worried about kidnappers. But here I am, safe and sound."

"You sure had us worried, son." Dad's pencil still hovered, as if to take notes on my testimony.

"We even called the police to report a missing person," Theo said with awe.

"But that's all over with," Mom said. "Now what I want to know is why. Why did you do it?"

"I don't know. I just did it, that's all."

"You set out on a crazy cross-country business and you have no reason?"

"It wasn't crazy."

"What would *you* call it, then?"

"Here in this room, it sounds kind of crazy. But out there, on that bus . . . I mean, until the very end, in Pittsburgh, it felt . . . destined."

"Destined?" Mom frowned. "Talk plain English, please."

"Should I get the dictionary?"

"Don't get smart."

"Destined. It was like the trip was choosing me." Dad's pencil descended slowly to the page. "You understand, don't you, Dad?" I asked. He stared at me.

"At least you weren't kidnapped," Theo said.

Mom set down her knitting and leaned forward, elbows on knees. "The police sergeant asked if you were in any trouble—at school, or maybe with a girl. Is there some problem with Ruth, perhaps?" She and Dad checked each other's eyes. "If you wish to speak alone to your father, you need only say so."

"What? No. Nothing like that." I rubbed my eyes, and behind my fists I could feel her eyes gliding between the buttons of my shirt, prowling beneath the elastic of my underpants. How long did I have to stand here? Heat began to throb across my face. I hadn't come home to answer all their questions.

"Why did you do this, Murray?" she said. "You can tell us the truth. We're your parents."

For a moment I couldn't hear anything but a furious roar inside my skull. "Do you really want to know?" I was standing above her now. "Do you really want to know?" I was shouting into the white crease of her hair. She raised one palm. "Do you, Mom?" She shut her eyes and shook her head as I stood rigid above her.

"Murray!" Theo wailed with his hands over his ears.

"Enough," said Dad.

"Goddamn it, I'm tired of this shit." I was shouting at all of them now. This was why I had come home—to shout in the middle of the living room. "You call yourself parents, but all you do is go around singing and laughing. Lies, that's all I get. Lies. Why the fuck can't you—"

"Don't you talk to us that way," Dad shouted. "Apologize, or else."

"What about *you*, Dad? Are *you* back for good?"

The pencil snapped in his hand, making a sound like a breaking bone. He squeezed the halves inside his fist as he looked up at me.

"Listen to me, Dad." I was talking terribly quietly now, with a furious little space between every word. "I left and I came back, and don't you ever again ask why."

The four of us watched each other. Dad's forehead was red and wrinkled. Mom's lips formed a narrow white line. Tears ran down Theo's cheeks. The radio hissed with static, and the sun burned into the rug. There had never been such ferocity in this room. It was thrilling. I stood above them and felt triumphant.

"I'm going to sleep," I said, turning away.

"Murray, wait," Theo called in a choked voice, scrambling after me, tugging my sleeve.

"No."

I fell asleep with one sneaker on and the music of loud words in my head.

■ ■ ■

I awoke at noon of the next day with my stomach gurgling. I looked over at the cubbyholes: CIGAR BANDS, COMICS, DODGERS YEARBOOKS. . . . What had I been dreaming about? I saw the torn paper bag on the floor, and yesterday's trip rushed in. I smiled. Who would believe what I had done!

On the kitchen table I found a note propped against the cereal bowl. *Good morning. Gone to Bloomingdale's with Theo for back-to-school clothes. Mom.*

School! Those cramped metal desks . . . multiple-choice tests . . . homework. I wasn't ready for school. I had gone to Pittsburgh. I had run away from home.

I ate Corn Flakes, toast and jelly, toast and honey—I was famished after all that sleep, but too restless to sit. The kitchen seemed small, or was I bigger? With toast in one hand, I did a little dance step around the chair, my elbows poking out like wings, the way Fred Astaire would do. In *Royal Wedding* you knew he wasn't really dancing up and down the walls, but you couldn't help believing he was. "All I want is kissing you . . ." I was still hungry, but nothing in the fridge enticed me. ". . . and music, music, music." Ruth and I had eaten cheesecake on our first date. Ruth. Her eager lips.

I brushed my teeth, humming between strokes. Ruth would love every minute of my trip. "You really did that?" she would say. My chin could have used a shave, but it showed that it had gone to Pittsburgh and back. I was so excited I put my right sneaker on the left foot.

Ruth. The sensible thing was to call first, but I didn't want to be sensible. Better to be standing there when she opened her door—surprise!

Visiting a friend, I wrote on the bottom of Mom's note. *Home by dinner.*

I took the bus, but even so, I was sticky with sweat as I walked down Sixtieth Street. What if no one was home, or only her mother was? I rang the bell, stared at the silver peephole, and was about to ring again when the door swung open.

"Mur-ray!" She smiled, and I saw that wonderful dimple in her cheek. "What are you doing here?"

I kissed her. "Surprise." I kissed her harder, longer.

"Do you want everyone in New York watching us?" she said, stepping backward. "Come inside."

I followed her into the narrow vestibule and closed the door behind me. In the sudden darkness, I smelled the sweetness of her hair. We hugged, she wiggled her hips against me, and before I knew it, my penis had risen and was pushing back.

"I'm glad to see you, Ruth."

"No kidding." She laughed. "You act like you've been off in the army."

"No, I was in Pittsburgh."

"What?"

"Only briefly. It's a long story."

She led me into the living room and tilted her head. "You're acting funny, Murray." She smiled. "I like it."

"That's why I came. I mean, you won't believe what I have to tell you."

"Come to my room, where my little sister won't bother us. She can be a pest when my parents aren't home."

As we turned down the hall, I heard Tony Bennett crooning at top volume behind her sister's door. We tiptoed past, into the sunshine of Ruth's room, and closed the door behind us.

"So tell," she said, taking my hands. "What was in Pittsburgh?"

"A bus station."

"Yeah. And?"

I picked up a glass globe from her desk and shook it, watching the plastic snowflakes swirl around the Statue of Liberty. "And then I turned around and came back." I held the globe to my ear, but I couldn't hear the snow falling.

"This is getting weirder by the minute, Murray."

"By then the police were looking for me." I set the globe down, pushed aside the fashion magazines, and sat on the bed. "Missing person. Kidnap victim. My parents were frantic."

She stared down at me, a vague smile on her face as she tried to decide if I was joking.

"I ran away from home, Ruth."

"You're kidding."

"Two days ago. Took the bus west."

"I don't believe this, Murray." She sat beside me, put her hand on my knee. "Why would you . . . ?"

"Because I wanted to. To see what it felt like." I pointed toward the pink curtains on the window. "Out there. Free."

We were so close I could see the green flecks in her brown eyes.

"I was riding alone through the night and I thought about you. I missed you."

Her breath fluttered against my face. I closed my eyes,

and we kissed. I touched the warm skin of her throat. We tipped sideways onto the bed.

Her fingers were in my hair.

I moved my hands along the slope of her behind, down her legs, and slowly up under her skirt, the unbearably smooth skin.

She squeezed my leg and said something I couldn't hear.

"What?"

"Lock the door," she whispered.

I stumbled to my feet, crossed the room, and swiveled the knob, heard the metal tongue click into the socket. Locking me in here with her. My heart hammered. When I turned around I saw her pale breasts, her pink nipples, her eyes watching me.

"Don't just stand there," she said.

I tore off my shirt, pants, shoes. Lay beside her.

Her nipples grazed my chest. We kissed so hard it hurt. I reached down between her thighs.

"Ruth," I whispered as her thighs clenched my hand.

Her thighs loosened, and my fingers inched upward, touched her panties. They were wet. She shuddered. I felt her hand on my swollen underpants.

We lay perfectly still, not breathing, reading each other's eyes. Then she leaned across me, and her hair tickled my face. "I want you, too," she whispered in my ear. "But don't get me pregnant."

Yes, of course! Bobby L.'s gold foil envelope. His "token of friendship" had been hiding in my wallet, waiting for this afternoon. "Don't worry," I said.

I rolled over and rummaged through the clothes on the floor, found my pants, found the wallet. So much work to do before . . .

I pulled down my underpants and shivered. Naked—no

girl had ever seen me naked. My fingers were so wobbly I could hardly tear the foil. Finally here was the thing I had heard about and never held: the rubber. What if I unrolled it wrong? Inside out? Could you roll it up and start over? I should have practiced beforehand. I held my breath and gently unrolled the almost weightless ring onto myself.

She kicked off her panties. Lay beside me. Someone else's nakedness, and I was allowed. Her stomach was soft, smooth. I rubbed the pillow of hair between her legs. She moaned. Slowly, not daring to breath, I inched lower and fingered that juicy warm pocket, the place I had never believed I would touch.

She was making excited noises.

I climbed on top of her. Up on hands and knees. How to do this? I felt her hand down there, guiding me. I slid in. Inside her! Moving to the rhythm of her hips, faster, all of me funneling down to that one dark place, wanting to . . . explode.

Afterward I couldn't stop trembling. She held me until my breathing quieted.

"How are you feeling?" she said in a husky voice.

"Great."

I rolled off her, slid the rubber off, held it at arm's length. I was no longer a virgin.

"There's the wastebasket," she said.

Pink wastebasket. The clock said 1:20. Half an hour ago I had been a virgin. Now I was . . . we were . . .

"How are you feeling, Ruth?"

"Sore."

"Oh God, don't be mad. I'm sorry. I thought you wanted to do it."

"I meant sore down there."

"Oh." I squeezed her hand. "I'm sorry."

"What's to be sorry for?"

A car honked outside the window. Voices from her sister's radio sounded faintly through the wall. All this time the world out there had been going on. Mom and Theo were shopping in Bloomingdale's without any idea that I was lying here naked.

"Wasn't it great?" I said.

She gave a nod.

I touched her breast. "Don't you feel, I don't know, different?"

"I feel happy."

"But also different, right?"

She shrugged.

"Come on, Ruth, you know what I mean. This morning we were virgins."

She looked at me with an expression I couldn't read, and then, almost imperceptibly, she shook her head.

"Ruth! You mean you . . . Who? When?"

"One night last summer at the beach. Somebody I cared about. Don't look like that. I'm still the same person."

I looked down at the dark triangle between her legs. So I wasn't the first. All this time she had been carrying around her secret. A night with someone I didn't know. A girl with a past.

"Did you hear me?" she said.

I nodded.

"What are you thinking?"

I rubbed her stomach. "I'm thinking about Friday night. My parents go out on Friday nights. So maybe—"

"We're going to Cape Cod for a week."

"How about the next Friday, then?"

"I don't know, Murray."

"But you said you liked it."

"I did. I do. Can't we enjoy this?"

She laid her head against my chest. I breathed through her hair, musky now with the smell of our bodies.

Entirely different.

■ ■ ■

I stood outside her front door, squinting in the sunshine. I wasn't ready to go home and talk about back-to-school clothes. Not yet.

I swung my arms high as I walked, whistling, smiling at people. I needed someone to celebrate with.

I called Sol from a phone booth. No answer. I called Foxx. No answer. I called Jeep, although I knew he was at his job on Long Island. Wasn't anyone home?

All right, then: Ferg. No time like the present to settle the score with him.

"Hello?" he said.

"This is Murray. Can I come over?"

"Fine. I've been waiting for you."

Fifteen minutes later we were sitting on his bed with a basket of fruit between us.

"Watch it!" I said.

"Oops, did my orange piss in your eye?"

"Curb that orange."

It went like that for a while, little jokes and silences while he ate and the air turned tangy.

"So, Murray," he said, "where were you this weekend?"

"Pittsburgh."

"What in the world were you doing there?"

I shook my head. "The question is, why did your mother phone my parents?"

"What? My mother?"

"Come on, Ferg. Why did she tell them I wasn't staying with you?"

"Because I told her to."

"You did?" My orange bounced to the floor.

"I thought they would believe her more than me."

"For Chrissake, Ferg, I told you to keep my secret."

"I was worried. You sounded kind of loony on the phone." Through the thick lenses his eyes seemed intensely small.

"You betrayed me," I said.

"No."

"Yes." A column of neatly folded socks and underpants leaned against his desk. I wanted to kick it down.

"Listen, one of the counselors up there asked me, 'If you were in trouble, which friend would you call for help?' You know what, Mur? I named you."

"Some friend you are. You ratted on me."

"You're missing my point. When you called from that phone booth, I heard you asking for help. *You* calling *me,* your friend, for help."

I remembered that phone booth with the perspiring fat man waiting impatiently outside, before I knew I was en route to Pittsburgh. Then I jumped to Ferg's apartment and listened to myself. *Hello, Ferg, this is me. Turds Mole to Turds Mole.*

"Wrong, Ferg. I was feeling great," I said.

"You sounded weird."

"I had wings on my heels, ready to fly."

"To Pittsburgh?"

"Anywhere. I was looking for . . . ecstasy. All I needed was your little lie to find it."

The bed creaked as he reached down for my orange. "Did you find any?"

I grinned. "You wouldn't believe me if I told you."

"Try me."

"I promised a certain someone not to tell."

"At least give me a hint."

"Let's just say I did what every boy dreams of doing."

He studied my face for a moment. Then the answer registered in his eyes, and a sly smile spread over his face. "You're kidding. Who was she?"

"I'm not kidding, and I can't tell. But believe me, it was"—I punched his arm—"ecstasy!"

He rubbed his arm. "Good for you."

"I'll say."

He nodded as he peeled a strip off the orange.

"It was unbelievable," I said.

"When did you fall in love with her?"

"Well, I'm not exactly in *love* with her." I shook my head as he offered me a section of orange. "I mean, I like her a lot. Otherwise I wouldn't have . . . done what we did. Actually, I love a lot of things about her."

"Hey, I was just asking."

"You ask too much."

Was I supposed to love her? She hadn't asked if I loved her before she took off her clothes.

I leaned back against the pillow and saw the bare white ceiling. "Ferg! What happened to the stars?"

"I tore them down."

"How could you? They were so beautiful."

"Yeah, but I don't want to feel the way I used to feel when I looked up at them." He placed the orange on my stomach. "Too small. Or else too large, the sun, burning up with importance."

For a long while we said nothing. It was difficult, patch-ing together our old friendship without Turds Mole. It was as if I had lived long enough to begin losing friends.

I lay there with my eyes shut, smelling the orange perfume. And then I was in Miss Moran's apartment listening to her talk about poetry in Ithaca. Writing names on the bus window's darkness. Trying to phone Mr. Silberman through the tears.

I looked up at the bare ceiling and said, "I didn't feel in trouble until I started west. That's when I began feeling lonely. That's when I called you for help, Ferg. From Pittsburgh. But your line was busy—maybe your mom was talking to my mom at that very moment—and the bus was about to leave for New York."

When the smile rose on Ferg's face, I was glad I had told the lie.

■ ■ ■

Halfway home, I was ready for the next half-truth.

I bought a bunch of roses at the florist's and hid them behind my back as I entered the apartment. Mom was in the kitchen, turning the handle of the egg beater, then pausing to peer into the bowl, then turning again.

I leaned against the refrigerator. "What are you making?"

"Whipped cream. At your father's request, apple pie *mit Schlag.*"

"Can I lick the beater?"

"I suppose."

The vibrations of the refrigerator were throbbing inside my chest. "Mom, there's something I want to say."

"One moment, until this is done." She churned busily. She still hadn't looked at me. "So! Ready now." She handed me the beater, its blades wreathed in white foam, and I gave her the flowers.

"Beautiful!" she said. "But what's the occasion?"

"It's my homecoming present."

She held the flowers at arm's length. "A bit late, don't you think?"

"That's what I want to say." A blob of whipped cream fell to the floor. "I'm sorry I shouted nasty things at you."

"Truly nasty."

"Yes, I—"

"And uncalled-for. Here we were, thinking you had been in some accident, only to find you were off on this . . . this joyride."

I laid the egg beater on the table, unlicked.

"We were worried to death about you," she said.

"I'm sorry."

"You don't sound it."

"I'm really sorry, Mom."

She took a breath for another tirade but then simply said, "Okay, you're forgiven."

There was one more thing to say. I opened my arms. "Never again."

As we hugged, the trembling flowers tickled the back of my neck.

28

At five-thirty in the morning it was hard to feel excited about anything, even about standing on top of the Empire State Building with the dim, silent city laid out beneath us and, supposedly, a lunar eclipse getting ready to happen above us (if the dirty gray clouds would ever let us see the moon). There we were, Mom, Dad, Theo, and I, along with a couple of hundred other crazy people with cameras and binoculars hung on their necks, all shifting from foot to foot, sipping coffee from thermoses, peering at the clouds, and yawning. As soon as I finished one yawn, another would begin. "Can a person sprain his jaw?" I asked Dad.

"An eclipse is worth losing sleep for," he said, slapping our shoulders like a coach with his team. "We're watching history."

"All I'm watching is clouds," said Mom.

"I'm cold," Theo said, pulling his sleeves over his hands.

"Come, Samuel, admit now this was a dumb idea," she persisted.

"Yesterday you didn't think so."

"Well, yesterday wasn't five o'clock in the morning."

Yesterday, which was a week after Pittsburgh, Theo had said in the middle of spooning whipped cream over his apple pie, "Let's have a family celebration tomorrow." At once the rest of us had repeated the words and clapped him on the back as if he had announced he was getting married or had found a cure for polio. "A family celebration!" we exclaimed to one another. Saturday would be Baumsday, Mom declared as she poured Dad's coffee. And he just happened to have a couple of little celebration ideas, Dad said, spooning whipped cream into his coffee: a lunar eclipse, for example, and the Giants-Bums game. It was as if he had been hiding tickets in his pocket for precisely this moment. Tickets to a double feature that stretched from the Polo Grounds to the moon.

"Well, what do you think?" he had asked with a huge grin.

At the time there had been only one thing to think, of course: ecstasy. What I had hoped to find on my own by going west, I would find here at home. That was what I thought on the eve of Baumsday.

Twelve hours later, here we were, ninety-six floors above Manhattan Island. The skyscrapers formed steep canyons checkered by lighted windows. At the bottom, toy-sized yellow cabs and green buses moved soundlessly, feeling their way with headlight beams.

"I'm cold," Theo said.

"Samuel, enough already," Mom said.

"Any minute now, the clouds will open up," he murmured, with the binoculars bouncing against his chest. "Any minute now."

"What time is it?" I asked.

"Five of six. Any minute now, I bet you a hundred dollars." Suddenly he waved the binoculars. "Look!"

"Hooray!" people shouted, tipping back their heads.

As the clouds split open, we saw the moon masked by the earth's shadow, a gray eye floating in a gray sky. A moment later, the clouds closed again.

"Was that it?" Theo asked.

"Ohhh," the crowd moaned, and people began shuffling toward the elevators. "How am I going to remember it," a man asked, "if I couldn't take a picture?"

"Happy Baumsday," Dad said, looping one arm around Mom's waist.

On the drive home, Mom and Theo fell asleep in the backseat while Dad whistled a marching song under his breath, drumming his hand against the steering wheel. "Do you know this tune?" he asked. "When I was very young, maybe four or five, my father took me to Unter den Linden, the big avenue in Berlin, to see a parade. For an hour we waited while bands marched by, playing this tune. Suddenly my father lifted me on his shoulders and said, '*Pass auf, Samuel, hier kommt der Kaiser*'—'Here comes the kaiser.' For a moment I saw him, riding a snow-white horse, shiny gold medals and braid on his uniform, a silver sword at his side. Just one moment, like a blink of your eye."

He braked for a red light and turned toward me. His one-day beard smudged the lower half of his face, making his teeth shine whiter than usual. "I was very angry you ran away to Pittsburgh like that. I was afraid you were hurt, kidnapped, God knows what. But now that you're safely home, let me tell you." He wagged his jaw. "I think it was wonderful that you, my sensible Murray, would do such a stupid thing." The light turned green. He worked the gearshift. Then he laid his hand on my knee and, one-handed, steered us home, whistling.

That afternoon, almost before we had got our breath back, we were up at the Polo Grounds. All four of us. Mom cheered when we cheered, booed when we booed, and asked lots of questions. Can each man spend the same number of swings? Why do you say that ball was "foul"? Why do the men all spit like that on the grass?

From the start, everything went the Giants' way: Don Mueller's blast into the upper right-field deck; Bobby Thomson's into the upper left-field deck; then Mueller's second of the day. Meanwhile, the best we could do was fill the bases in the third inning and score a measly run when Maglie nicked Robinson's wrist.

By the fifth inning, with Dem Bums losing 5–1, it was getting colder under those gray clouds, and so dark that the lights had been turned on. Abrams and Furillo were on base, thanks to an error and a single. "Are we having another eclipse?" I asked Dad. But he was looking through his binoculars at Maglie's windup and didn't hear me. On my other side, Theo was moving his lips in a prayer for Pee Wee Reese to hit Abrams and Furillo home, so he didn't hear me, either. Lucky for me he didn't, too, because he would have said I had jinxed us with "eclipse talk." Who knows, maybe I did. For at that very instant, Dark snared Reese's looping line drive, then tossed to second base, where Stanky leaned right to put the tag on Abrams as he scrambled desperately back and then leaned left to put the tag on Furillo as he pounded fatally ahead. Triple play. Three men gone in five seconds.

An entire inning had been wiped out as I held my breath. As forty thousand people held their breaths. For a moment we all looked at one another furtively, as if to check out whether we had really seen what we thought we had seen on what had until then been a more or less normal September afternoon. Then they all faced the field again and began to cheer, while I groaned a lamentation for my beloved Bums, who would be only six games ahead when the Giants finally let us go home at the end of this dark, cold day.

But Dad was cheering, cheering madly, as he stood on the wooden seat waving his Dodger cap. "Bravo," he shouted, "encore," the way he did after conducting Beethoven's Third in the living room along with Toscanini. I couldn't join him, any more than I could cry the way Theo was crying on my other side.

"What happened?" Mom asked, pulling Dad's sleeve.

"Lischen, you're a lucky lady. Your first baseball game, and you see a once-in-a-lifetime sight."

"But Dad," Theo said, "why couldn't it be *our* triple play?"

He shrugged. "Next time."

"Next lifetime," I said.

He gave me a look, and then he chuckled. "You need a little fatalistic optimism." I shivered inside my jacket and brooded about this season in which everything refused to obey the law of averages.

At home we were greeted by a pile of mail behind the door, including an envelope from Foxx. *My masterpiece,* he had scribbled under the newspaper photograph inside, this one of a traffic jam on Route 17. A trailer truck had tipped across three lanes at an infamous bottleneck near Sloatsburg, and for six hours fifteen thousand cars had been stalled over a stretch of sixteen miles. "The worst traffic jam in history," proclaimed the caption. Flattened Chihuahuas, a sixteen-mile traffic jam—what in hell was Foxx up to?

This wasn't the time for me to figure it out. Ruth was coming back from Cape Cod today. I phoned. No answer. Maybe an hour from now . . .

I didn't call again, though, because the postcard of the Eiffel Tower slid quietly through the flap on the door.

> Murray, *mon cher.* Next Tuesday I fly home, racing this postcard into your arms. *Toujours l'amour* and all that.
>
> Arlie

Tuesday. I wondered how steeply the island would tilt when she landed.

29

It didn't tilt at all, and I was relieved. Our reunion would not be as painful as I had feared.

We faced each other across the doorstep, her finger still raised to the bell, my hand on the knob.

She wore her hair in some complicated new way, folded over one ear and fastened in the back with a barrette. Her cheekbones stood out sharply, making her look older—or maybe it was the bluish eye shadow, or the way she contained the smile in the corners of her eyes.

"Do you recognize me, *chéri*?"

"You look wonderful. Older and more wonderful." But the island hadn't tilted, and this time I felt the twinge of disappointment behind my relief.

We kissed. "Murray, it's been so long." She tugged me along toward the living room. "I want to tell you all about my summer *tout de suite.* Oh, Murray, you can't imagine how strange it feels to be back. American accents sound so heavy, as if people had wooden tongues."

I stuck out my tongue at her. "If you don't like it here, lady—"

"Okay, okay, I didn't mean to hurt your feelings. Come on, let's look at my photos."

As one little glossy black-and-white picture after another passed across my palm, she told stories of her summer. Magnificent cathedrals; unexpected conversations; getting lost on the Left Bank; creamy *pâtisseries.* I listened to her voice more than her words—the familiar, flutelike voice of this girl who must have been composed by Bach (as Ferg had once said) because her mind moved like a fugue. Arlie, whom I had achingly desired on the ferry, and in the museum, and halfway across the cabled bridge (tuned in F sharp, she had said). Here she was, sitting beside me on the couch, wearing blue eye shadow, and I didn't ache for her. I touched her arm, which was so deeply tanned that the blond hairs seemed illuminated, and I didn't feel whatever it was I used to feel—that scary risk of making my claim upon her. A summer had taken place. There was air between us.

"Murray, you haven't listened to a word I've said."

"The bearded man in the Louvre told you he had studied with Matisse."

"Wrong, *monsieur.* That was fifteen minutes ago. Since then I've been to Versailles and kissed a Communist, and you haven't heard one word."

"How did you know he was a Communist?"

"Well, I don't really know, except that he was reading *L'Humanité,* which is the Communist newspaper."

"But you kissed him—*that* you know."

"Oh, come on, Murray. Only once—well, maybe twice—at the end of this long walk through the Père Lachaise cemetery. You should have seen it, Murray: acres of tombstones of the most famous people in the world. There we were, walking over Oscar Wilde, Modigliani, Gertrude Stein. It was thrilling."

I folded my hand around her wrist. "Arlie."

"What?"

"I just realized something. I won't ever again be hurt by you."

Gus chirped once, twice, and then swelled into a long warble. Arlie's eyes scanned my face. Her lips trembled. Then she pulled me against her. "What happened to us this summer?"

Her breath was rough, noisy. I stroked her back in slow curves. My fingers ran over the ridge of her bra, and I remembered Ruth's pale breasts. Had Arlie found some ecstasy one unmentioned night between the postcard from Notre Dame and the postcard from Versailles?

"Murray? Are you still my friend?"

"Of course."

"No, I mean it." She sat up and looked at me with teary eyes. "I know I hurt you last spring, but you came so close, wanted too much, and I just couldn't . . ."

"It's all right."

Gus fluttered against the bars of his cage.

"Sometimes, Murray, I think I'm going to end up a wrinkled old lady in a tiny dark apartment."

"With a French Communist?"

"Don't tease me," she said in a thin voice.

I touched her cheek where the eye shadow had smeared. "You're going to marry some exciting man and have three kids and be wonderfully happy."

She leaned over and kissed me on the mouth. "Thanks. Even if it isn't true." She stretched her arms in a wide vee above her head. "God, I'm starved. Feed me, Murray! Sandwiches, peaches, chocolates—quick, before I swoon."

After that, things happened quickly. Egg-salad sandwiches and pickles and quarts of Coke spread across the kitchen table, while Rosemary Clooney sang "Come On-A-My House," and, between juicy mouthfuls, I told about visiting Willy and Barbara.

"Was she wearing a long slinky dress," Arlie asked, "and smoking cigarettes with one of those holders?"

"Shorts. White shorts, and no cigarette."

"She doesn't sound much like a—what do you call it?—a seductress. Did I tell you I saw Edith Piaf?" As we munched on cookies, she described the nightclub, with the cigarette smoke so thick she could hardly see the stage, where Edith Piaf stood in a pink spotlight and sang until everyone was in tears.

I was going to tell her about Dashiell Hammett, but she said, "Believe it or not, I'm still a little bit hungry."

As we ate chocolate-covered raisins, she tossed one into her mouth, and then we tossed raisins into each other's mouths, and soon the game ended in a giggling avalanche.

"We're one hell of a team," she said on hands and knees, hunting raisins.

But in that case, why hadn't the island tilted?

"Edna and St. Vincent Millay. Remember?" she asked.

In the absence of pain, what was I feeling?

"Oh, God, I feel like a panda bear," she said. "Let's go for a walk around the park."

I shook my head.

"Well, how about a matinee movie?"

"I think I want to be alone now, Arlie."

"What's the matter?"

"I have some work to do."

Her face twisted as if she were going to cry, but then she gave a thin smile. "Getting a head start on homework for senior year?" She laughed a little, and I laughed a little, as we eased our way toward the front door.

"Yeah, homework," I said. "I'll call you when I'm done."

But this was no algebra problem or history quiz, this enigma of ecstasy. Do you cheer or boo a Giants triple play? I asked myself as I put the egg salad into the refrigerator.

"Can't we enjoy this?" Ruth had said.

I poured dusty raisins into the trash can and turned off the kitchen light.

I could have kept going, could have ridden the bus deeper into the homesick night. Could have and didn't.

"Happiness is failure perfectly spoken," the old Ferg would have said. "Happiness is perfectly ordinary," the new Ferg would say. I lay on my bed and stared at the ceiling, my blank ceiling. Ferg made ordinariness seem easier than it was. I had underestimated his summer's work.

I raised myself on an elbow, and in the yellowing afternoon sunlight, I read the labels: CIGAR BANDS. DIXIE CUPS. DREAMS. ELEPHANT TUSK. FIRST GAME OF THE SEASON. GREAT SAYINGS. No room for ecstasy. Not unless I did some rearranging. The cubbyhole for ELEPHANT TUSK seemed likely to remain unfilled forever. So I could change the label to ECSTASY. On the other hand, who knew how such things worked? An ecstatic cubbyhole might provoke the universe to kick back again—another Giants triple play.

Deadlocked. Stuck. I had run out of answers. After everything I had tried this summer—putting up "Speak Out for Freedom" posters, riding to Connecticut and Pittsburgh—here I was, lying on my bed, exactly where I had begun.

Only when I was standing by the desk did I realize that I had stood up. And only after I had crossed out ELEPHANT TUSK with a slash of the pen did I realize that I had made a decision. EMPTY, I printed on the label. And then I felt the smile loosening my face. Empty! With arms folded across my chest, I read the label again and again. Empty. Empty.

On September 5, 1951, the collection came to an end. For the first time in nine years, I would have to learn how to live without alphabetical order.

FALL

30

In new khaki pants and new blue shirt, after shaving whatever on my face needed shaving, I went off to school. The first day of my last year at Harrison High!

High above the front door I saw *Judy loves Frankie loves Jan,* the faded red message that no one had quite managed to paint over or figure out. Off to the right, the gym floor gleamed under golden varnish, awaiting the tread of the first Converse hightop in the first game of Horse.

"Hey, Mur, how was your summer?"

The sign on the south stairwell pointed down to what some Crayola artist had already renamed the barfeteria, while up the stairwell floated the smell of Lysol plus years of meat loaves and tomato soups.

"How was your summer?" everyone was asking everyone, hungry for fresh gossip.

I climbed toward the second floor. Mr. Sklar's voice resonated out of his room and down the hall, as if over the summer his vocal cords had been restrung. I waved, but he didn't see me.

In homeroom I took a desk by the windows, stashed my spiral notebooks under the lid, and waited for the 8:58 bell. The blackboards were really black for once, scrubbed and ready for another year of pompous student-government announcements.

''Aarons, Ron.''

''Here.''

''Adams, Gordon.''

''Here.''

''Albertson, Mary.''

''Present.''

''Andrews, Alice.''

''Here.''

''Baum, Murray.''

''Here.''

My thighs pressed up against the metal underbelly of the desk, as if I had grown or the desk had shrunk since June. Had all that running swelled my quadriceps? But the bell sounded before I could settle the question, and off we swarmed to assembly.

More or less in unison, five hundred students and teachers recited the Pledge of Allegiance and settled into the lumpy red chairs. Then we listened to the disembodied voice of Dr. William Jansen, superintendent of New York City schools, as it intoned from the loudspeaker on the auditorium stage (and the stages of a hundred other school auditoriums across the city): ''Our pupils must know the nature of the struggle between freedom and bondage. They must reach a full understanding of the issues at stake in the present crisis. They must understand the meaning of their heritage as free Americans and what we must do as a united people to preserve and perpetuate our way of life.'' It seemed silly to applaud for a speaker who couldn't hear us, but when Mr. Schorr, the principal, applauded, so did everyone else.

School had brought us together again. Sol's face seemed

to have grown an extra layer of flesh, happy flesh that folded and unfolded with big smiles. "Hey, Mur, good to be back, isn't it?" he said. Any minute I expected to hear him announce that he and Lianne were getting married, having children, and moving to Teaneck, New Jersey.

Ruth slipped her hand like a coin into mine as we walked from assembly. "Let's do something Friday night," I said.

"Sure," she said. "How about a movie?" She squeezed my hand and left me watching her rear end, which hitch-hiked behind her with a personality all its own.

A movie. She acted as if we had never been naked on her bed. Then again, if I didn't love her, it would be less confusing if we stayed inside our clothes. But what about ecstasy?

Jeep jogged my elbow. "I'm not ready for this. I've forgotten how to read. My mind is in shock. Help me, Mur. Sit next to me in class."

Foxx stopped me at the bottom of the stairs. "Got your brain tuned up and oiled for a new academic year, Baum?"

"Yeah." I took a step back, but he clung to my sleeve, pulling me into a corner.

"Hey, pal, where'd you vanish to last month?" he said. "If it was Paris with Arlie, don't tell me, because I'd rather not writhe with jealousy right here in the—"

"Tough shit." I shook off his hand. "Don't talk to *me* about vanishing."

"Uh-oh. You're still hurt, aren't you? Bruised down to your pinkie from that Hammett business. Hey, what can I say, man? I tried to make up for it with those newspaper articles I sent you. Tried to cheer you up."

"Dead dogs and traffic jams? You call that cheery? I call it very strange."

He turned the drinking fountain on and off, on and off.

"Well, maybe accident humor is an acquired taste. Like whiskey." The water gurgled into the drain. "Be glad I didn't send you the article about how my father broke a whiskey bottle on the living-room table. As a matter of fact, he also broke my mother's nose. With his hand."

"Jesus, Dan."

"Hey. Cheer up, kid." He pinched my cheek. "Anybody can live without a living-room table."

School had summoned us from Paris and Peekskill and Pittsburgh. In Advanced French, I didn't listen to Madame Boncourt tell the anecdote about arriving in *les Etats-unis* with her *cher mari* Jean-Paul, who was now, *hélas! mort*, and who at the time, with only fifteen hundred words of *anglais*, et cetera, et cetera—the same anecdote she had told the year before and the year before that. We were a small tribe that congregated in these large green rooms and spoke a special language: Eng Lit, Trig, Bot, Phys Ed, Gov. For nine more months we would know one another better than we knew anyone in the world, and then at graduation we would be sent out among strangers. I looked steadily at the side of Arlie's face until she felt my eyes and turned and nodded.

School had brought us all together, minus one. In the afternoon we went to our table at the back of Buddy's Grill and ordered a mountain of hot dogs, a sea of vanilla Coke, making up for months of deprivation. The jukebox was playing Johnny Mathis. The grease still streaked the wall like a Jackson Pollock painting. Buddy's glasses bounced on his nose as he warned us to pipe down. But this year Bobby L. was present only in the snapshot he had sent to Foxx from a photo booth somewhere outside Camp Lejeune. I barely recognized him; there was something strange in the way his chin tucked at a raw angle into his collar, or in his expressionless eyes, or maybe it was just the way the light from the flash flattened his face. Who was this man, I wondered? Then I turned the photo over. *Is their life after school?* he had written in pencil, and I pictured him perched on a toilet seat writing furious one-sentence essays on the wall. "Well," I said, handing the photo to Ferg, "we've lost a school author but gained some clean bathroom walls." He wrinkled his forehead. "Private joke," I added.

"Guys, you shoulda seen these girls," Jeep announced. "Beautiful blond girls, stacked to the gills, lying all over the beach like—like I don't know." He stroked his white T-shirt, where *Lifeguard* rippled in red letters.

"And each of them broad where a broad should be broad, I bet."

"Broad where a broad should . . ." Jeep grinned. "Hey, Mur, didja make that up?"

"Me and Rodgers and Hammerstein."

"Who? Oh yeah. Anyhow, there was this one named Margo who . . ."

The tribe minus one. Maybe Ferg would stand and make a toast to the empty chair. But Ferg seemed to be collecting the lush details of Margo, or at least he was leaning in Jeep's direction. And Foxx was laying pretzel upon pretzel, building a salty log cabin. And Sol was smiling at some private thought.

When Jeep was done, a silence took over—comfortable at first, then thin and uneasy. I looked around, but no one looked at me. Not even Ferg. Especially not Ferg. I understood now: Ferg had abdicated.

I could take his place. My friends, I could say, we are a small tribe of brothers, minus one, who have only nine months left. Friends, I could say, why has King Ferg, the first and forever Turds Mole, left us in the lurch by pretending to be just an ordinary guy? Or I could say, Listen! I'm no longer a virgin!

I let the moment pass, and the next moment, and the next, while the silence stretched too thin.

"Foxx," I said finally, "tell us a story."

He looked at me from under his eyebrows, shrugged, and cocked a pretzel between his teeth like a cigar. "Once upon a time, shortly before the dreadful giants invaded Earth, five brave pimple-faced lads gathered in Buddy's Grill."

As he commenced the Battle of the Third Avenue El, full of gallant teenagers with wounds oozing ketchup, I closed my eyes. There would never be another King Ferg of the Round Table.

After the last outer-space giant was killed by a barrage of poison-tipped paper clips and ground up into egg rolls for starving children in China, I raised my hand. "To the best friends we'll ever have." Paper cup bent against paper cup. "And to Dan Foxx, the new host of the Round Table."

"Our goalie host."

"Of the square table."

"Olé!"

"Oy vay."

■ ■ ■

"Stop by for a chat," Miss Moran said as we passed each other in the hall. For days I ducked into bathrooms, walked behind two-hundred-pound Joey Bartel, waved vaguely, and scuttled down stairways. What should I say to her? The last time we talked, in her apartment, I had begged her to take care of me, pitiful me, the runaway scared of going away. But the worst part was what had come next, my try for ecstasy. She had gone all the way to Ithaca and read her poems; I had barely reached Pittsburgh before turning back. Better to duck into bathrooms than tell her that.

One afternoon, though, I was walking by her classroom and she called out my name. She was eating an apple at her desk while grading papers.

"Eating lunch on the job," she said. "Not exactly good for the digestion." She gestured toward a chair. "Now that you're a senior, Murray, I never see you."

"Busy. You know how it is, the first week of school."

"It's an intriguing time. My classroom is full of new faces, and as I scan them I wonder which of them is a writer—a real writer."

"I'm taking The American Novel with Mr. Piersall. We're reading *Moby-Dick*, which seems pretty good even though it's seven hundred pages."

She took a bite and chewed slowly. I looked around this familiar room where I had first heard about Thomas Hardy and W. H. Auden. It seemed long ago.

She cleared her throat. "Did everything go all right after you left?"

"Left?"

"My apartment, that afternoon. You seemed kind of depressed."

I took a deep breath. "Actually, Miss Moran, things didn't work out at all. Not in the way you think they did."

"What do you mean? You went to stay with your friend Ferguson, didn't you?"

"No, I said I would, but I lied."

"Where *did* you go?"

"After I left your apartment, I got on a bus and began riding west."

"Oh, Murray."

"To the Pacific Ocean, that's what I had in mind, or at least as far as my money would take me."

She set the apple on the desk but kept her eyes fixed on my face.

"Somewhere in New Jersey I began to get nervous, or lonely. Scared. When I arrived in Pittsburgh, I phoned my parents and told them I was coming home." I shrugged. "Not exactly the great American novel."

She laughed. "Not exactly." She leaned back and laughed harder. "Pittsburgh? Oh, Murray, that's a wonderful story."

"You're making fun of me."

"No, I'm not." She put her arms on the desk, creasing the student papers. "I think it's marvelous. Off you go from my apartment with your Macy's shopping bag, heading west like a modern Huck Finn. Okay, you didn't get beyond Pennsylvania, but I bet you had one hell of an experience. The great American short story."

This time we both laughed, and I felt better. A short story. It wasn't much, but it was something.

31

My birthday began as usual, with Mom's poem hidden during the night inside my slipper.

Birthday Poem No. 17

You are my sunshine,
My number-one shine,

Although at times I think you love
The Dodgers more than me.
You are my Murray
Of whom I worry
That soon you'll grow too tall
To hear the words I sing to thee.
So I am learning
That you are turning
Into a mensch
And Mr. Baum-to-be.

Love,
The King and I

Then came the presents:

a framed print of the Picasso boy in blue, with a note from Dad: *Dear Pablo, enjoy your pink period;*

a bag of fifty nickels from Theo, *for 50 pinball games in a row at the Broadway Arcade;*

an electric shaver (*from your parents, before you stumble over your beard*).

Then came the breakfast of blueberry waffles, mine studded with seventeen tiny candles.

"Well, son," Dad said as he finished his second cup of coffee. "Are you ready to play checkers?"

"Ready to *win* at checkers?" I replied.

"Feeling like a big shot, are you?"

I soon discovered I wasn't feeling much of anything at all. Even though my kings were marching triumphantly all over the board, and Dad was smacking his forehead and muttering *"oy vay,"* I was barely interested. My right hand seemed to move on its own; the kings moved on their own. I watched them from my chair while I waited.

"Your turn, Murray."

Waited for something to make this birthday exciting, as birthdays used to be. The stuffed panda hiding under my bed. Pin the Tail on the Donkey. Musical Chairs. Candles fluttering hotly against my mouth as I wished.

"Murray, have you fallen asleep, or what?"

"Play with Theo. I think I'd rather read."

In my room I lay without reading, and dozed through a dream of careening buses, and finally turned on the ball game. In the bottom of the sixth, as the Dodgers were losing again—to the lowly Pirates, no less—there was a knock on my door. "Your father and I want to talk with you."

What now? Which bad news? He couldn't be going away again, could he?

They were sitting next to each other on the living-room couch. "We want to talk about college," he said.

College? Here I was, barely catching up to the present, and they were throwing me into the future.

"For years your father and I have been putting money into a savings account. That's your special birthday gift."

"Good colleges are expensive," he said. "I was talking with Dave Green at the office. His son went to Yale."

"And Mrs. Albioni's son," she added, "you remember him? Louie had so-so grades, but he went to Rutgers."

I tried to picture myself at college, and my mind went blank. Nothing. As if I wouldn't exist next year.

"Of course you have wonderful grades," she said.

"Although you may not want to go to Yale."

"Or Harvard. We don't want to be pushy."

Why were they doing this? Here I had just come home, and they were talking about my leaving again. Give me time. Give me time to get used to my ordinary life.

They were both leaning forward now, smiling in unison.

"Thanks," I said. "It's really nice of you. But let's discuss it later, okay?"

"Okay," they said. "Later." Their voices and smiles wound down to a halt. I had spoiled their fun, and I was sorry, but I couldn't do any better. Even though it was my birthday. An endless birthday.

After dinner the telegram from Cleveland arrived. At first we supposed it was a happy-birthday telegram, although nine o'clock seemed rather late. "The Silbermans are getting old," Mom said as she opened the envelope. "Old people forget things."

It wasn't a matter of forgetting. *Dear ones. This morning Franz went peacefully. A blessing. Too tired to talk. Love, Hannah.*

The flesh of my father's face sagged. "*Ach, mein Gott!* My oldest friend."

She took his hand. "I'm sorry, darling."

"I still see him in those *Lederhosen*. Franz!"

I left them sitting hand in hand and went to my room to cry. A month ago I had almost phoned the Silbermans, almost knocked on their door, almost eaten at their table and slept safely on their couch as I decided what to do next. Another few hours westward and I could have looked into his yellowed eyes and told him that my father, his friend, had come home safely. Now it was too late. The little man with cellophane skin had shrunk to nothing. Had departed without my good news. If only I . . .

The tears came faster, mixed with sobs, and I grabbed more Kleenex.

If only I could . . . But there wasn't anything I could do for anyone's grief tonight.

I used to close my eyes, reach out with one hand, and grope into a cubbyhole. Find the cool, translucent, blue-green marbles. Or the cigar bands with their turbaned princes. Or the Tom Mix Decoder Ring that glowed green beneath the blanket. But the collection had ended. All I could do was lie here with a damp wad of Kleenex inside my fist and hope that the day would end before I received any other news from the world out there: from Connecticut, or Korea, or God knows where. All I wanted was to wake up the next day and find things moving contentedly along.

32

When Callahan showed up one afternoon at Buddy's Grill, none of us thought anything about it. Ray was the kind of guy you didn't notice at first because he was small and polite, the kind of guy who got picked last for the team and played right field. When he showed up a second afternoon, none of us could think of how to say tactfully that he hadn't been invited. By the following Monday we had almost gotten used to his being the sixth Knight of the Round Table. Actually, it felt good to be back up to six, even if Callahan—who made quiet jokes that you knew were jokes only because he raised one eyebrow and waited—was nothing like Bobby L.

But it wasn't the same. Callahan, who planned on going to journalism school, proposed a "current-events circle." Every Monday we discussed the Korean peace talks, or inflation, or something important like that. No one stood up to give a prayer of thanks to Preacher Roe. Foxx didn't sing animal arias. One day Ferguson even ate a hot dog ("just out of carnivorous curiosity").

"What's going on with the Round Table?" I asked Ferg on the phone.

"It's going on. We're all going on. What's your problem?"

"What's wrong?" I asked Foxx in study hall. "You're our king, but you're not acting very kingly. No mad pronouncements or ostrich songs."

"First you give me shit about too much humor. Now you give me shit about too little humor." He pretended to pull out his hair. "They warned me about fickle critics." Now that I looked, I saw his hair was shorter. From the back he resembled everyone else.

"What's happening to us?" I asked Sol. He lifted one shoulder and said nothing was happening, things were fine. In fact, he wanted Lianne to come to Buddy's, too, "because she and I believe in sharing everything in our lives."

At first she held his hand under the table and looked intently at people. Soon she was complimenting Callahan on his deep voice, which she said sounded exactly like Edward R. Murrow's, and then she was teasing Ferguson about his hot chocolate and flirting with Foxx. Her laughter floated above ours; her perfume cut through the greasy smell of hot dogs; she made Buddy's Grill seem homey. "Come back," everyone said. "Don't let Sol keep you to himself," they said.

So it was no surprise when Arlie arrived and changed everything. Callahan addressed his questions to her, Foxx aimed his jokes at her, and Jeep turned his *goddamn*s and *asshole*s into *damn*s and *butt*s. Buddy even delivered her Coke personally to the table and stood there wiping his hands on his apron, like a waiter. I went over to the jukebox and thumbed my nickel into the slot. Under the rounded glass the record rose, flipped sideways, settled on the turntable, shuddered, and began spinning at 45 rpm. "They tried to tell us we're too young," Nat King Cole crooned sadly across Buddy's Grill. More sadly than I had ever heard.

A week later, Ruth came in with Callahan! Ruth! She sat beside him, ordered a cherry Coke, joined the conversation, and laughed at his jokes, as if she had done it all before. Ruth and Callahan!

I phoned her that night. "Well, I hope the two of you will be very happy."

"What are you talking about?"

"You and Callahan. The two of you seem to be chummy."

"I think Ray's interesting, and why are you being so nasty?"

"In case you forgot, you and I . . . that afternoon . . . didn't that mean anything to you?"

"Oh, Murray, it was swell, and I'll never forget it. Everything happened like magic."

"But?"

"But we're too young to make it a regular kind of thing."

I nodded.

"Did you hear me?" she asked.

"Yes."

"Are you mad at me?"

"Not really."

"Are you sure?"

"Want to go to a movie sometime?" I said.

■ ■ ■

Soon we had to sit at two tables because there were so many of us—Lianne, Arlie, Ruth, Jeep's girl of the week, and the six guys. "We don't even talk about baseball anymore," I complained to Foxx.

"Maybe so, amigo. But are the girls to blame?"

He had a point. Even without the girls, none of us had been talking baseball. Thinking about it, yes, but not talking aloud. Each day's news brought casualty reports from a war being fought in several American cities. Chicago, September 18: *Dodgers lose 5–3; Campanella hit by pitch, unable to play for indefinite period.* St. Louis, September 19: *Dodgers lose, 7–1.* Brooklyn, September 22: *Dodgers lose, 9–6.* Brooklyn, September 23: *Campanella returns, flies out with bases loaded in ninth; Dodgers are defeated 7–3.* Boston, September 26: *Dodgers win, 15–5.* Philadelphia, September 29: *Dodgers lose.* By the end of September we were only one game ahead of the Giants, and no one talked about what was happening. At breakfast Dad read the *Times* without any hoots of "Go, Duke!" from behind the page. At night Theo turned his radio low, so that Red Barber's voice sounded like someone praying at the end of our hallway.

"I can't stand it, Ferg. It's driving me nuts. And on top of everything else, my parents are holding their breath until I say I'm going to college."

"Tell them you're too busy to go to college."

"I'm serious, Ferg."

"Exactly!" He tossed popcorn toward his mouth and missed. "Serious. Delirious. Every senior is worried sick about turning into a Bowery bum unless he gets accepted by Harvard. Which is why I decided not to apply to college."

"You what?"

"At least this year."

"But what will you—"

"Travel. Work in my mother's gallery. Who knows?"

I looked hard at him. "Are you all right, Ferg?"

He smiled. "Check back in a year for your answer."

That didn't help me at all. I had enough uncertainty without adding a year of "who knows?" to my life. All evening I tried to do my history homework and kept mixing up the Jacobins and the Girondists. During my third run through the French Revolution, someone knocked on the door.

"I'm busy," I shouted.

"This is important," Theo said.

"That's what you always say, and it's always some stupid kid stuff."

The door banged open. He marched up to me and laid a fist on the page I was reading. "I'm no kid. I'm five foot eight inches tall and my voice is changing and you make me mad."

"All right, all right. I'm sorry."

"Say it again—this time like you mean it."

"I'm sorry, Theo."

Slowly he withdrew the fist. "We're too old to fight," he said, and I noticed that his voice was thicker than I remembered, almost a manly growl. And his nose was thickening, too, beginning to look like Dad's.

"What do you want to talk about?" I asked.

"Mom and Dad are worried about you. First because you pulled that Pittsburgh stunt, and now because you may not go to college. Mom thinks you're in some kind of trouble, and Dad says no, you're only in a stage." He shoved his hands into his pockets. "They asked me all these questions that I couldn't answer."

They were talking about me. I felt discovered. "Thanks, Theo." I punched him gently on the shoulder. "Don't worry, I'll be all right."

"I know that. But they don't, 'cause they're parents. So will you talk to them?" He turned toward the door. "Hey, Mur," he said without looking back, "*are* you going away to college?"

"Maybe. I don't know. Why?"

"'Cause I'll miss you, that's why," he said over his shoulder.

I couldn't seem to find enough air for my lungs. "I'll miss you, too, Theo." It came out shakily, so I tried harder. "You can visit me on weekends, sleep in a sleeping bag on the floor, go to the football game."

"Sounds like fun. Kind of like camp in the winter."

College camp? Maybe so, maybe so.

33

Had there been an election on Monday, October 1, Jackie Robinson would have been elected president of Brooklyn, the first black president in Brooklyn's history.

He earned it on Sunday, the last day of the regular season, when both the Giants and the Dodgers were clinging like crazy to first place in the National League. At Ebbets Field the game with the Phillies was tied up 8–8 and stretching unbearably into the tenth, the eleventh, the twelfth. Two outs. Things look grim as the Phillies load the bases. And grimmer yet when Waitkus hits a screaming line drive over second, sure to drive in one or maybe two runs. But then out of nowhere Robinson dives through acres of air and snatches that ball in the webbing of his glove high above the infield. He falls, he dusts himself off, he trots toward the dugout with that pigeon-toed gait, as if saving the pennant in the last game of the season is just an average day's work.

Thirteenth inning: still tied. The Giants have won their game in Boston, so we must win ours or lose the pennant. Fourteenth inning: still tied. Robin Roberts on the mound, and who else but Jackie Robinson at the plate. Jackie takes a ball, a strike, and hits the third pitch into the upper-left-field stands. With one swing he has granted the Dodgers and their million desperate fans a reprieve. Bless you, Pope Jackie the First.

The play-off series would start on Monday. Suddenly the 1951 season was to begin all over again, shrunk to three games between two teams.

"Now, Samuel, what is this, you are suddenly such a holy Jew?" my mother asked at breakfast.

"But *Süsschen*, it's Rosh Hashanah, the highest of holy days, a day to think about our sins in the year gone by."

"How come you never stay home all the nineteen Rosh Hashanahs I have known you, only this one, which happens to be the day the Dodgers play this run-off game?"

"Play-off game." He put down the paper and looked wide-eyed at Theo and me. "By golly, boys, does the play-off start today? By golly, what a coincidence. In that case, maybe I'll tune in for a few innings while I'm home."

"Me, too," Theo shouted. "I'm a Jew, aren't I, so I can skip school?"

Mom shook her head."A Jew, yes, but not yet a big enough Jew to get away with your father's mischief." She twisted Dad's ear. "You should have shame, Samuel, but you never do." Dad pinched her bottom. "Never!" When I left for school, the two of them were hugging in the kitchen while the sink overflowed with soapsuds behind them.

I took a pocketful of dimes to school to call ME 7-1212, the special number that would tell the latest score. But Jeep had brought something better than dimes: his portable radio. At the beginning of math class, which was ten minutes before the game began, he complained about a stomachache. Twenty minutes later he laid his head on his desk.

"Are you feeling ill, Baker?" Mr. Jackson asked.

"No score. I mean, no *sir*." None of us breathed. "I mean maybe a little sick, sir." He was actually turning pale as Mr. Jackson scrutinized him. Through the silence we heard a peculiar sound, as if a tiny electric train were racing around inside Jeep's desk, or perhaps—yes—as if a crowd of Lilliputians were cheering for a two-run double.

"Mr. Jackson." Foxx was waving his hand. "Mr. Jackson, I have a question about the sixth problem," waving his hand while giving me the elbow. "Make noise," he muttered. "Make noise." And I did, we all did, shuffling feet, clearing throats, camouflaging Red Barber and saving Jeep's ass.

We couldn't save the Dodgers, though. They went down 3–1.

Nine innings short of death. The only ones who could save them now were Robinson and Campanella and Furillo.

As I waited for the Third Avenue express, newspaper pages blew against my ankles. The train was late, and I was getting cold.

Actually, it was not only Robinson, etc., who would decide it. Maglie and Irwin and Thomson would also play a part. And so would accidents—a pebble in the infield, a wind blowing in from left. "Ordinary accidents."

"You talking to me, kid?" A man standing next to me on the platform give me a quick, suspicious look.

"I was, uh, talking to myself," I muttered. The train rumbled to a halt, and I found a seat in the far corner.

Plain ordinary chance. Tinkers to Evers to Chance.

So Mr. Sklar was wrong. You explain and explain and explain, lining up causes and effects in a straight line, until one afternoon you find yourself whistling into a funny wind that blows your straight line crooked.

No wonder I had never finished the JRP. I had been working against the quirky laws of the universe. Mr. Sklar should have told me what I was up against.

I whistled quietly all the way home.

"Where's Dad?" I asked Mom.

"He's in the living room pretending to be holy."

"I'm not pretending," he shouted from the hall.

"*Ja,* sure," she shouted back. "You better believe God can tell the difference between holiness and baseball."

"Smart God." He was in the kitchen now, rumpling my hair. "Happy New Year, Murray. Of course you heard the news. We lost, three to one."

"I know. Listen, Dad. I have something I want to say. To both of you."

She was stirring the soup. He was eating a piece of cheese. The two of them waited amiably.

"I decided: I'm going to college."

Mazel tov! *Wunderbar!* They made all kinds of glad noises. Mom put down the wooden spoon to hug me. Dad waited until it was his turn, and then, after a moment's hesitation, he shook my hand. For what seemed a wonderfully long time, we stood there, shaking hands.

■ ■ ■

My own laughter woke me from the dream. Red Barber had sat down beside me during history class and scribbled on a yellow pad, *Explain the World Series.* I pondered it for a long time, like an exam question, and then wrote *Turds Mole to Evers to Chance.* I was handing him the paper when Mom snatched it away. "You boys should be studying instead of passing foolish notes," she shouted, marching us to Mr. Sklar at the front of the room. But he wasn't there. On his desk a yellow piece of paper leaned against a book. *Gone to the play-offs*, it said, and I awoke laughing.

The next morning I looked cautiously around the doorway of Room 411. He was there. "Well, Baum, what's on your mind?"

"I've got something to discuss with you."

"Baseball, no doubt."

I pulled out the familiar pages, heavily wrinkled by now. "Actually, it's about what you wrote on my JRP."

"You never give up, do you?"

I looked down at the pages and began to talk very fast. "'Dead horse; loyalty oath; sunny Siberia. Step back and think about how to explain this history. As accident or choice?' That's what you said about my father. Well, sir"—I paused for my mind to catch up with the little speech I had rehearsed during breakfast—"all this summer I tried to find the cause of every action and every event. But now I think accidents play a part, too. Sometimes you have to explain things in terms of chance. Sheer chance."

I stood on the balls of my feet, ready to run if he exploded in anger. But he sat motionless, hunched in his chair, chewing a pencil, waiting for something more. I took a breath.

"Consider baseball, for example," I said. His eyebrows flicked up. Suppose, the day before yesterday, Jackie Robinson had been standing ten inches to the left. Then he would have missed Waitkus's line drive and the Dodgers would have lost the pennant. Ten inches of historic chance.''

I had never heard Mr. Sklar laugh. Soft bubbles of sound. ''Great God in heaven, Baum, what have I done to deserve you?''

At the end of the hall I dared to stop running. I stood still for a long time, until my heart no longer boomed its terror and joy.

NEW YEAR'S EVE

34

''Why is it we never see your friends anymore?'' Mom asked again one evening in the middle of dinner. ''That girl Arlie, for example, such a pretty girl. And Foxx, he made me laugh that time he told about his grandfather in the Jewish vaudeville.'' She leaned over to collect our plates. ''Why don't you invite them to a party here?''

''A big party,'' Dad went on. ''Big-band music on the phonograph. Big plates of salami and cheese.''

''And my punch bowl,'' she added.

''A New Year's Eve party,'' he said.

''The party of the year,'' Theo chimed in. ''The party of the decade. With helium balloons on the ceiling.''

Against that kind of momentum, I didn't have a chance. Even if I had said no, I think they would have had the party without me.

''The party of the century,'' Theo continued. ''Of the . . . of the . . . what's bigger than a century?''

''Put a lid on it, Theo. And you're going to stay in your room.''

''Unfair. Mo-om!''

''All right, you can watch,'' I said, ''but you can't talk to anybody.''

"My voice won't crack, Murray. Honest, it's almost all changed. By next week it'll be done."

"All right, already! Talk. Drink. Dance with Arlie, for all I care. Just wear a mask so no one knows who you are."

And he did—dance with Arlie, that is. Not just once, but twice. When she took off her heels, he was even a little taller than she was. That was the kind of party it turned out to be: unbelievable.

People who hardly knew each other danced together: Arlie and Theo; Callahan and the tall husky-voiced girl who came with Jeep, I never caught her name; Ruth and Ferg, cheek to cheek (Ferg! cheek to cheek!), his glasses fogging up, and then a second time, without his glasses, blind to my incredulous smile; Susan Powers, elected "Miss Student Body" in 1950, and Callahan ("Old Edward R. Murrow's feeling ballsy tonight," Jeep whispered).

People who weren't invited came. People who were invited didn't come. Zoe brought her brother, a senior at Cornell, who spent the evening smoking English cigarettes disdainfully in a corner. Simon Carson, Simple Simon, came, even though no one could ever figure out how he had heard about the party. Frankie Aurelio, who was practically a hood, came with some girl named Candy and a flask in his side pocket. By this time I was ready for anyone at all to appear at the door: Tante Lotte, or Mr. Sklar, or Bobby L. with one sleeve folded up neatly and fastened with a safety pin. But they didn't come. Sol and Lianne came very late ("Sorry, Mur, we were . . . busy"), exchanging moist touches, moist glances.

People who inevitably said the same things at parties said them. "*Excusez-moi, mademoiselle,* do you know how to French kiss?" Jeep asked five different girls. Other people said things they had never said before. Susan Powers, her voice thick with Mom's eggnog, whispered in my ear that she had always found me sexy, and in my excitement I said, "me, too," and then "you, too," and desperately, "thank you," but by then she had moved on.

"Murray," Arlie said with a little kiss, "you look like Gregory Peck."

I decided that my hormones were secreting invisible juices into the air when Lianne pulled me aside and said, "What am I saying if I tell you I love your tochus?" Oh, Lianne, this is so sudden and unexpected, but of course it cannot come to anything because your fiancé is, after all, my best friend, but if you want to touch my tochus, just one quick firm touch, here in this dark corner, whom would we really be hurting?—all this I thought in a tumescent instant with a stupid grin on my face. "That's what Sol said," she went on. "He said, 'I love your tochus,' and I didn't dare ask him what *tochus* meant. But I decided I could ask you, Murray, because it sounds Hebrew." Whereupon, in a voice that sounded like Gregory Peck's, I whispered, "Yes," and cupped my hand over her shy Protestant ass, and fled.

People disappeared and appeared, or never moved all evening. Big Brother from Cornell smoked himself into an English fog. The twins, Ned and Jed, sat identically on the couch for an hour. When they at last stood up, I was sure they would dance with each other, but they went over to the window and, side by side, gazed solemnly into the night. Mom hustled in and out, filling the punch bowl, adding fresh trays of sandwiches, watching us until I caught her eye and she hustled back into the kitchen. "Not to worry," she had said at dinner, when I made them promise not to intrude. "Dad and I will hide in our bedroom."

"No one will guess you have parents," he had added.

But Ruth needed a safety pin for her hem. When Mom took her to the bedroom, there was Dad, wearing that Hawaiian shirt with the orange-green palm trees ("Just in case I have to answer the doorbell," he had said with a wink). He was taking apart the hall clock and whistling a marching song. Whether it was him or the clock, something kept Ruth back there, and kept her, and kept her, until shortly before midnight she was tugging him into the living room. "It's almost the magic hour," she announced, "and here's the magician."

Dad didn't dare meet my eye. He swept the black silk hat from his head, bowed, and waited for the crowd to form a semicircle. "Friends, Romans, countrymen. My name is Maestro Hocus Pocus, and I ask you to watch verrry carefully. Does anyone happen to have a rabbit?"

First the rabbit-in-the-hat trick, then the nickels from the ear, then the rope that you cut in half but that always emerged unbroken between his fingers, and finally the handcuffs. I knew how it would go. I also knew the joke about "sawing my sister in half, so now I have two half-sisters." Everybody else had fathers who wore three-piece suits and said nothing but "Good to meet you." Why was I singled out to have a Hawaiian magician father? As my face blushed hot, I looked down at the floor and wondered how to disappear.

"Well, if you give me no rabbits," he said, "I must find my own."

No one noticed as I slipped down the hall to my room. I lay among the coats heaped on the bed: a scratchy woolen coat with square buttons; a thick fur coat; a wrinkled brown trenchcoat with a few raindrops still crouched on the collar like stowaways; tweed jackets, plaid jackets, jackets with sleeves twined loverlike with sleeves of other jackets;

Arlie's silver coat of some material so glossy my fingers could hardly feel it; a black leather jacket that creaked under my elbow.

I tunneled among the smells of my friends. I lay beneath the weight of them, and their textures, and the tiny conversations of their buttons and zippers. All of them were collected on my bed like children playing Sardines, where someone hides and the first kid to find him curls beside him in the hiding place, and then the next kid does the same, and the next and the next, a gang of tickling breaths and stifled giggles, until the very last kid, who has grown frantic with loneliness, discovers all the others. Everyone was collected on my bed—everyone but Miss Moran, and even she could easily have joined the heap. Perhaps she would have been the last, her hands groping in the dark against our bodies, until she shouted "I found you" and brought us all back to the light.

I was ready to return to the party.

No one had noticed my absence. Dad was holding them hypnotized. "Please, I beg you, watch my fingers verrry carefully," and the German *r*s purred through the room. "This one I learned from Harry Houdini himself one afternoon." Harry Houdini or Harry Truman? Looking at that orange-green shirt, one had to wonder. Dad, up to his old tricks.

They laughed and clustered around him, my father. Ruth's mouth hung open with astonishment. Ferg's glasses twinkled with light. Lianne bit her thumb, laying her head on Sol's shoulder. Arlie was smiling the way she used to smile when we took a breath between kisses. "And now we must all say the magic word: *Mashed Potato*." They closed around my magician father.

"But Mr. Baum," said Foxx, "*mashed potato* is two words."

"Not if you say it fast enough," replied my father in handcuffs in a Hawaiian shirt.

"Mashedpotato, mashpotato, mashtayto, mashtayto," we said in a chorus.

"Hooray," we screamed as he raised his uncuffed hands.

Over the heads of my friends, our eyes met. I winked, and he winked back.

Someone turned on the record player, and we started dancing. "I think your father's cute," Ruth said.

"Thanks," I said, just before Callahan cut in on us, and then I cut in on Sol to dance with Lianne until Foxx cut in on me, whereupon I cut in on Ferg to dance with Arlie, and so on, and so on.